## ALSO BY C.K. CRIGGER

### *The Woman Who Series*

*The Woman Who Built a Bridge*

*The Woman Who Killed Marvin Hammel*

*The Woman Who Wore a Badge*

*The Woman Who Beat the Odds*

*The Woman Who Inherited Trouble*


### *Western Short Stories*

*Aldy Neal's Ghost*

*Ask Parrot*

*A Deal's A Deal*

*Double Deal*

*Left Behind*

*Memory of Blood*

*The Whereabouts of Miss Nellie Thistlewaite*


### *Novels*

*Ault's Heir*

*Black Crossing*

*Hereafter*

*Letter Of The Law*

*Liar's Trial*

*Lost Girl Lake*

*Madame's Daughter*

*The Yeggman's Apprentice*

*Yester's Ride*

*The Winning Hand*

# THE WOMAN WHO INHERITED TROUBLE

## THE WOMAN WHO: BOOK FIVE

### C.K. CRIGGER

**WOLFPACK PUBLISHING**
— EST 2013 —

**The Woman Who Inherited Trouble**

Paperback Edition
Copyright © 2023 C.K. Crigger

<u>Wolfpack Publishing</u>
9850 S. Maryland Parkway, Suite A-5 #323
Las Vegas, Nevada 89183

wolfpackpublishing.com

eBook ISBN 978-1-63977-741-9
Paperback ISBN 978-1-63977-740-2
Library of Congress Control Number: 2023931555

# THE WOMAN WHO
# INHERITED TROUBLE

# CHAPTER 1

Delbert Avery, who considered himself Spokane's preeminent attorney, was a dapper little man whose short beard helped conceal a rather prominent underbite. Contemplating his client, he pushed the prepared document across the desk for the man's final perusal and folded his hands on a slight paunch.

"Are you certain this is what you want to do, Joseph?" He indicated the document. "This is a lot of money at stake. Money and property."

His client, a mining magnate by the name of Joseph C. Flowers, choked on a laugh. Unfortunately, the laugh deteriorated into a harsh cough, one that bent him over and turned his face white.

"I have a lot of money, as you well know," he rasped when he could speak again. He wiped blood from his lips with a snowy monogrammed handkerchief, wadded the cloth and stuffed it in his coat pocket. "But it's not just about the money. You know that."

"I do. I also know your grandsons..." The attorney

hesitated, pretending not to notice his client's distress. "They will not be pleased."

The client snorted. "Bunch of soft do-nothings, the lot of them, who think they can buy the world with my money. Lord knows I've spent thousands on them and not a one is worth the powder to blow'im to hell. Now they can't wait for me to die. I may've disapproved of the man my youngest daughter married, but at least she had the gumption to live her own life. And so did her husband." His brows drew down. "For as long as she lasted. And he. Neither of them asked me for a penny. Ever. As for Anita's own child?" His harsh laugh came again. "Gumption doesn't begin to describe this one. Looks to be worth a hundred times more than the other three if you put them all together."

The attorney, who'd played a large part in ascertaining the worth of this particular grandchild, couldn't deny his friend Joseph's conclusion. He nodded. "Nevertheless, the boys are not going to be happy. You don't think they'll...er...do anything about your final disposition, do you?" Personally, he had no doubts they'd put up a fight. And they were dangerous. Weak men, especially those with enough money at stake to prod them into action, always were. Surely Joseph realized that.

"Depends on what you mean by 'do,'" Joseph said. "Fight the will? Of course. Use other means? Maybe. A word or two of warning might not come amiss."

Flowers read slowly through the rest of the document, finally grunting his satisfaction. He looked up into Avery's worried eyes. "Don't matter what they do as long as you made this watertight and legal."

"The document is sound," the attorney said. "I'd wager they'll try to contest it, but they won't get anywhere. Not even with the codicil we added." A smile flashed across his face. "Not even if they kill their cousin."

Flowers's breath caught again, sending him through another coughing spell. "I wish you hadn't said that," he told the attorney, "because I've got it in my head they might give it a try."

Avery didn't verbally agree, but inwardly, he did. In these hard times it would be easy for the Flowers grandsons to find men who, for the right price, would kill whoever they designated. There being nothing he could do about the potential danger to Flowers's fourth grandchild, he called in his clerk and his law intern to serve as witnesses to the documents, and with something of a flourish, passed his favorite Waterman pen to Joseph.

They all stood about, watching as Flowers signed his name with a trademark scrawl in need of a magician's abracadabra to decipher. Finally, the deed was done.

When Avery's employees went back to their stations, Flowers pulled a sealed letter from his pocket and shoved it toward the attorney. "For my heir," he said. "Hand it over personally, if you will, Delbert."

Mute now, his objections already voiced, Avery merely nodded.

Four days later, Joseph Flowers was dead, his tuberculosis having caused a massive bleeding episode. On the day of the funeral, the attorney wrote a short letter with his Waterman pen, addressed the envelope and affixed a two-cent stamp. He put the letter in his secretary's mail to be sent the next day.

Back in his office, he poured a measure of Tennessee's finest high malt whiskey into a crystal glass and waved the libation in the air in a salute to his dead friend.

"I watched your grandsons at the funeral." He lifted the glass, peering through the clear amber liquid as though looking at a ghost. "Oh, they acted sober enough and sad when they thought somebody might be looking. But I knew and so did some of the others. They couldn't hide their glee from me. Sorry, old friend. I know how disappointed you are."

He drank the whiskey in one go. "But not half as disappointed as they're going to be."

# CHAPTER 2

JANUARY BILLINGS KNEW AT A GLANCE SOMETHING WAS stirring her part-time ranch hand into a regular tizzy. Johnny Johnson had knocked on her door this morning a half-hour early, then stood in front of her with his hat in his hands, his face a curious mix of red splotches on his tan cheeks. She might've thought it was funny if she hadn't been so concerned.

She didn't have to be clairvoyant to know he considered whatever he had to say a serious matter and the cause of his nervous dithers. Johnny's hat was only a couple months old, but caught up in his troubles, he had inadvertently squeezed the brim into a tight curl.

She bit back a smile. He'd be upset when he finally noticed what he'd done. She hoped it would be after he finally acknowledged her dog Pen, who sat in front of him waiting to be greeted with her usual scratch behind the ears.

Growing impatient at being ignored, the big black dog whined and tried putting up a paw to be shaken.

Johnny's failed to respond.

"Come on to the kitchen, Johnny. Have you eaten? I'm just getting breakfast on the table." January kept her voice cheery although he was making her a little nervous.

On an ordinary morning, he would've jumped at the chance of breakfast due to cinnamon-laced plum syrup spreading its aroma throughout the house. The apple, plum, and pear orchard her late husband Shay had started when he first settled here produced like wildfire nowadays and she had an abundance of fall fruit.

But even as she started toward the kitchen, he continued to stand. Pen, doing her job, nudged him with her nose.

"Johnny?" January's voice rose. "You're scaring me. What's wrong? What's happened? Is it Bo?" Bo Cobb was the other of Johnny's employers as he and January shared Johnson's services.

Johnny's Adam's apple bobbed as he swallowed and finally looked at her instead of the floor. Not that it wasn't a perfectly nice floor with its clean, polished boards, but she considered it only polite when talking to people to aim the words at their face.

"Bo is fine," he said. "Nothing is wrong. Don't be scared. It's just...just..." He stopped and started again. "I've got news. Good news. I hope. But I got a favor to ask. Or I don't know if it's a favor, but maybe just a question."

January's mind raced through any possible grounds for his overwrought condition, until finally, it came to her. She thought she knew what caused his awkwardness. "Johnny Johnson—" Her voice caught. "Did you ask Evie Langley to marry you?"

His eyes widened. "How did you know?"

*He's only nineteen. Evie is only seventeen.* Those were the first things to flash through her mind, right up until she remembered how responsible they both were. Young, but hardworking and wise.

"Well, you have been courting her for a year."

In fact, ever since Evie nursed Johnny through a bullet wound he'd taken on January's behalf.

"Did she say yes?" January laughed and answered her own question. "Of course, she said yes. Anybody can tell she's head over heels for you."

Shades of pink covered Johnny's face in a vivid wave of color. To her mind, it looked better than the previous blotches. "They can? She is? Head over heels?"

"Yes." But then she sobered. "Now you're wondering if you've done the right thing. Wondering how you're going to support her and where you're going to find a place to live. Am I right?"

He nodded. "You're a doggone mind reader. How'd you know that?"

She tapped the side of her head. "Mind reader, you said it yourself."

"Aww, Miss January." He grinned.

A little more coaxing got his feet under her table and a fork in his hand.

"Now," she said, sitting down across from him, her plate not quite so laden as his with flapjacks, fruit syrup and fried eggs fresh from her buff Orpington hens, "when do the two of you plan on getting married?"

His blush bloomed again.

Going by his reaction, one could be prodded into believing the word married was slightly off color and not respectable. January held back a laugh. Well, he'd soon get over that. She sure enough had, when she'd married Shay Billings. And Lordy! how she still missed him, murdered only six months into their marriage.

"Evie will be eighteen in February." Johnny spread butter on his flapjacks and poured plum syrup over all. "We thought then."

"Ah. You have a few months to get things settled then."

"Yeah." Here he turned glum. "But do you know how hard it is to find someplace to live? We don't want to pile in with her folks and brothers. Don't want to live in some rat infested hovel, either. Or in your barn, no disrespect intended. The barn is fine for me, but it's no place for my wife." He had space in the tack room in her barn where he slept when he stayed over. Not bad, but he was correct in saying it wasn't fit for a new wife. Evie Langley deserved better. "Whatever I find, it's got to be near enough I can work for both you and Bo. Unless I can find one job that pays as much as the two put together."

January felt a sharp pang at the thought of him quitting. "I agree, even though I'd hate to lose your help. You're the reason I'm sometimes able to do different things."

By *different things* she meant building houses, bridges, and the occasional piece of fine furniture. And that wasn't even mentioning stuff like bringing murderers and shysters to justice and chasing down kidnappers, bank robbers, and horse thieves. Not activities she planned in advance, but jobs foisted upon her because there was no one else willing or able.

Or, she often thought, anyone stupid, stubborn and wild enough but herself to take it on.

"Trouble is," she said to Johnny, "the wages Bo and I

together pay may be enough for a single man, but not for someone with a wife. And what if you start a family?"

He blushed yet again. "We'll manage, Miss January."

"I know you will." A big smile lit her face, puckering the shiny S-shaped scar on her cheek. "And congratulations to you both, but I wish better for you. Let me think on this, all right? I'm sure we can figure something out."

"Yes, ma'am." Placing his knife and fork across his plate, Johnny stood up, reclaimed his coat and hat and went out to do the chores requiring heavy lifting, like emptying sacks of grain into barrels and mixing special food for the livestock according to their needs. A man of boundless energy, he'd clean the barn, too, and scrub scum from the watering trough. He liked to stay busy.

But nothing to alleviate his problems occurred to her over the next couple days. Johnny told her he was going to apply at the feed store in the next town over, and set off early one morning, hopes high, with her blessing. However, the only thing high was his temper when he got back in the afternoon.

"The place was filthy dirty." He shook his head in disgust. "Be a wonder if every animal fed his stuff ain't diseased. Had so many mice running around you'd crunch them underfoot if you didn't look out, and to top it off, he don't pay no more than I'm making now. A big waste of time."

He grumbled something else under his breath; something not fit for a lady's ears. January, by her own definition not much of a lady, wasn't offended. Not by his language, at least. Just by the thought of someone pawning sub-standard feed off onto the stock of hardworking ranchers. She'd never stand for it, and you could take that to the bank.

Still pondering Johnny and Evie's problem, on Friday afternoon she hitched her team of Belgiums to the wagon and drove the seven miles into town. Pen sat proudly panting on the seat beside her. They were picking up a 50-gallon drum of Portland cement ordered from Sears Roebuck with the intention of finishing a stone foundation for the barn she was building at her almost finished new house. Although, considering how cold it had gotten, that might have to wait until spring. Depended on if they got a fall warm-up.

In town, her business finished and the problem of how to unload the concrete now occupying her mind, she stopped the team outside the post office on the way out of town. Not that she expected to get mail. Correspondents were few and far between, but she figured she might as well check as long as she was here. Besides, folks often posted help wanted ads, or items they wanted to sell, on the cork board covering a full half of the post office wall. It was worth taking a look on Johnny's behalf.

Leaving Pen to guard the wagon, she climbed down and entered the small, boxy building. Always one to think ahead, she'd prepared a poster stating Johnny's qualifications to hang there. She was sure he'd soon find something suitable to his growing talents. But oh, how she'd miss him.

"The Johnson kid quitting? Or have you fired him?" Eldridge, the postmaster, had questions.

"He's got plans," she said, refusing to say what they

were. "But you may be sure I haven't fired him. He's an excellent worker and a friend."

"Hmmm," he muttered, as if doubtful.

January hoped she hadn't ruined Johnny's reputation by posting the ad on the post office wall.

This accomplished, she almost forgot to peek into the little box she rented for her mail. It took Eldridge saying, "You've got mail, Mrs. Billings. It's in your box. Got your key?"

All the little windowed boxes required a key. She shook her head no.

"I'll get it," he said.

To her surprise, a couple letters were waiting, both postmarked Spokane. And, something that set her nerves on edge, one struck her as official. Important, with a typewritten address. The other? She frowned, looking at it.

She could tell the postmaster, hovering near her hoping to have his curiosity satisfied, had questions as well.

"That's a real important man, writing to you," he said, pointing to the typewritten letter's return address. As if this comment would lead her to tell him all.

"Is it? I've never heard of him."

Disappointment showed on his face when she shrugged and stuffed the letter in her pocket to read when she got home.

She gave him a mocking flutter of the hand and left in a hurry.

Nosy old poop, she thought, pleased at thwarting him. She hadn't forgotten Postmaster Eldridge had been in Marvin Hammel's pocket when the rancher had been plotting to kill Shay and her. Though not, in all honesty, an active participant. Since then he sometimes went overboard in trying for atonement. Still, she found it hard to trust the postmaster, although he seemed honest enough nowadays. Besides, he always stared at her scarred face.

For years, from the time she was a kid until she met Shay and he convinced her the scar on her cheek was not her shame to bear, she'd hidden her face within the depths of an outmoded, outsized bonnet. One-half scarred, one-half beautiful—beautiful according to Shay anyhow—nowadays she went around uncovered. Not that she flaunted the S her own grandfather had carved on her cheek when she'd been a ten-year-old. Crazy old coot. But she didn't hide it, either. Mostly.

The route home led past her new, almost finished house at Kindred Creek bridge. As a plus, she'd erected a small shed at the back. Shelter for her horse on bad weather days when she worked inside. Thinking to save herself some labor when it came time to use the concrete, she backed the wagon into the shed and left it there, riding one of the Belgiums home and leading the other. Pen pranced alongside, cavorting like a puppy after being cooped up on the wagon seat for hours on end.

At home, spraddle-legged from riding the big dray horse bareback even if it wasn't but a couple miles, January got the critters brushed and fed. Cold from the ride, she called to Pen and hurried into the house. This had been one of the days Johnny worked for Bo, which meant the house was chilly, the fire long out. Sighing, she left her coat on as she built up the fire in the cookstove, and put a pot of bean soup on to heat.

It was only when she felt comfortable enough to

hang the coat on a backdoor hook that she heard something rustling and remembered the letters. Staring down at the slightly crumpled envelopes, her uneasy feeling returned. As Eldridge had pointed out, one letter was from a Spokane attorney, someone whose well-known name showed up in the newspaper quite often. The other bore no return address, just her own name and general delivery to The Falls, printed in pencil in a childish-looking hand. Both puzzled her.

In no hurry in case they happened to be bad news, she ate her soup first, feeling she might need the fortification, and washed her few dishes. Only then, with Pen snoozing on a rug at her feet, did she settle into the armchair with the letters in hand. Slitting open the envelopes, she dug out the one from the attorney, it having struck her as the more important of the two.

First she scanned the salutation.

*Dear Mrs. January Billings (nee Schutt):*

How odd to see her maiden name added.
And then the opening sentence.

*I am writing to notify you of the death of your grandfather, Mr. Joseph C. Flowers...*

January gasped. Her eyes froze on that one word. *Grandfather?* Your, as in *her,* grandfather?

She read another line, upon which her world spiraled. Her vision blurred and everything turned dark.

Dimly, she heard Pen bark a question, and bark again when January didn't respond.

Then she didn't hear anything for a while as her eardrums reverberated with the beat of her heart. With her anger—no—with her fury.

Joseph Flowers was her grandfather? *The* Joseph C. Flowers? Why hadn't she known this? Why hadn't her father ever told her? Why hadn't anybody ever told her?

Why hadn't she ever asked?

If what this letter said was true, why hadn't this grandfather gotten in touch when she needed him.

Because, and here she crumpled the letter and threw it across the room, she blamed well didn't need him now.

# CHAPTER 3

JANUARY COULDN'T SAY HOW LONG SHE SAT THERE, PEN'S head a warm spot resting on her thigh. The only warm spot on her entire body, truth be told.

After a while, Pen's soft whine urging her, she got up, walked over and retrieved the letter. As she unraveled the paper, it rustled between her clenched fingers. Of thick paper, an expensive stationery grade, the letterhead announced Mr. Delbert Avery, Attorney, and his place of business blazoned across the top. The scent of tobacco, bay rum, and money clung to the paper. She hadn't imagined it then.

Was she impressed? Maybe a little.

All of which did nothing to stop the shock still roiling through her. And, not to be forgotten, the anger. All from just the first paragraph. She read it again, mostly to reassure herself it wasn't a figment of her imagination.

Sure enough, the words were the same.

*Dear Mrs. January Billings (nee Schutt):*

*I am writing to notify you of the death of your grand-father, Mr. Joseph C. Flowers, a gentleman of whom you may have heard as news of his exploits have often appeared in the local newspapers. You may also have heard him mentioned as Fireweed Flowers.*

*I am told this relationship may come as a surprise to you, but be assured your connection to Mr. Flowers is well-researched and indisputable.*

*Per Mr. Joseph Flowers's last will and testament, as well as separate instructions he's left in my care, I will need to speak with you in person at your earliest convenience. Please telegraph ahead to arrange a meeting. The reading of the will is Friday next at 11 a.m. Your presence is impera-tive and to your best advantage.*

*I look forward to meeting you.*

*Your servant,*

*Delbert Avery, Attorney-at-law*

Could she believe what the letter said? Was any part of it true? Questions rattled and tumbled through January's mind. Surely it was all some kind of joke. A prank meant to embarrass her. But it didn't strike her as funny, and embarrassment was not her prime reaction. Who would do such a thing, anyway? No one came to mind.

Is this how rich people act? She'd only known one really rich person before, and he'd tried to kill her which, anyway you looked at it, was aberrant behavior. Now this.

January snorted, a sign of disgust so loud her dog cocked her head in question. So sad to discover the kind of people she came from. One grandfather she never knew existed and another who'd carved her up like a Sunday roast. What a pair! Depressing, to say the least.

She eyed the date on the letter. The meeting Attorney Avery spoke of was scheduled for this coming Friday. Only three days away, if it was even real. And if it was real, why get in touch with her now? Why, after he —Mr. Joseph C. Flowers—was dead?

She needed someone to talk to. Someone who came from money and could, if he would, tell her if this was indeed how rich people might act. Well, she knew of someone, didn't she? A face rose up in her mind's eye. Granted, a face she'd spent the last month trying not to think about, but there it was. Planted like a weed seed.

Oh, he was not as rich as anyone connected to Flowers Enterprises. She didn't think so, anyhow. But he still possessed a background that included more wealth than anyone else she knew. At one time, he'd moved in circles where upon occasion men dressed in tuxedoes and ladies wore evening gowns while eating their dinner. Or no. They didn't eat. They *dined*.

She needed to talk with Eli Pasco.

The mere thought of seeing him again set her innards to quaking.

She'd gotten to know Pasco in the spring, when his horse had been stolen by a young girl who, in her turn, was kidnapped by a very bad group of people. When Eli asked the sheriff for help retrieving his horse, and before anyone knew the girl was in danger, January had been called upon to dust off her deputy's badge and investigate. Both the girl and the horse had been recovered, but it hadn't been easy. Not for Eli and most certainly not for her.

Breaking out of her shell, January had danced with

him at the sheriff's wedding, and she'd thought...he'd indicated— Well.

But then there'd been a mix-up last month that concerned his father's ex-wife. Eli and she had argued. It hadn't ended well and January hadn't seen hide nor hair of him since.

Pen, sensing January's indecision, snuggled closer and licked her hand.

"What do you think, Pen? Do you think he'll talk to me if I go see him?"

The dog looked up at being directly addressed.

"Do you feel up for a walk? He likes you, you know. He took good care of you when... well, you know when. You could be a go-between. Are you agreeable?"

The dog made a little sound of what January decided to take for assent.

"All right, then. We'll go first thing in the morning." Although, if she hadn't known such a thing just wasn't done, she'd rather have put on her coat and gone right now.

Settling this much made it possible for January to open the second envelope. The untidy printing on the envelope had led her to believe it might be the hand of one of the local schoolchildren. In only a few months, there'd be a Christmas party for the students and folks were asked for small donations to buy nuts, fruit, and candy to put in brown paper bags and hand out. She'd donated to the cause before, though never been a part of the bag-filling squad. A party in itself, from what she understood.

This was no such letter. Quite the contrary.

No salutation.

*Stay away. You aren't part of the Flowers family. You're a*
*nobody and an interloper. Show up here and it is apt to*
*prove bad for your health. Stay away.*

No signature, either, although the first two words
were a clue not to expect one. The one thing she got
from the note was that she evidently had more relatives
than just the dead grandfather, and he, she, or they had
no interest in meeting, let alone sharing even their
names with her.

Prove bad for her health, eh? January snickered. A
clumsy little warning. Obviously, they didn't know who
they were dealing with.

What would Eli have to say about this?

If he'd even speak with her.

* * *

UNABLE TO SLEEP, January got an early start in the
morning. By the light of a single lantern, she milked
Bossy and put the milk through the separator, then
saddled Hoot, Shay's silvery gray gelding. This wasn't
one of Johnny's regular days at the ranch, but she left a
note in his room in the barn in case he showed up
anyway as he sometimes did. The note didn't give much
away. Certainly no mention of whom she meant to visit.
Simply a terse little missive saying she'd be home by
afternoon. If he wasn't here when she got back, she'd
tear up the note. No need for him to know she'd been
gone or to wonder about her absence. This development didn't seem like anything she wanted spread
about and discussed. Not by anyone, even amongst
friends.

With Pen prancing at the gelding's heels, they passed through town before many were awake. Most businesses were still closed, although lights in T.T. Thurston's mercantile gave notice he, and maybe his wife, were at the store doing housekeeping duties before opening for the day. Squirt and his helper Sam at the livery were already shoveling out stalls, and the café was open for business. She noticed the silhouette of two men at a table inside. One was probably Adam Southbrook, the town marshal.

Ignoring the fragrance of coffee and fresh-baked goods the café emitted, she heeled Hoot into a lope and with Pen panting to keep up, soon was heading toward the forested foothills where it was noticeably cooler. January could see her breath.

A long ride for this early in the morning, and cold. January didn't allow herself to think of the reception she might get, glad to concentrate on keeping fingers on the reins from going numb. And then, perhaps before she was ready, she arrived.

As had been the case the first time she rode up to the Winkler, now the Pasco, ranch, a cat sat in the open barn door washing its face. Smoke rose from the brick chimney, and a glance showed the front porch had new board steps up to the door. Hoot stopped and she dismounted, flipping the reins over the rail at the front of the house. A vastly improved house from the first time she'd seen it. Pen, tongue lolling, at her side—she knew the old dog was tired and ready for a sleep—she stood a moment before drawing a deep breath and raising her fist to knock.

The door opened before her knuckles touched wood. Eli Pasco looked out at her, his face curiously blank. He stared down at her for what seemed minutes, but which logical thinking decreed must only have been seconds. Then he swung open the door and moved aside.

"It's cold out there. You'd better come in." He made a sweeping motion with his arm in invitation. "The dog, too."

Gulping, she stepped into the small entry hall, whipped off her hat before thinking how mussed her hair must be and smashing it back down until it touched her ears. Her mission here seemed stupid. Why had she ever thought he'd help her? Why should he, if he even could?

"I'm sorry to bother you," she said in a rush. "But I couldn't think..." No. The rest of that sentence sounded rude. "You...I need advice and you..." She fell silent. No. That didn't sound right either. Why hadn't she thought out what she needed to say? Lord knows she'd had plenty of time on the ride out here.

Clearly, he wondered the same.

"Has something happened, January? Another band of kidnappers or horse thieves bothering you? Bank been robbed? Somebody gunning for you?" His voice flowed around her, cool and sounding vaguely amused. But his eyes, dark as bitter chocolate, bored into her. Intense, as if he sensed her distress.

It struck her that he was nervous. Not as much as she, but still not as comfortable as he let on. Somehow reassured, January, digging deep, gathered a mantle of calm and finally managed a complete sentence.

"If you're too busy and want me to leave, I understand," she said. "No kidnappers or horse thieves to worry about, and the bank hasn't been robbed. Not that I've heard, anyway." She tried a tentative smile.

His expression lightened, but then his brows drew together over narrowed eyes as he cocked his head. "You left one out. Is somebody gunning for you?"

Oh, he was quick, all right.

"I don't know. Maybe." She drew the word out slowly. "Or if not right now, there might be in the near future. It depends."

"On what? No. Wait." He closed the door behind her with a decisive slam. "Come in. We'll go into the kitchen where it's warm and you can tell me what's got you in an uproar. And don't tell me it's nothing. I can see it is. You wouldn't be here otherwise."

Did that last sound kind of regretful? She thought maybe so.

He led the way, calling Pen to come along with him —which she willingly did—and offering a bowl of water and finding a rug for her to lie on near the kitchen range.

January studied him as he tended the old dog, noticing he could've used a shave and that his dark hair was a trifle long. But his house was in order and truthfully, he didn't seem in a hurry to run her off. Her innards eased as several, though not all, of the knots in her stomach came untied.

As in any well-run household, coffee warmed on the back burner. He poured some into a pretty cup and offered sugar, which January refused. Over on the rug, Pen's eyes closed as she settled into a nap.

Eli sat at the table across from her. Glancing around, she saw his Mauser Broomhandle C96 semi-automatic weapon in its cross-draw belly holster hanging from a hook near the back door. Handy, but at least he didn't feel called upon to wear the rig in his own house. Not today, at least.

Maybe, like her, he didn't feel comfortable talking about their last meeting since he got right down to business.

"Have you turned in your deputy badge?" he started off. "Or is there another trail you need to follow? If so, why come to me?"

She couldn't decide if he meant the questions as mere conversational gambits or if they were a warning he didn't want involved. "I've still got the badge. I don't even know who I'd turn it in to, but I'm not on anyone's trail. Not since...since Holzer and Peel." There was another name she didn't mention, even though it belonged with the other two outlaws. The name that hovered between them. Ruby Pasco. His father's ex-wife.

The woman he and she had come to a sort of cross-roads over.

Staring at him like he was staring at her, she figured they both were remembering the last time they'd seen each other.

Eli blinked. She blinked.

"I'm here about something completely different. Something personal," she said at last. "Saying I'm in a state of astonishment is an understatement and I don't know what to do."

His head cocked. A silent question.

In answer, January got the letters from her pocket and held them toward him. "I need advice about these. Please, will you read them?" They dangled from her fingers as he hesitated. A second passed. Then more.

She snatched the letters back and turned to go. "You don't want bothered. I understand."

She knew her face had turned color. Her eyes felt hot. There was only one thing to do. "Come, Pen," she told the dog, and for the first time ever, Pen simply sighed.

Startled, January looked back to discover Eli holding the old dog by her collar as Pen struggled to rise. "She's tired," he said. "Let her rest. Let me see what you have. It's no bother." He hesitated. "You took me by surprise, is all. I didn't think you..." He let the rest drift away.

Glancing at the clock ticking on a shelf over the sink, he said, "It's early yet. My guess is this is real important."

Slowly, she nodded. "Maybe. I just don't know what to make of it. Or if any of what this letter says is true. I hoped you might be able to tell me."

"Why me?" he started, then waved the question away as if erasing it. "Never mind. Let me see."

Not sure whether she felt relief or embarrassment, January handed the attorney's letter to him. Maybe she'd show him the other note, the threat. Or maybe not, depending on his reaction to the first.

Eli took his time, examining the outside of the envelope before extracting the sheet of paper inside. His fingers rubbed the stationery, feeling, as she had done, the quality of the paper. Then he read, eyes widening just a little, and it seemed as if, just for a moment, he quit breathing. His eyes flicked toward her. His mouth moved but made no sound. *Flowers?*

He looked up. "Well," he said. And then again, "Well."

January nodded. "Is this real? Can you tell?"

The corner of his mouth ticked upward. "I'm familiar with the attorney's name and reputation. He took over the defense of a man I brought in a year or so ago. Won the case, too, so he's good. And if there's anybody in this part of the country who doesn't know of Joseph Fireweed Flowers, I can't imagine what rock he lives under. You didn't know he was your grandfather?"

She shook her head. "So it is real."

"I'd say so." He watched her, his brows drawing together. "There's only one way to find out for sure. Show up at that meeting."

Her stomach roiled and unaware, she pressed a hand against her middle. "Oh." It came out small, like a child's whimper.

"Sit down," he said. "I'll pour more coffee. You're not going to tell me you're afraid to meet with this attorney, are you? January Billings, who'll track down murderers and face the guns of a whole outlaw gang, afraid?"

He sounded teasing, but January wasn't in the mood as she passed him the letter with its childish penciled scrawl. She plopped down in the chair again and gave a sigh. "Huh. Laugh after you read this one. It's bit different."

Eli perched on the table's edge, his perusal making quick work of the unsigned message. Slowly, folding the letter and returning it to the envelope, he handed it back. "Just thinking aloud, January, but maybe you should thank whoever wrote this."

"Thank him?"

"For giving fair warning. You'll know to watch your back."

"If I go to the meeting. To my advantage, the

attorney says, but could be the warning is the true message."

"That's what you need to find out. I'd say it's a bad idea to let this pass. The Flowers family—the Flowers organization—is too important to ignore. Any tie to them at all, let alone this, well, you'll have to follow up. Before they follow up on you."

"Important?" January heard something in his voice. "Or do you mean dangerous."

His answer didn't hesitate. "Both."

"I'd rather pretend I didn't get this."

"Which one?"

"Either. Both." This time when she rose, Pen came when called and ambled behind her to the door.

"You'll go," Eli said when they were outside and he'd lifted the tired old dog into the saddle in front of her. He sounded certain.

January looked down at him, into his dark eyes. "I will?"

He chuckled then. "Sure you will. If your curiosity isn't running away with you right now, I miss my guess. You'll have to attend the meeting and see what it all means."

* * *

ELI WATCHED as January passed from sight, her back straight, head held high. He couldn't help wondering if he should've told her what he knew about the Flowers family. It hadn't seemed his place. He had his own prejudices, but didn't want to spread them to her. If this all worked out, she'd have to deal with the family on her own terms. Come to her own decisions.

Anyway, he hadn't dealt one on one with any of the grandsons, although he'd heard about one of them from Mimi Jonque. She came to Spokane from the same town his father called home. The same place Ruby Pasco had scorned. Except Mimi's name hadn't been Mimi Jonque then. Mimi told him once she had reason to be grateful to the Flowers family, but sometimes he wondered if her gratitude was misplaced.

He might finally find out.

What he'd been able to tell January about the Flowers family had made her see she needed to attend the meeting Delbert Avery had spoken of. No matter what she decided to do about the clan, the situation needed clarified. It needed settled.

And he intended to be around when it was.

# CHAPTER 4

Eli had the right of it when it came to her burgeoning curiosity. January had always wondered about her mother's family. All her life she'd known Anita Schutt died when January was only two years old, but nothing more than that. She had no memory of her. Up on the hill above the new house, Anita had been laid to rest with no mention of her maiden name on the headstone.

When she'd asked her dad about her mother, he spoke with fondness, but never with details. And most definitely, never of Anita's former life. To January, Anita had been simply, "Your mother."

It seemed clear to January, in possession of the little the attorney had said in his letter, that Anita must have run away from the Flowers family. And they had let her.

Also, in retrospect, January realized she'd always been discouraged from asking questions. She wondered now if the reason her father and she had hidden themselves away had been not so much about him hiding from a possible murder charge, but from the reach of Joseph Flowers. Her other grandfather.

"Well, Pen, I'm going to ask those questions if I ever get the chance." She patted the dog who lay across the front of her saddle. Pen's head rested on January's thigh as they rode home from Eli's ranch. The horse's gait was not, she supposed, the most comfortable position for either of them. "Or maybe I'll *make* the chance. What do you think about that?"

The dog blinked sleepy eyes at her.

A brief stop at the train depot on the outskirts of The Falls gave information on the most timely train to Spokane to attend the Friday appointment with Mr. Delbert Avery. But what she didn't do was send a telegraph to the attorney. Rude of her, she knew, as well as posing a problem for Mr. Avery, but somehow, simply appearing seemed a better choice. A safer choice.

Based on the contents of the letter warning her to stay away, Eli had raised several more questions in her mind. Best, he'd advised, if she made time to scout the area before meeting any of the people concerned. See what she could discover about the Flowers family members in advance. For instance, pinpoint which one most likely to have written the words, *show up and it's apt to prove bad for your health.*

What might they do? How far would they go? And what would she do about them?

Needless to say, Johnny Johnson whooped with surprise over her announcement when she asked him to look after the place and keep Pen company while she was gone.

Johnny's jaw dropped. "Joseph Flowers? You mean

that rich guy from Spokane who owns a bunch of the Silver Valley? And a good section of the Palouse? And half of Spokane? He's your grandfather?"

"Apparently. He's dead now."

"Well, yeah. Come to think of it, Bo mentioned something about an obituary two or three or four weeks ago. He said he read it in a newspaper announcement."

The newspaper! January thanked him for the idea. She figured it gave her a place to start when looking up the Flowers family history.

"Does this mean you're rich now? On account of him being your grandpa, I mean. If this attorney wants you to come to a meeting, I'll bet it's the reading of the will. Your grandpa probably left you something." Johnny's enthusiasm overflowed. "Wait till I tell Bo."

January snorted. "More likely it means he wants me to sign a paper saying I won't stick my fingers into the Flowers's pie." She had no intention of mixing in their business, certain the only result would be trouble. Trouble for her, anyhow.

"Would you?" Johnny asked then. "Sign a paper, I mean."

She started to say yes, then hesitated. Would she? "Maybe. Probably. It depends."

"On what?"

"On what best serves the interests of the people involved."

Johnny's brow puckered. "Such as?"

"Such as making sure people who work for the company don't lose their jobs. On whether the business does good or bad." She'd had experience with a rich man riding roughshod over the little guy, after all. Marvin Hammel provided a perfect example. "Besides, I don't know anything about any of this, which is why I'm asking you to look after this place while I try to find out."

"Well, sure," he said, as if offended she might think he'd turn her down. "Me'n Pen'll get along fine."

"I know you will."

Thursday morning found her at the depot prepared to depart, Hoot having been safely housed with Squirt at the livery for the duration of her absence.

"No worries, Mrs. Billings," Squirt had said when she dropped the horse off and gathered up the carpet bag carrying, among other things, her good walking dress. Her only walking dress, in fact, which was termed a suit in the fashion world. Or so Pinky Langley had said when she persuaded January to buy it. Seeming an indulgence at the time, January was glad to have something decent to wear on this occasion.

Squirt gave the gelding a friendly slap on the neck. "I'll take good care of this fine fellow. How long you gonna be gone?"

She shrugged. "Not too long, I trust. A couple days, maybe three."

Squirt gave her a look. "You thinking there might be trouble?"

At this she smiled a little. Squirt, obviously reading more into her travels than she intended, always kept his eyes open and on the lookout for trouble. "I hope not," she said, and left it at that.

Not having been on a train for some time, January took a seat feeling a measure of trepidation. She huddled into a corner with her scarred cheek to the window. There were only two passenger cars connected to the engine on this day, neither very full. The train also hauled two flat cars laden with cedar logs, three cattle cars, and a caboose carrying the daily mail. A toot of the whistle, a jerk of the locomotive wheels and they were off.

She filled the time watching the land change from forests to ranches to farms, and making mental lists. When they reached Spokane, she left the station not only with a destination in mind, but a list of things to accomplish before she met the attorney. First off, a hotel, right in the downtown area where she could drop off her carpet bag and leave her hands free. She'd left her .38 at home, but as always, had her pocket gun secured in her boot holster. It did not, as she soon discovered, prove comfortable walking for any distance, the holster seeming determined to rub a blister.

At the hotel, chosen upon Eli's recommendation, the clerk looked askance at her meager luggage and the simple clothing she wore. One item was the brightly colored Norwegian cap Pinky had knitted for her. The one with earflaps that when pulled down covered most of her scarred cheek. Fortunately, it was cold, providing an excuse.

The clerk arched a questioning brow when she asked for a room, looking her up and down as if doubtful of her provenance. "This is an expensive hotel, madame. You might be better served to find another..."

January didn't wait to hear more. "I think you'll find my money spends as well as anyone's," she said crisply. "This hotel was recommended to me and I like the location. I just hope the cleanliness is satisfactory and the food edible. I'm a bit picky with where I lay my head or with what I put in my mouth." She reached in her pocketbook and pulled out a fistful of cash.

He hadn't expected this. "Clean? Of course. And the food," he added stiffly, "is exemplary. You'll see." Left with the choice of expelling her without cause, or of her questioning the quality the hotel, he chose to go with the money.

Of course he did, she thought. Was it any wonder she avoided cities?

Barely glancing around her assigned room, January deposited her carpet bag onto a folding stand and trudged off to find the newspaper office. She found it in a triangular-shaped building sitting on a busy street corner. Upon her request, a middle-aged female clerk brought a stack of back issues to her. The ones where Joseph Flowers' death had made headline news were easy to find. She settled in at a table and began to read.

Lung disease had killed him, apparently. Tuberculosis. His history, dating from his first mother lode and the development of underground mining—possibly the start of his lung problems—to his expansive land acquisitions, building projects, and everything in-between, was repeated over and over in several issues.

So, January thought, smiling a little to herself, he'd been a good businessman and rich. But she read nothing to say whether he was a good man or not. Yes, he supported the local orphan's home and a soup kitchen, but she was given to understand that was often more a political ploy to enhance one's reputation than purely charitable.

In the later issues, a few articles had expanded and began listing his family and the surviving members. Here her breath quickened. This was the most important thing for her to learn.

He'd had four children, she read, the newspaper

rattling as she held it in front of her face. Two sons, two daughters. The newspaper put names to them, Joseph Jr. being the first born son. Of course, she thought with an inner snort. Did men, especially very rich men, ever give their eldest son anything other than their own name?

The other son was Cameron. Next was the eldest daughter, Beverly. And then Anita, the baby of the family who had, according to the newspaper, eloped with an unsatisfactory suitor and died young.

Anger flared. Unsatisfactory suitor? Her dad, who'd ruined himself and killed his own father in order to save her, their child? There was nothing in the paper about that. The reporter had one thing right, however. Anita had died young.

So, evidently, had all the other of Flowers' children, along with their mother. Joseph, the report said, had never remarried.

Impatiently, she shook the paper.

As it turned out, all the children had lived long enough to spawn one child each.

Joseph Flowers III, John Byerly Flowers, Calvin A. Masterson, and, she read, rumors of another unnamed heir. Did that mean her? Plain old January Schutt Billings?

She thought so. She feared so.

Joseph III, according to a reporter's implication in the newspaper gossip section, had every intention of making a power play to sweep the others off the table and take over running the whole business for himself. Easier said than done, perhaps. She'd be interested to see how that played out.

John, whom the reporter called John B, was often in

trouble with the law. Unpaid debts connected with a certain entertainment palace mostly. Of course, no charges ever stuck for long, victims eventually being bought off by the Flowers money. Or so the implication went, cautiously stated.

Calvin was a gambler who'd had more than one lawsuit filed against him and, as witnessed by his cousin John B, been in at least one gunfight. He'd killed a man and served a few months in jail.

January wondered if Eli knew anything about him? Or any other of what seemed to be a fine set of cousins. *Fine cousins. A joke.*

Eli. She wished he was with her now. He had considerable experience dealing people like this although, if she read between the lines, they were no different than the common criminals she'd dealt with in the past.

Casting the idea from her mind, she decided she'd read enough and had plenty to think about. Besides, the newspaper's clerk was fidgeting like a six-year-old in need of the privy, all signs indicating she should leave. Evidently, the woman's shift was over and she wanted to go home.

January, not being an inconsiderate person, thanked the woman and, tipping her a dime, left the news office and headed toward the hotel.

Minutes later, still mulling over all she'd learned— provided she could take the Flowers family stories as truth and not a combination of some sort of lurid scandalmongering mixed with whitewashing—January was quite surprised to find herself standing still and staring through the plate glass window of a ladieswear boutique.

That's what the sign said. *Mamzelle's Parisian*

*Boutique.* The large window in itself looked expensive, and beyond the glass, the gown displayed on a headless form was certain to be outrageously priced. But, maybe for the first time in her life, January coveted an item beyond her normal attire. Her split skirts and simple shirtwaists had always satisfied her. They were neat, comfortable and inexpensive. For the most part, her undergarments did not include corsets related to armor. Her wardrobe suited her life and work.

She started to walk away. One step, two.

Still—

She stopped. Turned for one last look...and came face to face with a woman peering back at her through the window. An exotic woman with shiny black hair piled atop her head, and very dark eyes set on a slant.

The woman smiled and crooked her finger.

Unable to resist the invitation, January entered the store. *The boutique.*

"You like the dress?" The woman pinned her with a steely gaze, which paused at the scar then moved on. "I think it must have been made just for you. You should try it on."

"Oh no. I don't need a dress like this. Not at all. I just wanted...that is, it's very pretty. I simply admired it."

"Exactly." The woman winked. "It's not a question of need. Sometimes a woman just wants what she wants."

Noticing the woman's French accent had slipped a cog, January resisted, but couldn't stop herself from touching the delicate lace of the overskirt. Except for the sleeves and the skirt, the dress was quite plain, without the train often seen on stylish gowns. It struck her as the perfect dancing dress, being a little shorter than some. The gathered sleeves and a flaring, fluid overskirt made of lace set the style apart, but the color was what drew her. A deep forest green she believed might match her eyes.

What would Eli think if he saw her wearing such a gown? Or would he even notice?

Another thought of Eli Pasco to be cast aside, yet somehow she found herself standing in a tiny private room wearing only her unmentionables, with the dark-haired woman slipping the green dress over her head.

They stood together in the dressing room, staring into a large mirror.

"It's perfect." The exotic clerk nodded in satisfaction. "I'll have the gown delivered to your hotel."

January kept blinking. *Is that me? The color really does match my eyes.* She glanced at the woman. "How do you know I'm staying at a hotel?"

The enigmatic smile gleamed. "You have a certain look. I can tell you're not a city woman. That's all."

January smiled, too. "You're right. I'm not."

Dressed once more in her ordinary clothes, she dug in her pocketbook yet again, this time for an astounding amount of cash, compounded by the addition of a pair of dainty dancing shoes, silk stockings, and a pretty little doo-dad to wear in her hair.

"You'll knock him off his feet," the clerk said. "Count on it."

"Hmmm." January grinned at the idea, at the same time wondering why Eli Pasco rose up in her mind. Why not Squirt?

Well, maybe not Squirt.

"More likely I'll end up dancing around my parlor by myself. Or just me with my dog as a partner."

The woman laughed, possibly in disbelief.

January was almost to the hotel before it struck her that the woman hadn't seemed to mind the scar.

* * *

THE SPOKANE HOTEL, a modern miracle of hospitality, boasted a telephone in every room. When its peal summoned her only a few minutes after she'd unlocked the door, she didn't know what to think.

Cautiously, she lifted the handset. "Hello?" Embarrassed at how timorous she sounded, she reminded herself this was, after all, only the second or third time in her entire life she'd spoken on a telephone.

"Mrs. Billings," the snooty clerk from earlier said into her ear, "a package has arrived for you from Mamzelle's Parisian Boutique. Do you wish to accept the package? I can have a bell boy bring it to your room."

He sounded a touch more respectful than upon their first meeting.

"Yes, please do," she almost whispered. A strange relief filled her. For a moment she'd thought the Flowers family had somehow tracked her here and knew she wasn't ready to meet them. Not yet.

"Thank you." The man hung up.

January didn't leave her room that evening. She'd brought a book and read it, and when her stomach calmed enough to feel hunger, with a sense of triumph she called down to the clerk's desk and asked for her supper to be sent up.

Although she felt quite accomplished using the telephone on her own, the boy who brought her meal put her wise regarding leaving the dishes on the floor outside the room.

Morning seemed as if it would never arrive but, in the nature of the universe, it did. And time rushed toward the eleven o'clock meeting as if it rode on wheels.

# CHAPTER 5

January, dodging around a sleeping hotel clerk, went out early, while it was still dark. She easily found her way along the mostly deserted Spokane streets. A lowering sky threatened an early snow before the day advanced much further. She could taste the coming snow, and smell it on the cold air.

Few pedestrians shared the streets with her, although the streetcars were already running. Men emerged from boarding houses carrying lunch pails and headed toward the river. Millworkers, she supposed, both saw and grist, working the day shift. Dray horses hauled laden wagons to and fro, teamsters calling and urging them on. New buildings, brick to replace wooden ones destroyed in the great fire of '89, filled every block.

January, nose wrinkling, was astonished to find the city streets smelled more strongly of horse manure than her barn at home, where fresh straw was laid down every day. As if that weren't enough, the sheer size of the buildings overwhelmed her, and she felt almost dizzy in the midst of so much activity. And yet, all the strangeness excited her, too, like a tingle along her nerves.

No one paid her any mind, although she watched them. It never, as she knew all too well, hurt to scout the terrain when anticipating trouble. Only a fool would walk unprepared into a situation like she faced today, and January Schutt Billings was no fool.

She hoped not, anyway.

Or, she admitted a second later, maybe she was. Likely she should simply have ignored this whole thing. Pretended she never received the attorney's letter with its hints of reward. Ditto the clumsy letter of warning.

Curiosity drove her. After all, who wouldn't want to know about their roots? The well from which they'd sprung? One side of her family wasn't particularly savory and she had the scars to prove it. Would this side be any better? Any worse? Considerably richer, at any rate, from all accounts.

Choosing by what she gleaned from the newspaper stories she read yesterday, she suspected her cousin Calvin had authored the warning.

But what did she really know? She was sure all three cousins would prefer she never showed up. Any of them —or all—may have had a hand in the writing.

She sighed, watching her breath's condensation dissipate ahead of her as she walked and took note of her surroundings.

Ignoring the letter wasn't in the cards, she had decided. At some point, whether she wanted involved or not, she'd be forced to face the threat. Apparently, nothing could be settled without her participation, and it was certain the Flowers heirs wouldn't allow their inheritance to float in the wind.

When she'd seen what she needed to see, which mainly meant searching out the attorney's office, January went back to the hotel. In the dining room, she choked coffee and something called Eggs Benedict down her throat before returning to her room to get ready.

At any other time, she would've quite liked the eggs.

\* \* \*

JANUARY HADN'T BEEN this nervous when facing down an outlaw shooting at her point blank. But then she'd had a gun in her own hand and her aim had been better than his.

She'd donned her good walking dress—no, fashion folks were calling the garb a lady's suit—and to tell the truth, it was mighty uncomfortable. Made of a fine wool, it was too hot since it consisted of a plain, slim-fitting woolen dress with a long, heavier woolen jacket over it. The jacket had a nipped waist and was held closed by fancy black frogs. The suit itself was a very dark red with black trim at the neck and cuffs.

January knew she looked pretty fine in it, but couldn't wait to get outside and cool off. The wool was making her sweat and the dress itched in places she couldn't reach.

Finally, it was time to leave. She pinned a plain, curled brim hat over her hair, checked the pocket pistol in her boot, and left the room without a second glance in the mirror.

In the hours since her earlier outing, a wet snow had

begun falling, covering the ground to the point she had to watch her step. The wind, blowing strongly out of the northeast, stirred the snow and forced her to hold her hat on with one hand as the pin threatened to come loose. So occupied, she didn't pay much attention to the man standing outside the office building where a sign announced Delbert Avery, Attorney-at-Law, in gold leaf letters. Not until he opened the door for her and she got in out of the wind.

"Eli," she said then on a gasp. "You're here. I mean, what are you doing here?" Then, on a tiny gasp, "I hardly recognized you." He wore a suit, well-fitted and as suave as any of the important looking men who were passing through the spacious hall. His chin was closely shaved and he'd gotten a haircut. One thing different. The bulge of his shoulder holster barely showed, invisible unless you looked for it, which she did. Not his Mauser Broomhandle, then. Something of a smaller caliber.

He took her arm and led her toward an oversized, glass-fronted door near the front of the hall. He'd evidently arrived early and already knew where to go. "I thought you might need someone to provide moral support. And watch your back. Am I wrong?"

"I don't know. I guess we'll soon see." Relieved beyond measure to see him, she smiled a bit timorously. "But I don't think you're mistaken. I'm just sorry to bother you. Thank you for coming."

"No bother. Later on, I'm meeting a man who wants Windswept to service one of his mares this spring. This is just a little something extra as long as I'm here anyway."

It didn't feel like a little something extra to January.

Some of the butterflies were already settling in her stomach thanks to Eli's presence.

Avery's office space, they discovered, took up a good half of the building's ground floor. Bolstered by Eli's confidence, she went through the fancy door, entering a reception area containing a sofa and a couple upholstered chairs set ready to put anyone who had to wait at ease. A thick rug lay underfoot. A middle-aged male secretary, or maybe a clerk, was speaking loudly into a telephone receiver, covering Eli's whisper in January's ear.

"May I say you're looking very classy today, Mrs. Billings? I want you to know and remember that. Don't let anybody buffalo you," he said.

She widened her eyes. "You think they'll try?" *Classy?* A little shiver swept through her.

"I'm sure of it."

So was she. The note from one of the cousins proved the intention. Taking a deep breath, she stepped toward the secretary as he hung up the telephone handset and rose to greet her. Maybe he thought she looked classy, too. "I'm January Billings," she said to him. "I believe Mr. Avery is expecting me."

"J...Mrs. Billings...we hadn't heard from you." It sounded like an accusation. He stared at her, blinking rapidly as he took in her scarred face. "We thought you weren't coming."

She wasn't surprised when he included himself in the *we*. He had the look of a man whose boss spoke to him in confidence. January supposed that made him a clerk then, not just a lowly secretary.

"I almost didn't," she said.

"We weren't sure..." he continued. "That is, hold on.

Mr. Avery will be right with you. Let me just go apprise him of your arrival. He'll be most relieved."

He sprinted through one of the doors off the reception area.

January's eyes rolled upward. "Apprise him of my arrival?"

"Tell him you're here." Eli explained, as if she didn't know. He grinned. "So he'll be relieved."

"Ha." It wasn't really funny, but the wordplay helped her relax.

In seconds, the clerk had returned, holding the door for the attorney to precede him. Delbert Avery walked in, a greeting already on his lips. For a second he appeared nonplussed at seeing Eli, then his eyes brightened as he took in January's appearance.

Was she not, perhaps, the disaster he must have been expecting?

"My dear lady," he gushed. "How wonderful to see you. When I had no reply to my letter I was afraid you might think it all a hoax and refuse to respond."

No sense beating around the bush, January thought. "It crossed my mind. If it hadn't been for a note I received at the same time, I would have."

Avery cocked his head like a curious bird. "A note?"

"A warning to stay away."

He was quiet a long moment. "I see," he said at last, and turned his attention to Eli. "And you are...?"

"A friend," January answered.

"A friend and bodyguard." Eli coolly expanded on the answer, surprising her.

Avery's pale eyes narrowed. "You look familiar, sir. Have we met?"

"Not formally. We were in the same courtroom a couple years ago. I'm Eli Pasco."

"Pasco." The light dawned. "You're the bounty hunter who brought in my client for the Landro versus Pendergast trial."

"I am."

January, her gaze going from one to the other, formed the quick opinion Mr. Delbert Avery was not entirely displeased by this revelation.

He sighed. "Well, Mr. Pasco, I pray your services as bodyguard are never required. Mrs. Billings, if you would come with me, I have some details regarding this situation with your grandfather to explain. Joseph asked me to speak to you privately, before you meet your cousins at the reading of the will."

She looked at Eli, but he merely nodded. "I'll wait. If there's trouble, January, just give a holler."

The attorney's gray brows arched. "I'm not expecting trouble. Not here, at least. Meanwhile, Benjamin will bring coffee," Avery paused, "after he brings some for Mrs. Billings and me."

It was a hint, one that sent his hovering clerk off into yet another room at the trot.

Avery led the way down a hall to the furthermost office, where he invited January to sit.

The leather chair was too big; uncomfortable in that she was forced to perch on the edge, her back stiff. Although on second thought, she didn't mind the discomfort. It kept her alert.

"First of all, I have in my possession a letter Joseph left for you," the attorney said when they'd settled in with their coffee, so promptly served by the secretary January knew it had already been prepared.

January frowned. "A letter from my grandfather?"

"Yes. But he wants you to have it after the reading of the will. He thinks...thought...it would help you understand the motivation behind the dispositions he's made to the family more fully."

"Did he?" Her comment came out dry. "And did he expect me to comply with whatever he's dictated?"

"Of course." Avery sent a wary glance toward her. "That's why you're here, isn't it? Because of the..." He paused as if unsure of how to phrase the rest of the question.

January thought she knew. "Because of the sentence that said I could expect something to my advantage?"

He sat back, his chair tilting as he nodded. "Yes."

Her heart thudded. "Then it may interest you to know I have no need of anything that belonged to Joseph Flowers. No need and no desire. I inherited what was left of the Schutt estate, and also a fine, working ranch from my husband, Shay Billings. I'm satisfied with what I have."

"Within my experience," he said, dry as a desert, "I've found people prone to say more is always welcome."

"Do they?" Knowing her face was flushing, she picked up her coffee and took a sip. It was very good coffee, rich and mellow, its fragrance stimulating to the senses. "Tell me something, Mr. Avery, did Joseph Flowers learn of my existence recently? Or did he always know about me?" Her cup clattered hard back into the saucer, making the attorney wince.

He swallowed, Adams apple jerking in his throat. "I believe Anita—your mother—sent him an announcement when you were born."

"You believe?"

"She did."

"So he always knew of me. And did he know when my mother died?"

"Yes. Your father sent a notice. Joseph was still angry with her. I'm sorry to say he didn't respond."

"So all these years—" January stopped and took a long breath. "What a wretched excuse of a father he must have been." She touched her scarred cheek. "And to think I always thought my Grandfather Schutt was a poor specimen of manhood. Turns out he was simply mentally diminished. What was Flowers's excuse?"

Avery switched his gaze from her cheek and, unwilling to meet her furious glare, raised his eyes to the shiny tin ceiling overhead. "He realized at the last how mistaken he'd been. This is his way of trying to make amends."

"Is that what he's doing?" January forced a snort of something resembling laughter. "Or is he trying to punish the cousins by introducing me as a scapegoat? From what I've read about them they're an unsavory lot, as well. I just can't wait to meet them. I suppose they all take after him." It wasn't a question. Glancing at a large wall clock, she stood up. "It's eleven o'clock. Time for the grand reveal."

Avery, perforce, rose, too. "In the conference room, across the hall." He paused to collect a thin file from his desk as well as a pen from a marble holder.

She beat him to the door, sweeping across the spacious hall to the room Avery indicated. Three men sat inside. They'd been talking, but went dead silent as she appeared in the doorway with the attorney hovering at her heels.

Pausing there, she took a moment to examine the men. She figured she had each one's identity pegged. Joseph III must be the one who wore an expensive looking suit. His legs were crossed, his swinging foot showing off a highly burnished shoe. He'd taken the seat at the head of the table, no doubt figuring it his right as he was now the head of the family. He was blond, both of hair and mustache, the latter which blended so thoroughly with his skin as to be almost invisible. She had to look twice to see it.

John Byerly Flowers—John B—was sartorially attired with a slightly cheaper suit than his cousin, and wore custom-made boots. In a lapse of manners, he'd failed to remove his hat, a Stetson, January thought, although later she discovered more than likely he kept the hat on to conceal a burgeoning bald spot.

The third man had to be Calvin Masterson. He sat crosswise in his chair, a leg thrown over the arm. His collarless shirt was unbuttoned at the top, his jacket open. He had dark hair and a dark beard that could've done with a trim. A strong odor of liquor emanated from him.

One thing they had in common—aside from none making a move to rise from his chair. As if to prove kinship, they all had the same color of eyes as she did. The dark, woody green of a pine forest.

As they watched, January selected the nearest empty chair and sat. "Howdy, boys," she said. "I'm January Billings. I can't say as it's a pleasure to meet you."

None of them uttered a single word. Instead, each made a point of gaping at her scar.

Something inside her hardened.

The silence dragged on. Avery arranged the folder at

the opposite end of the table from Joseph III, smiling faintly. After a full minute—maybe more—January turned her back on the Flowers cousins and spoke to him.

"What's wrong with them?" she asked Avery. "Are they all simpletons?"

# CHAPTER 6

Calvin twitched and sat up straight, his feet thumping to the floor. Joseph III's crossed leg dropped down with a thud. John B reached toward the inside of his jacket in an involuntary movement, quickly halted. Oddly enough, Mr. Avery mirrored the motion.

January's intuition screamed at her. *Gun,* it said. She forced herself still, to not reach toward her boot. This was not the time to let them know she was armed and prepared.

"I think I'd like Mr. Pasco to join us," she said to Avery, calmly, though her heart pounded. "To bear witness to what is said here today." She glanced at the men. "If anything."

He nodded and said, sounding choked, "Not a bad idea." He poked a little bell to summon the clerk and passed on her request.

In seconds, Eli entered, taking in the tableau in a quick scan. He sat in the chair next to her and cocked a brow.

Her mouth twitched.

The attorney cleared his throat and began. "Our first order of business is to introduce everyone. Mrs. Billings has been polite enough to start." Avery's small rebuke seemed loud and authoritative, maybe not just in January's imagination since they all jumped. He went around the table, pointing. January's guess as to her cousins' individual identities proved correct.

Then he came to Eli. "This is Mr. Eli Pasco. You may have heard the name, gentlemen. He is here to keep an eye on Mrs. Billings's interests."

"And, due to a certain unsigned note she received, her safety," Eli added. They'd been warned.

January, watching carefully, was a little surprised when the person who showed a response was John B. His face froze, except for his eyes flicking quickly toward his feet, then at his cousins. His male cousins, that is. "Bounty hunter," he said.

Eli, she knew, had caught the guilty start as well.

Funny, really. She'd thought it would be Calvin who reacted.

III sat up straighter. "Let's get to this, Delbert, so we can send this interloper and her hired gun on their way. My grandfather has been dead for over three weeks. The business needs attention."

His use of the attorney's first name was, January felt certain, some kind of play for power. An attempt to assert control.

Avery, who'd slipped on a pair of round-lensed glasses and hooked them over his ears, glanced at III above their rims. After a moment, he smiled. "Let's."

Taking his time, he broke open the seal of a large envelope, jostled the papers to straighten them and placed them on the table in front of him. His voice sonorous, he began reading.

"I, Joseph C. Flowers, being of sound mind..."

January lost what he was saying as she concentrated on Joseph III. He waited impatiently for the good stuff to begin. If he'd been a hound dog, she thought, he would've been panting, his flews drooling and fluttering in anticipation.

Then her eyes opened wide as Avery read, "To Joseph Flowers III, I leave the house he is living in and the sum of $5000.00. Over the years my grandson has traveled the world, received an exemplary education, and experienced the business world. He's also spent a lot of my money. From here on he needs to make his own way."

"What?" Joseph III's bellow could probably have been heard all the way to The Falls. "That can't be right! What do you think you're doing, Avery? I'll have you disbarred."

The attorney looked up. "Will you?"

Flipping over the page, he went on reading over the top of III's fury, until John B said, "Shut up, Joe, and let's get to the rest of this."

"To John Byerly Flowers," Avery read, "I leave a half-share in the Mullan Road Saloon and $6000.00, in hopes he will listen to and leave the day-to-day running to Mimi Jonque Sheridan, who owns the other one-half share. With my goodwill, they may continue in their present living arrangements over the saloon, just as they've been doing these last three years. John B has also received a good education, and while not as prolif-erate at spending my money as his cousin, has still benefited beyond all expectation. I hope he does well in the future."

Avery paused as if waiting for an explosion, but John B held his hand over his mouth as though to force himself silent as his face turned an alarming shade of red.

"Well," Calvin said, sitting up straight. He was smirking. "That just leaves me, don't it? Sorry, fellas, looks like I'm the last man standing. Guess the old man knew who could handle the reins after all."

The attorney stared at him for several seconds before picking up the next document, leaving just one more on the desk.

"To Calvin Masterson, I leave $4000.00 and the suggestion he depart for South America. Bolivia is, I believe, the preferred stopping place for American outlaws. You see, Cal, I know some of the things you've done. You've skated because of my name. No more. A steamship ticket will be purchased using estate funds when you take me up on the offer."

There were collective gasps. Out of nowhere, tension gripped January, as an uneasy feeling crawled wormlike into her mind.

"Dammit, Cal, is this your fault?" Joseph III demanded. "What have you done now?"

"Are you the one who—" John B stopped before going any further.

"Then who inherits?" Calvin jumped from his seat, the chair tipping over with a loud clatter. His hand was on his gun, only to halt when he spotted Eli's pistol already out and centered on his chest. Not that Eli's was the only gun in sight. Mr. Avery now held one as well, held almost as steady as Eli's.

"Right that chair and sit back down," Eli said coolly. "I figure you're about to find out."

Eli, January realized, was not playing around. And her cousins knew it. Scowling, Calvin complied, slamming the chair upright. He didn't sit, but stood with his white knuckled hands gripping the chair's backposts.

The attorney, tucking his derringer away, nodded his gratitude—and relief—and picked up the final paper.

"To my granddaughter, January Schutt Billings," he read, "I leave the rest of my holdings; money, property, shares and most of all, responsibilities. All of it. She need not be beholden to anyone, least of all me, and after one year, may dispose of the estate as she likes. Whether she runs the outfit, as I feel certain she is capable of doing, or decides to follow her own path, I want her to know I regret never having met her. My apologies."

January felt the blood drain from her head. Black spots appeared before her eyes.

*NO!*

The silent shout resounded only inside her head. Had this grandfather just signed her death warrant?

Avery looked up. "There's a letter for each of you. The letters hold complete copies of the will. He asked that you read your letters, think about the will's contents, and abide by what he has to say. He wanted me to tell you all he had your best interests at heart and, anticipating your reactions, suggested you each, after thinking the disposition over, independently contact your own attorneys if you must. Yes, even you, Calvin."

Sitting back, the attorney removed his glasses. "That is all. This meeting is adjourned."

The cousins, snatching the envelopes from Avery's

hand, stormed out. Their voices resounded in the hall outside the conference room where they stopped, venting their rage.

"I'll fight it. He can't get away with this. Leave me out? I'm the firstborn! It's mine. It should all be mine." Without a doubt it was Joseph III speaking, and the loudest by far in his protest. "How could the old man do this to me. To us. All of us. A scarred nobody not fit for polite society? My wife will be appalled if this...this... farce holds."

"Farce? Seems more like a disaster to me. My guess is your wife will scream loud enough they can hear her at the mine in Murray." John B spoke more quietly, stating, perhaps, the obvious.

"Like the fishwife she is." The drawl, January figured, had to belong to Calvin.

John B laughed. "Cal's got it right. Everybody knows Bethany, aside from telling you what to do, Joe, is easily appalled, if that's even the right word, when things don't go her way. She's gonna be worrying about the money, that's for sure. And actually, the little cuz ain't that bad."

"Keep your mouth shut in regards to Bethany, John B. You, too, Cal. Both of you. You don't know what you're saying. All the liquor you drink has skewed your judgement." Joseph defended his wife hotly. "It always has."

"Yeah, and now this is over, I reckon to get drunk today." John B actually laughed. "Roaring drunk. Maybe I'll just stay that way, all six thousand worth."

"I'll kill her. I swear. I'll kill her." Calvin spoke last. He was the quietest, January noted, but also the most chilling. She had no doubt who the "her" he referred to was, after all.

Then the clerk spoke. "Gentlemen, please. Take

your quarrel outside. You're disturbing the other partners."

Oddly enough, the Flowers cousins complied. Their voices faded. The outer door slammed.

In the conference room, Eli holstered his pistol. January sat shaking, unaware of her hand seeking Eli's. Under the table, he grasped her cold fingers, squeezing as if to pump blood back through her veins.

Sighing, Avery stood. "That went about like I expected it would. About as I warned Joseph it would. Let's return to the office, shall we? I believe we could all use a drink. Even you, Mrs. Billings."

"We should go," she said, but he shook his head.

"There's more. Information just for you. Things your cousins didn't need to hear as they don't directly change anything about the estate."

Eli, still holding January's hand, helped her up. "Do you want me to go?"

January shook her head. "No. Stay with me, please."

Back in the office, Avery splashed very good whiskey into heavy crystal glasses and passed them around. His hands, January noticed, trembled more than her own. So he hadn't, she realized, been as sanguine as he'd appeared during the ordeal. The Flowers's reaction worried him.

"I'm glad you were with us, Pasco," he said. "Calvin is hot-headed, uncontrolled. I don't know what he would've done if you hadn't stepped in. And Joseph. I wasn't sure how he'd react. Or how he will react in the future." A clear warning.

Eli shrugged. "Every once in a while my reputation serves me in good stead."

"When it doesn't make you a target," Avery said

dryly. He unlocked the middle drawer of his desk and retrieved a couple large envelopes, one stuffed to the point of a strained clasp. He pushed them across the desk to January.

"You'll need these to make sense of the situation, Mrs. Billings. It lists the properties, contracts, deeds, all the documents pertaining to your grandfather's estate. He's expanded on what the will said, and he's recommended people who can help you. He didn't want you to face it alone." A second later, he added, "There's a lot to face. A lot to consider."

Eli twitched. "Best then," he said, "if everyone—meaning those grandsons—knows she has friends and people of her own she can rely on."

January's mind raced. "You're talking possessions, Mr. Avery, but something Joseph III said raised yet another question. Or more questions, I should say."

"It did?"

"What is it?" Eli asked.

"He mentioned—and so did John B—someone named Bethany. Joseph's wife, I believe. What about her? Do they have children? What about John B and this Miriam—no. Mimi—something or other? Where does she figure in? And Calvin. Does he have a wife? A family? Same questions. Are there old retainers? Workers? Friends I need to consider?"

Avery gestured toward the envelope. "These should provide answers to most of that."

"And does it say anything about the biggest problem?"

"Biggest problem?" A frown creased Avery face. "What is that?"

"Can I just walk away?"

Avery grinned, widely, with a show of teeth. "With a considerable amount of trouble, yes, but you might want to think twice about doing so, Mrs. Billings."

She shook her head. "I doubt that."

He was adamant. "I suggest you look at the bottom line of the financial report before you make any decisions."

January looked over at Eli to find his jaw set, his dark eyes narrow with speculation. What did he already know that she didn't?

"Eli?" she said.

To her surprise, he nodded. "My gut says it's best to count all your chickens, January, right down to the last feather, before you let go of anything."

Avery nodded. "Wise advice."

It seemed all too clear to January that her inheritance consisted of a great deal of money along with the gaggle of angry relatives. And trouble.

* * *

Joseph III waylaid her outside the office building. His skin, seen under the lowering sky, was paler now than his beard and mustache, making him appear ghostly. January supposed the impression due to his revision of fortunes. A most unwelcome turn. In plain fact, if asked, she would've said he was downright scared.

He grabbed her arm, stopping her with a jerk. "Send this man away." He meant Eli. "I need to talk to you."

It was a demand, not a request.

Eli reached over and plucked Joseph's fingers from her sleeve. "Touch her again and you'll lose some fingers."

"You..." Joseph began, but January cut in before the situation escalated.

"Make an appointment," she said and swished on past him. She made certain her head was high and her back straight.

Already a fellow had stopped to stare, possibly recognizing Joseph and wondering at his angry expression.

Eli, forced to go with her, chuckled softly. "Make an appointment?"

January had to smile, turning just a little so she could see Joseph. He stood stock still, watching them. If that wasn't murder she saw on his face, she didn't know what it was.

Her smile faded.

The Spokane Hotel, a most respectable hotel suitable for ladies who wished to avoid risking their reputations, had a policy of no gentlemen visitors. Although, when January thought about the policy, she supposed the edict easy enough to circumvent.

With the clerk watching closely, Eli made a funny sort of half-bow and without argument, left her in the lobby. But she hadn't been wrong. Fifteen minutes after entering her room—and locking the door behind her in an excess of caution—there came a tap on her door.

"Who is it?"

"Your secretary," Eli answered, which made January grin.

Once inside, he glanced around the room. "Looks comfortable."

"It serves."

The bed was in a large alcove, with a table on each side, and a commode with a fancy basin and pitcher. No private bathroom. Given the choice, January would've traded the telephone for one. In the outer room, a couch, a table with two armchairs, an armoire, and a desk with a chair on wheels crowded the space. The much vaunted telephone took pride of place where it sat on the desk. A large potted plant blocked light coming through the window above the bed. January had immediately ascertained the plant was in dire need of water and doused it well.

Eli was looking for something other than furniture or bathrooms. "One way in, one way out," he said. "I don't like it."

"It's a hotel. I'll only be here tonight. I'll be all right."

Eli shook his head. "I don't like it," he repeated. "It's too easy to get at you. All I had to do was wait until the clerk was busy with an old lady and her dog to slip past him and mount the stairs. He never saw a thing. He's not exactly the kind of man I'd put in charge of your safety. Somebody wave a gun at him and he'd probably faint."

She didn't think he meant to frighten her. He knew she didn't scare easily. No, his intention was to warn her. He did both.

"I've got my boot gun," she said. "Don't worry. I'm used to taking care of myself, you know. I live alone on a ranch. I've gone after outlaws by myself. Why would this hotel be any worse than riding my own land or sleeping in my own bed?"

"Because these are men who want you—you, January Billings—dead. They've got a whole lot at stake. With those outlaws, you were just someone who got in the way of whatever they were doing at the time."

He wasn't entirely wrong, but not entirely right,

either. She had most certainly been directly targeted before.

She had already laid the documents from the file Avery had given her on the table. All except the letter from her grandfather. That she intended to keep for herself, when she was alone. Maybe she wouldn't read it today. Or maybe not even next week. Time would tell.

Because Joseph III had been glaring at her so venomously, his was the first file she pulled forward. Each of the cousins had his own file, some thicker than the others. Somewhere, probably in Delbert Avery's office, January was willing to bet there was one on her, as well. She'd like to read that one, too.

Or would she?

Shrugging the thought aside, she seated herself opposite Eli at the table and flipped open the folder. "Here we go."

Eli claimed a document and began reading. Before long, a snort indicated disgust. January, who was perusing Mr. and Mrs. Joseph III's most recent itinerary through Europe on a furniture buying trip for their palatial home, looked up. The list of purchases totaled some $20,000. "What?"

"Did you know Joseph Flowers III is thirty-five years old?"

She blinked. "Really? He doesn't look it."

"Born in 1867. I guess if a man never labors a day in his life, he doesn't wear down like other folks."

"Hmmm," she said.

Eli's family had been well-to-do, she knew, but he'd always worked. And become a bounty hunter, then a rancher. Neither were passive occupations.

She read off her own document. "This says he met

Kaiser Wilhelm II while he was in Germany on his grand tour, and he and his wife both met with the Pope while in Rome."

But in the end, they found nothing to indicate her cousin was a man of violence. Only a hint he might not be above paying someone else to do his dirty work.

"This also doesn't mean he won't become violent," Eli warned. "Only that he hasn't so far. Not anybody has noticed, anyhow. When a man used to living like Joseph has loses his easy money, he's apt to do most anything."

"Especially if his wife eggs him on." Another circumstance within January's experience. Elvira Hammel came to mind. And Ruby Pasco as well. "And provided she doesn't take the matter into her own hands. I believe I'd like to meet Mrs. Flowers III."

"I doubt you two would get along," Eli said, tossing a document onto the table and picking up another. "And I don't figure she wants to meet you."

January only laughed.

# CHAPTER 7

PAIN ARCHED OVER JANUARY'S HEAD. IT STARTED AT HER nape and traveled all the way to the crown before settling in her temples. Not because she was going blind, or so she hoped, but because her eyes hurt from reading the jumble of words Delbert Avery and her grandfather had documented about her cousins. At least, the words were a jumble even though she got their import clearly enough. It was what they meant that made her head ache.

Eli, when she glanced across the table at him, appeared as disgusted as she felt. Reaching up, her fingers scattered the pins that had been holding her brown locks in a coil and let her hair flow onto her shoulders. *Better.*

"Enough reading?" he asked, watching her with a concerned expression.

"More than enough." They'd been poring over the mass of papers for three hours. "I don't believe I learned anything I didn't already suspect from reading about my cousins in the *Chronicle* and *Review* articles. And from meeting them today. Just more details. What do you think?"

He regarded her soberly. "Joseph III is still a puffed-up do-nothing filled with overwhelming self-importance."

She smiled slightly and cocked her head.

"But," he added, "he's also dangerous and unpredictable. As for John B..." He frowned. "I don't know what to make of him."

"He's not a wise gambler for one thing," January said, tossing Eli a stray piece of paper that added up some of his gambling debts. "Takes too many plunges into the unknown and loses. If it weren't for his partner Mimi Sheridan, he'd be in real trouble."

Eli nodded. "And on account of that, also unpredictable. Last, there's Calvin." He leveled his dark gaze on her. "Watch out for him. He's got all the earmarks of a killer."

Her eyes opened wide. "He does?" And yet, she thought, Eli should know. He'd made his living by capturing men who were killers or, putting the best light on some of their actions, careless of other people's lives.

"Try not to be alone with him. Him especially," he added.

"I'll beware of them all until I know any different. And more than likely after I know them better, too."

"Good." Eli stretched his arms over his head, tendons and joints audibly popping. "I should go." But even as he stood and shrugged into his suit coat, he hesitated. "When do you plan on going home? After reading through these papers, it looks like you might have to stay in town a few more days and meet with Avery again. He's the one to guide you through introductions to your grandfather's managers and foremen and the business of the estate. It's going to be a lot. Don't depend on any help from Joseph, even if he did think to take over. Don't depend on any of them. Individually or together, they're ready to take everything."

"I know."

Truth be told, although she knew he was right, the whole process frightened her and gave her the willies. When Shay died, she'd known about the ranch and how to do things. If she needed help, Shay's friends had been willing to help her. She'd been able to take control if not easily, at least ably, and soon, comfortably. But this? The scope of the Joseph C. Flowers holdings terrified her.

There was nothing easy or comfortable about any of it. And that part about having to hold the estate together for a year? What did that mean, exactly? So far, she hadn't found mention of the stipulation in any of the paperwork Avery had given her. The idea of living in a city gave her the vapors. Plus, it surprised her Eli hadn't mentioned it, while she found herself reluctant to bring the subject up. Maybe he knew that.

"Let me know your plans?" Eli said. "I'm staying at the Holliday Hotel. You can call them. They'll see I get your message."

Sighing, she nodded. "I can't imagine how long this will take. First thing in the morning I need to find the telegraph office and send a message out to Johnny, asking him to stay on until I get home." She smiled, a real smile. "He'll be glad of the extra money. He and Evie Langley are getting married next year."

"Johnny married? He's just a kid."

"He's young, but I wouldn't say he's a kid. He's been on his own for a long time. He told me Bo Cobb took him under his wing when he was thirteen and helped him grow up."

Speaking of Johnny apparently served to remind Eli of something, although January didn't know what. But he glanced at the clock ticking away on the desk, which acted to get him moving.

Puzzled, she followed him.

At the door, he turned. "Don't forget. Be careful who you open the door to."

"I will." They'd been through the precautions already.

He looked down at her, his suave demeanor melting a little as he said, "About Ford Tervo..."

Her innards chilled at his unexpected words. "Ford? What about him?"

Ford Tervo, Shay's friend and a U.S. deputy marshal, had died last month, murdered by an outlaw who'd not only been trying to kill January, but take over The Falls while planning a bank robbery. The outlaw failed, of course, but he and his gang had done real damage to the community. At one time she'd thought something might come of her own friendship with Ford, but distance helped the interest peter out and she was glad of it.

A muscle in Eli's jaw twitched. "Did you end up burying him at your place? I heard mention of you taking charge."

She hesitated. Had Johnny told him as much? She

and Johnny had discussed doing so. Why did it matter to Eli? "I would have, but as it turned out, I didn't need to. He had family who requested his body be shipped to his home."

"Oh," he said.

She paused. He seemed to be waiting for her to say more. "Which I did. A relief, as you can imagine," she added.

His face, granite hard, relaxed and he nodded. "Yes. A relief."

She had the thought they might not be speaking of the same kind of relief, but why would he care?

Then he was gone, the door closing quietly behind him. Still frowning over their last exchange, she stepped forward, turned the key in the lock and a second later, heard the floor creak outside as he walked away.

*What in the world had that been about? Why ask about Ford?*

She sighed and busied herself straightening the papers and restoring them to the envelopes before sitting back and closing her eyes. After a while, as her headache abated, she got restless. Squirmy. Accustomed to hard work and ceaseless activity, sitting motionless in a hotel room—comfortable though it might be— allowed anxiety to find a way in.

Time crawled. The letter from her grandfather beckoned, although she wasn't ready to read it just yet. The list of his properties kept appearing before her closed eyes. Two mines in the Coeur d'Alene mining district. They had made him rich and enabled the other properties. Those included three commercial buildings in Spokane, a hotel in Kellogg, and one in Coeur d'Alene

City. Plus, a farmer held a longtime lease on land located in the Palouse country.

She'd take a look at that. It might be an arrangement she didn't want to disturb.

Her grandfather had lived on a horse ranch in the valley to the east of Spokane until just lately. As his health worsened, the attorney had said, he moved to the top floor of one of his commercial buildings here in town.

Avery had given her a key. "Take a look," he'd told her. "I think you'll be impressed. You may want to live there."

Impressed? Maybe so. But comfortable? Want to live there? The answer to that would be a resounding 'no.'

Her eyes popped open. She'd told Eli she'd stay in her room with the door locked, but really, that sort of behavior wasn't in her nature—as he well knew. And she didn't like hotels, not even hotels like this one. No matter how luxurious it might be, she still felt as though closed up in a box. People came and went at all hours of the day and night. Why not take a look at where her grandfather had lived? She remembered walking past the street during her perambulations this morning. The building was only a block or two to the south. Not far at all. If it suited her, she'd let Eli know she'd moved. She needed no one's justification in doing so.

A glance out the window showed the snow had stopped. The street was muddy, with pedestrians watching where they placed their feet. They weren't looking at anyone else. She'd be unremarkable. Unnoticeable.

Quickly, she stripped out of the pretty suit and donned her split skirt and heavy coat. Her pistol went in the pocket within easy reach. Before she could change her mind, she left the room, locked the door behind her and crept unseen down the stairs.

The afternoon had drawn down, heading quickly toward dark. January appreciated the dusk, feeling safely hidden in its depths. Her body appreciated the movement, although she wished for her dog. Pen would've given warning if danger loomed ahead.

As it happened, she reached the building in short order and without a lick of trouble. A name carved into the bricks above the door read, *Flowers, 1898*, making the building hard to miss. Evidently her grandfather had been a prideful man to display his name on his holdings.

The well-trodden walk up to the building's entrance had been turned into mud despite the graveled path. January hoped that only meant the place had many tenants who'd be leaving for their homes soon. The edifice itself was imposing, not that she knew what style to apply to it. Structured of dark brick—after the great fire of 1889 almost all Spokane commercial premises were of brick—it had lintels of almost white sandstone. Looking up, she saw the building had three stories, the uppermost floor with sandstone half-walls around the edge. Crenellated. That was the word she was looking for, although she doubted the battlements were there for more than decorative effect. They made the building more imposing and, if her grandfather had walked about on the roof, possibly more secure.

A set of wide double doors invited her in. Choosing the one on the right, she entered.

Once inside, she saw offices opening off the dark and quiet main hall/lobby. January imagined all such commercial buildings were much alike. At least she couldn't get lost. She mounted the first set of stairs—wide stairs, probably at least three times as wide as found in a private residence. The dimly lit interior had walls wood-paneled to half-height. Electric light sconces prevented one from tripping over the dark blue carpet running across the middle portion of the stairs. It served to silence her footsteps, making her ascent seem almost furtive. At the end of the second story, the stairs became narrower, though still quite broad. A landing at the top of the stairs sported a wide heavy door—the only one on this floor—which sealed off Joseph Flowers's abode. The lock gleamed brightly, made of brass, she thought, so highly polished as to look like gold.

Or maybe it was gold.

January inserted her key and twisted. Well oiled, the lock turned with a soft click. The door, at her touch, opened without sound.

But that didn't mean the apartment was quiet. Or empty. Far from it.

She froze, head cocked, listening to a woman sobbing loudly. Curses interspersed her fresh wails. A man murmured, then finally, voice rising over the sobs, snapped, "Do be quiet, Beth, and keep looking. Your infernal caterwauling is not helping."

The woman hiccupped. Something made of glass shattered.

"Well," the man said. "That was unnecessary. And a waste of good Florentine crystal."

Stepping inside, January left the door open. She reached in her coat pocket and grasped her .25-caliber Smith & Wesson, the butt slapping into her palm in a reassuring sort of way.

The entry hall where she stood contained an ornately-framed, beveled-glass mirror set above a stand where she assumed a hostess might tidy her hair, or a host check his beard for biscuit crumbs before opening the door. Provided they, and not a butler or perhaps a hired girl, even opened the door to callers. The mirror's angle served to show January who had invaded her inherited space.

In truth, she wasn't at all surprised to see Joseph III leaning against a carved fireplace mantle. He stood scowling at a woman whose curvy figure had been crammed mercilessly into what must've been a torture inducing corset. Her appearance reminded January of an over-stuffed, tightly packed sausage. The woman stood beside a small mahogany table, its drawer half-open, and one hand placed as if to support her while she looked down at the shattered glass at her feet. The woman must be Joseph III's wife, January concluded. He'd called her Beth. Short, no doubt, for Bethany, whom the other cousins seemed to view with reserve.

That they were looking for something valuable went without saying. Why they were so careless of the mess needed explanation.

Returning her .25 to her pocket, January reached behind her and swung the door shut. It latched with a thud.

"What was that?" Joseph said. "Who's there? Speak up." Then, before she had a chance to open her mouth, he began berating his wife. "Fool woman. You left the door on the latch."

"I..." Bethany started, but by now January had figured out what she planned to say.

She strode into the room.

The moment he saw her, Joseph's complexion turned bright, angry red. "What are you doing here?"

"Who is this, Joe?" The woman's nose turned up at January's shabby country attire. "Is this one of your floozies?"

Now January knew something new about III. His wife thought him a womanizer. Unable to stop herself, she laughed. "Hardly. I'm the owner of this fine..." her gaze drifted around the opulent room "abode. The question is, *Joe*, what are you doing here?"

The woman sucked in a breath. "You? You dare—"

January cut in over the beginning of what she recognized as a tirade in the making. "You two seem to be looking for something. Committing a crime as you ransack the place, turning everything upside down. What is it?"

"None of your business," Joseph answered, then clamped his mouth shut. Bethany glared at him.

January figured they weren't about to tell her anything. Not by choice, at least. "The door is right there. I suggest you depart through it. Both of you. Before I call the police."

Joseph's lip lifted. "You have no right to any of this. *You* leave. You're the interloper. Stay and something bad will happen to you."

"Is that a threat?" she asked, smiling with the merest quirk of her lips.

He straightened. "Take it how you wish. Clearly my grandfather was out of his mind when he made that will. I intend to have him declared incompetent and the will invalidated. Perhaps, if you go without a fuss, I can see you receive a little something. A memento."

"She shouldn't get anything, Joe," Beth put in.

January ignored the woman, which she could see didn't set well with Bethany, and cocked her head. "You might want to rethink what you just said, Joseph. You know no part of that is true. Your grandfather expected you to make trouble, and I'm told he took steps to make it impossible. Leave before this goes any further. You are not welcome in what now belongs to me." Deliberately, she turned her back on the couple, and waited. The emphasis on the word "me" would do the trick, she figured.

True to expectation, the rush of footsteps and the rustle of Bethany's taffeta skirt gave plenty of warning. She stepped aside as Bethany launched herself toward January, intent on flattening her with her considerable weight. Instead of January being crushed, Bethany's heel caught on the carpet. She landed in an ignominious heap on the floor.

January looked down at her and shook her head. "A mistake, Mrs. Flowers. A truly foolish mistake."

"Get up, Bethany." Joseph ignored his wife's reaching hand and glared at January. "As for you, the mistake is yours. I'll see you dead before you take a single thing."

Sighing, January groped in her pocket. "Mr. and Mrs. Joseph Flowers III, I'm sorry it's come to this, but you're both under arrest." An outright fib. She wasn't sorry at all.

"What?" Bethany screeched.

"Don't be ridiculous." Joseph forced a laugh, even as his eyes narrowed to pinpoints. "You can't do that."

"Actually, I can. It so happens I'm a duly appointed deputy of the county and I'm placing the pair of you

under arrest. A night in jail might cool your tempers."
She didn't say which county.

"You can't," III repeated.

"I assure you, I can. The charges are unlawful entry
into a private residence and threats of bodily harm."
She nodded toward Bethany. "If you insist on more, it
will be attempted assault."

"Nobody will believe you," Joseph said.

"You wouldn't dare," the woman said, a trace of
apprehension showing itself. "My reputation..."

"I'm warning you," Joseph said.

January shook her head, eyes narrowing.

Joe jolted toward her, fist raised. He stopped in mid-
stride when January pulled her pistol from her pocket
and aimed it at him.

"I'd be justified in shooting you," she said, as if the
situation didn't bother her at all. Inwardly, she was
quaking in her boots. "You may have read some of my
history. You know I will do whatever is necessary."

She'd spotted the telephone mounted on the entry
hall wall as she entered, and stepped toward it now.
Lifting the handset, she gave the crank a quick spin.
Immediately, a telephone girl answered. Gripping her
pistol again, barely stopping Joseph before he made
another try at her, January asked for the police.

"They'll ignore you," Joseph shouted.

But they didn't. News regarding the Flowers family
and the reading of Joseph Flowers' will had gotten out
and already spread like a forest fire on a windy summer
day. A new heir to the Flowers fortune was in town.
Even the most recent police constable had heard.

Joseph and Bethany were taken into custody, loudly
protesting the whole process and vowing a retribution

they didn't seem to realize only made their position worse. In fact, it appeared to January that the officer in charge took pleasure in fitting handcuffs onto Joseph's wrists and escorting them away.

At last January stood in sole possession of the apartment, appreciating the blessed quiet as their voices faded.

Until Eli, seething under his breath, showed up before she could get the door closed.

# CHAPTER 8

ELI RAN INTO POLICE SERGEANT MILT FERGUSON AS HE left January to her paperwork at the Spokane Hotel. Or, turning it around, Milt ran into him, which resulted in the full cup of boiling hot coffee the policeman carried spilling down the front of his uniform jacket.

"What the..." His face angry, Milt whirled, from all appearances unaware of his guilt in blundering into the path of foot traffic without looking. A big burly man with a round jaw and fair skin, Ferguson appeared fearsome at first glance, although Eli would contend he wasn't nearly as ornery as he looked.

Eli recovered from the jolt first. "If I'd been a female, Milt, you would've had her sprawled on the ground and the department forced to pay her doctor bills." He refrained from adding, "It wouldn't be the first time." And it would've been the truth.

Ferguson's demeanor changed in a flash of big white teeth as he grinned. "By the Lord Harry, if it ain't Eli Pasco! I ain't seen you in a coon's age. Where you been? I heard you retired from the bounty collection business and went to raising horses." He leaned near to Eli. "Listen old pal, horses ain't the way to go. Mark my words, automobiles are the coming thing. What are you doing in the city, man?"

In view of Milt's opinion of horses, Eli was half reluctant to answer. But he did—partly. "I'm here to see a man about a horse."

Milt's guffaw shook the door of the nearest building. It also drew the attention of everyone within range of hearing. "Now that's a put-together tale if ever I heard one."

The stares they got weren't what Eli preferred. He'd as soon his presence went unnoticed. "No law against a man visiting the city, is there? Is it legal for a cop to drink coffee laced with bourbon while he's on the job?" Taking Milt's arm, he guided the city policeman away from the hotel. He didn't want the clerk spotting him and remembering the questions he'd asked.

Milt flicked the last of the coffee from his jacket front. Without further discussion, he followed Eli. "I reckon it is when we get a cold spell like this. And at least it ain't rotgut whiskey. It's the good stuff, imported from Kentucky. Anyhow, I just added enough for a little flavor. Now, are you going to tell me what you're really doing here? Doubt you came to town just to see the sights."

To Eli's recollection, the last time he'd talked with Milt was when he'd brought a safecracker with a thousand-dollar reward on his head to the jail and Milt had been the man in charge of the lock-up. The yeggman had put up a fuss and it had taken the two of them to subdue him when he went into some kind of fit.

"Two things, one being the deal concerning a horse

or two." He decided it never hurt to discover what the boys in blue were saying about folks in their territory. And from what he'd read in the attorney's paperwork—more of a dossier than simple introductory paragraphs—regarding January's new relatives, the police probably already had the Flowers cousins in their sights. "I'm looking out for a friend with a serious situation besides. Might be you could help me with that."

Milt, who sometimes acted the buffoon but was far from being one, shot him a look. "Yeah? I hope that help don't require shooting anybody. We got laws against gunning citizens down in the streets or back alleys nowadays."

Eli believed they had always had such laws, though some folks weren't prone to pay attention. Besides, gunning wanted men down in either place had never been his working method, and Milt knew it.

Looking up and down Sprague Avenue and finding nothing to worry him in the shift of traffic there, Milt said, "Walk with me. I'm late on my rounds. I guess if you can talk and walk at the same time, the least I can do is listen."

They started out, the wind buffeting their hats. Eli envied the strap holding Milt's tall-crowned headgear securely on his head. "This friend," he said, "recently received a letter about an inheritance." The odd idea of January Billings being someone as simple as a friend passed through his mind. He shook it aside. "A pretty substantial inheritance that came as a total, gobs-macking surprise," he went on. "It appears there are cousins involved. Unhappy cousins, as they weren't expecting another family member to appear on the scene. Words have been bandied about."

Milt, his blue eyes narrowed to slits, glanced sharply his way. Their gleam appeared to Eli like one of Edison's light bulbs turning on. "Words, eh? Threats like your friend continuing to live?"

Eli nodded. "I'd like to know if my friend—or I—should be worried. How serious these cousins might be when they're riled."

"I'd say that depends on who these people are, and how much of an inheritance is at stake."

"They're a trio who are used to having their own way and of buying themselves out of trouble. The inheritance, like I said, is substantial. The biggest to come around in a while. Maybe ever."

Face turning red, Milt grabbed Eli and shoved him into a convenient doorway, out of the wind. His voice dropped. "Eli Pasco, are you telling me you're here because of Joseph Flowers's missing heir? I hear tell it's a woman."

Taken aback by Milt's quick reading of his story, Eli gave an assenting jerk of his head. "What can she expect from the three of them?"

"Murder, if there's the slightest chance of getting away with it. That Calvin—" Milt broke off. "Word is, he's done it before. Shot an unarmed man down in one of Joseph senior's logging camps during an argument over a woman. Got away with it by saying the man threatened him. John B don't seem like such a villain. The woman he lives with mostly keeps him in line. Not to say he can't be persuaded by Calvin when the stakes are this high. As for Joseph III, he's a dark horse. Things mostly go his way around here, but if he was pushed out of what he thinks he's entitled to? I don't know. I say don't trust any of them and keep a real close eye on your friend."

"Personal experience got anything to do with the lack of trust?"

Milt didn't answer, his attention seeming caught by something going on down the street, although when Eli turned, he saw nothing aside from normal folks trying to get in out of the weather. It struck him Milt wanted a moment to think before he answered.

"Things have happened," Milt admitted at last. "Evidence disappeared from the lock-up. Charges dropped. Sergeant Sullivan got invited to take his dinner with Joseph senior and the judge. Favors exchanged."

"Hellfire." Eli's temper flamed. "Senior is dead. My friend—" he still wasn't saying her name "—is taking the reins. That kind of thing isn't going to happen on her watch."

Milt leveled a stare on him, the cop's round face somber. "Huh. Might depend on if she lives long enough. But for now, Pasco, I suggest you keep that fancy Broomhandle Mauser of yours handy."

They parted then, Milt promising to check for reports of the Flowers cousins wrong-doing and get back to Eli. But first he had his foot patrol to complete—without coffee, he complained.

Eli trudged on back to his hotel where he had an appointment with the man seeking a Windswept sired foal. Maybe two. A couple drinks in the hotel bar, and the promise of Windswept covering a pair of the man's best mares settled him down and gave him something to think about besides January's situation. Until, as the man with mares got up to leave, they were disturbed by a messenger boy with a funny flat hat on his head. He rushed into the lobby yelling out Eli's name and carrying a thin envelope.

The message was from Milt.

*Got problems at Joseph Flowers apartment,* it read, and gave an address only a few blocks from Eli's hotel. *You might be needed. Your friend already has some of that trouble we was talking about.*

Eli tended to the business of tipping the messenger, paying the tab for their drinks and shaking hands with the client. *Flowers apartment, eh? What in Satan's breath is January Billings doing there? What happened to her promise to stay in her hotel room with the door locked?*

\* \* \*

THOSE WERE the same words Eli growled, spotting her as he strode down the hall toward the open door of old Joseph Flowers's apartment.

"What are you doing here?" He demanded, and added, "What happened to your promise to stay put in the hotel? Why didn't you let me know you were on the move? I would have come with you."

Guilt stopped the pithy answer January had on her tongue. She had to admit he had a legitimate complaint since when the idea struck, she had rushed over here without thinking. She felt her face turning red, and guessed the scar was shining like a beacon.

And that made her angry with herself, some of the anger spilling over onto him.

"I know. Sorry. I'm used to doing for myself when I take the notion, you know." She looked up at him in a defiant sort of manner. "I remembered how Joe complained about the will being faked. I had another look at those papers and it occurred to me he might take it in his head to search this place. When I realized the address was nearby, I thought I should see for myself."

"And?" he said, unbending.

"I was right. Joe and his wife were already here going through the place, throwing things around. I suppose the situation got a little out of hand." Her mouth pursed even as her eyes danced. "The police took Joe and Bethany away."

"Yeah. I saw them being loaded in the transport wagon as I walked up. Then I waited until they were gone."

"Loaded in the what?"

"Transport wagon. They use it to haul criminals and drunks to the hoosegow."

"Oh." She couldn't help the wicked smile wreathing her face. "Well, I'm pressing charges. They've got to learn I won't stand for their shenanigans."

Eli's wry smile broke through at that. "I can't fault your thinking. I'd do the same. But, January, you don't know them or how they'll act. It's unwise to take them on alone. They're apt to have friends who'll take their side."

"Huh. Paid friends."

"Maybe. Some, anyhow. Maybe most. I don't know as that makes a lot of difference if they're shooting at you."

She knew he was right. "Come in. See for yourself what they did."

Gesturing him inside the apartment, she directed him to consider the manner of destruction. Most obvious were the broken crystal vase, ripped pillows tossed to the floor, and a couple desiccated plants overturned and spilling their dirt onto a dusty tabletop. Drawers in tables and chests had been rummaged through and left open; a corner of the thick carpet torn up; pictures hung askew. "They were searching for something. A different will, is my guess."

"Or maybe a good place to hide one, then insist it was legitimate and they happened to find it. Even if disproved, they could tie the estate up in court for a long time, meanwhile draining the accounts."

A faint smile touched her lips. "You don't have much of an opinion of my relatives, do you?"

"No. Do you?"

"No." She didn't even have to ponder the question.

By fortunate chance, January had gotten to the apartment before Joe and Bethany had time to completely wreck the interior. They'd begun their search in the main room. The rest of the apartment appeared untouched.

Eli walked through the rooms with her, and she was glad of his company. The place ached with an unnatural silence, the air smelling, if such a thing was possible after almost a month, of stale death. Or maybe it was her imagination run wild.

Two bedrooms opened off a hall located under some stairs. The stairs, she surmised, led either to a loft or to the roof and whatever her grandfather had up there. She wasn't about to investigate tonight. Dark had fallen and with the snow and wind causing unsteady footing, she figured exploring the roof could wait.

But she and Eli went through the two bedrooms, the largest having obviously belonged to her grandfather. The bed was made up with a lavish satin comforter, the room in apple pie order. In a fine, fine bathroom she stood for two full minutes with her mouth hanging open, admiring the fixtures, the space, and the warmth rising from a steam heat register. Immediately, she began making plans to copy the design for the bath she planned to build in her own new house.

Then she remembered *this* apartment, this whole building, was hers, and broke out laughing.

"What is it?" Eli asked, looking at her in alarm, but she shook her head and they went on to the kitchen.

"I think someone must've cleaned in here after Mr. Flowers died." She gazed around at the fully stocked room, wondering if it had ever been used. Even the copper pots hanging over a large preparation table appeared new. Not one bore so much as a scorch mark on the bottom.

Eli opened a door into a small room off the back of the kitchen and found a pantry, another sink, and a tiny maid's room. He took a quick look inside. "Avery probably hired someone. Or maybe there was a maid or a valet. If so, they don't appear to be living here now."

"A valet?" January came to peek over his shoulder.

"Like a lady's maid, only for men."

Her eyes lit. "Have you ever had a valet?"

He shrugged, leaving her to wonder.

They made plans to search more thoroughly in the morning, but after locking up, Eli insisted on escorting her to a nearby restaurant and making certain she got dinner. Sadly out of place in her riding skirt and plain white shirt, January hardly tasted a thing, although Eli said his steak was cooked just right and the fancy mashed potatoes were tasty. It was as appetizing as shredded paper in January's mouth.

If she'd had her druthers, supper in her room would've been more comfortable.

News of Joseph Flowers's heir had apparently made the rounds. So, judging by the stares and whispers happening behind hands cupped over mouths, had the identity of the heir.

Eli was better at ignoring the gawpers than January, although more than one, proving too intrusive to ignore, called for his dark glare.

January had a whisper of her own. "How did they find out? How can they know it's me?"

More than a little exasperated, Eli brought up several possibilities. "Could've been someone in Avery's office. Probably unauthorized, but this is pretty important news in a town like Spokane. Hard to keep to yourself, especially for someone wanting to impress friends."

January made a face.

"Or, and this is more likely," Eli said, "a reporter for one of the papers has been trailing the cousins and heard them talking this afternoon. They weren't being quiet, if you remember. Or someone from another office in Avery's building may have overheard the news and passed it along. All I know is, Milt knew about it."

"Milt?"

"Milt Ferguson. A Spokane police sergeant I know from my bounty hunter days. He sent me a message when he heard about the trouble at the Flowers apartment." He snorted. "I figured I'd find you smack dab in the middle of it."

This, January thought, staring down at a puddle of gravy on her plate, was not the way she wanted to live. To have people staring at her, probably begging her for favors or, as time went on, for money. All of it made her vastly uncomfortable. And knowing there were people watching her every move just about scared the britches off her.

She looked up at Eli. "I want to go home."

Only later, when the uncomfortable supper ended, did another possibility occur to her. There probably wasn't any other woman in the area who bore an S-shaped scar on her cheek. A scar that made her all too recognizable.

## CHAPTER 9

RISING EARLY THE NEXT MORNING, A HABIT INGRAINED IN childhood, January spent an hour with pen and ink, so that Delbert Avery, when faced with a large list of her questions clearly written out in surprisingly beautiful penmanship, evidently didn't know what to think.

She'd gotten to his office before his usual 8:00 a.m. arrival hour, and although his secretary fussed—discreetly, of course—about having to put other clients off, Avery made time before his first scheduled meeting to see her in his office.

Avery's distrust of the cousins, made clear after the reading of the will, had been renewed by yesterday's clash and by the charges pending against Joe III and his wife.

He couldn't quite hide his disapproval of the situation, although January sensed it wasn't her actions earning his distaste.

She had no idea how he'd learned of the fracas already, but had a suspicion he had people all over the city who reported out-of-the-ordinary goings-on to him.

"Joe knows this was his grandfather's final will. There is no other." He tapped his finger on the desktop. "Joe is tilting at windmills, simply trying to frighten you off." Reaching into his desk drawer, he handed her a hefty ring of keys. "I didn't forget these yesterday. I just didn't think you would want to bother with them the first day. However, under the circumstances, you'd best have them all in your possession in order to check the locks."

January blinked. There must've been at least a dozen various keys. Some were shaped in brass, some in silver, others in steel. There was even one—an old one —hand-formed in iron. They jangled on the ring like sleigh bells.

"These are the keys to his office." Avery pointed to two steel ones as she reached out to take them. "This silver one is the ranch house in the valley, the brass is a duplicate for the apartment. I don't know this one." He fingered the iron key. "It looks antique. These others all fit various buildings and a safe or two. You probably won't use them much. I think except for the antique they're all marked. If I were you, Mrs. Billings, considering what happened last evening, I'd have the locks changed on everything. Immediately. Today. My secretary can give you the name of a reliable locksmith."

Nodding, she blurted out the main question that had kept her awake last night. "If Joe knows there is no other will, what do you suppose he and his wife were looking for?"

"You think they were looking for something specific?" He'd begun to rise but sat down again. "Or were they simply being vandals? I know..." He shut off the sentence.

"You know what? You'd best tell me, Mr. Avery."

Apparently, her steely gaze and firm voice convinced him.

"Joe has a bit of a reputation for having temper tantrums, which are apt to turn destructive if he doesn't get his way. That's all. They may have thought to hurt you by destroying these possessions."

She scoffed. "What a fool. But I don't think hurting me was his primary intention."

"No?"

"No. I think they were looking for something. Something worth breaking the law to find. Why else look behind picture frames and under sofa cushions. Or in vases. Bethany smashed what Joe designated 'a valuable vase'. They even turned one of the sofas upside down and ripped off the backing, presumably to see inside it. If it isn't a different will, what could it possibly be?"

Avery took a deep breath. "Money, I expect. Everything boils down to money with Joe and..." He omitted whoever else he'd started to name. January suspected that someone was Bethany.

"Money is power," he went on. "Joseph wants both and so does his wife. Her greatest desire is to be one of the leading ladies of Spokane right alongside Mrs. Clark and Mrs. Campbell." He smiled weakly. "Or so my wife tells me."

January, having had some experience with wicked leading ladies, emitted a most unladylike grunt. She might not know who Mrs. Clark or Mrs. Campbell were, but certainly wasn't impressed with Bethany Flowers and her societal ambitions. Nor her attempt at bullying. When she thought more about the confrontation, she was probably lucky Bethany hadn't had a gun. "Did you know she attacked me last night?"

"Attacked you? Physically, you mean?"

"Yes. I can't imagine what she hoped to accomplish, but she tried to knock me to the floor." January couldn't stop her chuckle. "She missed and landed there herself instead. I'd bet she has bruises this morning."

Avery touched his mouth as if to smother laughter. "The mind boggles," he said on a note of wonder. He paused as if thinking. "But one thing does occur to me to account for their presence at Joseph's apartment. A couple days before he passed, Joseph withdrew a considerable sum in cash from the bank. I don't know whether it was in bills or coin, but if Joe and Bethany know about it, they may have been trying to take it for themselves." He paused and frowned. "They're often cash strapped, you see."

The information gave January a starting point when it came to figuring out these strange and violent Flowers cousins she'd been saddled with. She left the attorney's office with Avery's advice filling her mind, her pocketbook bulging with the set of keys, and a yet another bag containing files on all aspects of the Flowers estate. Avery had warned her there'd be more paperwork coming in the following days. The idea horrified her.

Before stepping into the sunshine, welcome after the storm of the previous day even though it raised a stink in the streets where piles of horse manure steamed and trash rotted, she paused to scan for anyone showing untoward interest in her. There were plenty of people walking about. Enough she supposed her safety would lay in those numbers. Her attention was caught by a woman gazing into the window of the large dry goods store across the street. A store January had determined to visit in the near future. No time like the present, she decided.

Avery had mentioned something about "keeping up appearances." She'd interpreted that to mean disapproval of her riding skirt and plain blouse.

"You don't want to give folks a reason to disparage you," he'd said, and she supposed he was simply stating a fact. Hadn't Eli mentioned something along the same lines? But she didn't want to be so flamboyant as to feed the flames of jealousy, either. She'd leave that sort of thing to Bethany.

On the other hand, and here a strange new feeling passed through her, what woman didn't feel empowered when she bought a new outfit. A vision of her green dancing dress flitted through her mind. Simple, everyday clothes might not feel the same, but even so, how lovely to not give the cost a single agonized thought.

Distracted, she stepped off the walk to cross to the store, dodging horses, wagons, and people on foot. At the halfway point, an itchy feeling gripped on and wouldn't let go.

Someone had eyes on her. She knew it. Just watching? Or focusing on her through a rifle's sight? Was she about to be shot down in the middle of Riverside Avenue?

Her pace quickened.

A mistake to think she could walk about the city and blend into the background. Her scar, this new Flowers kinship, even her reputation, though she hoped it unknown here, worked against her. The sensation of hot breath on the back of her neck made her nerves tingle.

But she reached the other side of the street unscathed and stood beside a woman also squinting a bit nearsightedly into the store window. Companionably, they looked together, discussing the display of lady's clothing, until, turning toward her, the woman said, "Is that man over there looking at you?"

She indicated a scrubby-looking fellow standing at the corner.

"I suspect so." She hadn't imagined eyes watching her, his method so obvious even a stranger noticed. He was tamping tobacco into a pipe even as he gaped avidly at her.

January smiled at the woman. "Perhaps we should move away from each other. I'm afraid—"

The window shattered. Glass flew everywhere. A gunshot echoed. A tug pulled January's hat from its pin as a female-shaped mannequin set on a platform showing off what January assumed was a fashionable dress, spun on an axis inside the store.

The woman cried out as a shard of the glass struck her face.

January pushed the woman aside. "Run."

Wisely, the woman, hand cupping her cheek, ran.

Fumbling at her boot, January drew her pistol. "Stop him," she yelled at a surprised quartet of fellows closest to the man who'd been watching her. His pipe. It had been a way to signal whoever fired the shot.

But the bystanders refused to move. And she didn't dare trust her aim with people darting this way and that. The ones to the left tried to go right; the ones on the right tried to go left. Stupid as they were, like her chickens in a windstorm, she didn't want to shoot one by accident. Meanwhile, not only the person who'd shot at her got away, but so did the pointing man. It struck her she'd seen the man with the pipe before. He'd been standing outside the Spokane Hotel when she left this morning. One of Joe's stoolies, she'd wager. Apparently, he had control of a whole gang.

Seconds later, the street was empty but for her and a few folks still milling in circles like cattle stopped mid-stampede. Prudently, she'd tucked her pistol back in her boot as soon as the pipe bearing man disappeared down a narrow opening between buildings. Prudent because of the pair of policemen who converged on her when a man pointed at her.

"You," said the patrolman in the lead. He flourished the heavy looking black baton in his fist. "What's going on here? Did you do that?" He pointed at the window. Without waiting for her to say a word, he pinned her arms behind her back. "You're under arrest."

January made herself go flaccid although her natural inclination was to fight his rough grasp. "You're making a mistake," she protested, trying for calm. "Ouch. You're also hurting me. Someone shot at me. They missed and hit the window."

"Feh." He made a sound somewhere between a laugh and a snort. "A likely story. Who'd want to shoot at you? What's the matter? A country girl come up from the sticks thinking to steal yourself some pretties?" The man had an Irish brogue.

He also poked her with his baton hard enough to leave a bruise.

"Ouch," she said again. "Sir, that is unnecessary. I'm not resisting you."

"Looks to me like you are." Grinning, he pushed on one arm and pulled on the other at the same time, making it appear she was fighting him. "Get to moving, girlie. I'm taking you in."

January barely kept on her feet as, evidently intent on making a show for bystanders, he hustled her along. One raised his hand as if in protest, which the policeman ignored. Her hair, tucked neatly into a coil under her hat when she had met with Delbert Avery, straggled down her cheek. The hat had been lost, trampled under the patrolman's foot and left behind.

Reasonably certain she'd be able to escape if she tried, January stayed quiet. That's not to say her respect for Spokane police didn't waver, though making a scene struck her as unwise. Apparently, the town's acceptance of her status as the Flowers heir—a point Mr. Avery kept trying to impress upon her—would be even less accepting if this struggle became known.

Not that she particularly cared. She didn't plan on making friends here. Get in and get out as quickly as possible. That was her goal. At that, she almost laughed. Would have if she hadn't been struggling to get her breath after the policeman jabbed her in the ribs again.

Did she, or did she not, sound as if she were plotting a crime of some sort? If so, this buffoon of a cop hadn't a chance of catching on.

Despite the glare January bestowed upon him, the policeman must've sensed her amusement. It earned her another swat with his baton, this time on the hip, that paralyzed her leg for a moment. She stumbled, nearly falling. It caused both of them to slow.

"You, sir," she said, gasping with pain and tilting her face toward him, "are going to be very sorry for striking me. I guarantee it."

Perhaps for the first time, he saw the scar. His eyes fixed on the S, an indiscriminate murmur rising under his breath.

"Lynch," someone roared from behind them. "Rory Lynch. Hold on, you idiot. Don't take another step."

The patrolman, his name evidently being Rory Lynch, stopped and turned. His face slowly drained of color. Perforce, January stopped, too, and was grateful for the respite. A man clad in a blue uniform with sergeant stripes strode toward them.

She watched the big sergeant approach, his stride long and forceful. Beyond him, a block down and standing on the corner across the street, Delbert Avery stared after them. When he saw her looking, he raised an arm and waved. Jerking away from Lynch, she waved back.

"Oh, hell and damnation." Lynch sounded pained. And maybe disappointed. "Would have to be Sergeant Ferguson. I'm in for it now."

January was unmoved. "I tried to tell you," she said, frost in her voice. "Someone shot at me." *Ferguson?* Last night, Eli had mentioned a friend named Milt Ferguson on the police force.

"Sure." Lynch's attempt to appear sincere failed. "All I'm doing, ma'am, is escorting you to the station so's you can file a report. That's all. We needed to hurry, ya know, in case that feller came back."

The new policeman had caught up, close enough to hear January's reply.

"Liar," she said, so nobody could mistake his excuse

for anything else. "Wait until your boss sees the bruises you inflicted."

"You can't show—" Lynch started but her glare stopped him.

"You don't know what I can do." She whirled toward Sergeant Ferguson who towered over her head. "And you. What are you grinning about?"

"Me? Grinning?" Milt Ferguson wiped the grin from his moon face. "Why," he said slowly, "I am. I guess it's because this sad excuse of a policeman is finally gonna get fired."

Lynch balled up his fist and swung a haymaker at Ferguson. The sergeant, being a whole lot lighter on his feet than one would expect for such a large man, slid back out of range as Lynch, propelled by his own momentum, stumbled past him. Stepping in closer, Ferguson landed one short punch to the ribs.

Lynch, air gusting out, collapsed like a kiddie's balloon.

And that was that.

"Well," January said, her upper lip curling. "All bluff and bluster and folded up like a wet sheet."

Milt laughed. Offering January the support of his thickly muscled arm, they started off, leaving Lynch still fighting to regain his feet. "Mr. Avery says you'd best file charges against this lout before word hits the papers."

"You mean before he rouses any of his compadres who might back him?"

"Smart lady. It's exactly what I mean." He stared straight ahead. "But then," he added, "Pasco told me you was smart."

"He did?" She smiled. "Do you know Eli well?"

"I do. A good friend but make no mistake, you don't ever want to get crosswise of him."

\* \* \*

BEHIND THEM, Lynch scuttled away. He had to report right away. Good thing he knew where to find the boss man. And he'd better get to him fast, before news of this blunder spread. At least it wasn't his fault. Just bad luck.

# CHAPTER 10

AT THE POLICE STATION, MILT FERGUSON INTRODUCED January to a detective who took her statement. Whether overworked or suffering from too little sleep, much to her disgust he yawned repeatedly, mouth opening into what looked like an empty pit. He was, she noticed, missing a good many teeth. His bored attitude convinced her nothing would come of the effort she made in making her report at the city hall. Lynch would no doubt remain on the force to bully other women, regardless of Milt Ferguson's claim, and whoever had shot at her would go free.

As to the store window, she supposed businessmen were forced to consider breakage by persons unknown as part of the cost of doing business. T.T. Thurston often complained of such costs.

The detective made no promises. Not to look for the culprit, and certainly not to catch him.

Back at the hotel, feeling unclean and in need of a soothing bath, she found the clerk hovering around a thin, fiercely erect gentleman seated in one of the lobby armchairs. He wore his graying hair, almost the same dull color as his suit, slicked back from a center part. A tray with a coffee service and a plate of pastries—untouched—sat on a table beside him. The bulging leather briefcase propped against the armchair's leg at his feet indicated his presence meant business, not pleasure.

The clerk, whose name she'd learned by now was Mr. Farley, greeted her with what appeared to be relief.

"Here you are, Mrs. Billings," he called to her. "You have a visitor." He nodded toward the armchair's occupant.

January, who'd had some experience with bank executives in the recent past, guessed the visitor's identity right away. Not the entity he was associated with, exactly, although Mr. Avery had given her a list of several men important for her to meet. A banker had headed the list. Power and authority oozed from this man's very pores. The smell of money, as if embedded in his clothing or on his skin, wafted to her from all the way across the room.

Sighing, as she wished to wash the police station's odor out of her nostrils in the worst possible way, gritted her teeth and obeyed the call. Smoothing her mussed hair behind her ears, she headed toward him, feet dragging.

"Mr. Salter?" she said, taking a chance on his identity.

He rose to his feet. As tall as Milt Ferguson, he towered above her, but his thin form didn't quite *loom* as the policeman had done.

He made a controlled half-bow, his gaze drifting

over her countenance. "Yes. And you are Mrs. Billings, I presume."

Was that disapproval she heard? And saw in the twitch of his right eyelid.

"I am." She offered her hand. Her grandfather, she thought, most certainly had a lot of money if the banker came to meet her. Ordinarily, she would've been summoned to meet with him in his office at a time he stipulated. A second thought followed the first. *What does he want from me?*

Instead of a handshake, he waved her toward the other armchair. The motion struck her as more of a command than an invitation. Coolly, she took her time perching on the edge of the seat, shoulders back, booted feet neatly crossed. He sat and leaned into the chair across from her, at ease.

"May I pour you a coffee?" he asked.

She hesitated before saying, "Please."

"Cream? Sugar?" He already had the creamer ready to pour.

"No, thank you. I take my coffee black like a true westerner." Inwardly, she laughed. Taste was taste. "Now, what can I do for you?"

Her words had come too late. He'd already diluted the coffee with cream, dropped in two sugar cubes, and pressed it insistently toward her. After a moment, she accepted the cup and saucer, looking down at the swirl of cream distastefully.

A frown crossed his brow, quickly erased—or maybe just hidden as he dipped down to retrieve the briefcase. "I have some papers with me for you to sign, Mrs. Billings. We need to take care of shifting at least one account immediately. It will enable the funds necessary to attend to current domestic expenses. Or I—the bank, I mean—can do all those things for you upon a simple signature, and you won't have to worry about what they're for or if they're paid on time. We'll see it's done. I suppose you are inexperienced in monetary matters, as are most young women. It will take time and schooling for you to catch up."

A shaft of pure fury bolted through her. Self-important condescending ass. She'd about had her fill of them for one day. "I beg your pardon? Time and schooling?"

He frowned again in a genteel sort of way. "Did you not understand? I'm afraid I don't have time right at the moment, but I can send one of my assistants over to explain the process."

January felt her scar burn as her blood settled into a simmer. She had a hunch he was worse than a simple condescending ass, but at this point, it would probably be best not to call him out. She already had enough enemies in this town.

On the other hand, did it even matter?

Setting her untouched coffee cup aside, she rose to her feet. "Not necessary. Leave the papers with me, please. I'll read them when I have a moment. Have your assistant call me here tomorrow morning and, if I deem it advisable, we can arrange a meeting at a mutually convenient time."

He stood because she did, his lips compressed as if annoyed. He had light, almost colorless eyes. Right now they were flashing like electric lights. "Madam," he said, frost in his voice. "I'm a busy man. I don't have time to coddle an ignorant country girl's whims. Perhaps, if you asked nicely, your cousin Joseph would help you with the business."

She sighed. This was twice in one day she'd been called a country girl in a tone that implied it was something to be ashamed of. Loudly enough to reach Mr. Farley who was still lurking nearby, and enunciating each word precisely, she said, "To make certain *you* understand, sir, I repeat. Leave the papers with me. I will read them when I have time. You may have your assistant call tomorrow to make an appointment for us to meet—if necessary."

So much for not making enemies.

His nostrils flared at the dismissal. They fluttered like an enraged bull's though he kept his voice low. "You're being foolish, young woman. As you will soon discover. You don't know who you're dealing with. Joseph and the other legitimate Flowers heirs will not stand for this."

"Understand this, Mr. Salter. It will be a cold day in hell that I consider Joseph Flowers the third in any way except as someone to avoid. And I'm a busy woman who has neither the time nor the inclination to deal with a pompous ass." There. She'd said exactly what she thought. She held out her hand, watching as the import of the insult suffused his face. "The papers, if you please."

He had to give them to her. Reading the expression on his face, she could see he would rather have ripped the documents into a million tiny pieces. Fortunately, or at least January hoped it was fortunate, there were too many witnesses in the hotel looking on with avid interest.

It appeared as though her identity was becoming known and spreading quickly around town. It didn't make her feel one whit better. If anyone had overheard their "discussion"—and she thought they had—the news of it most likely would travel through town as though sent by telegraph.

Thrusting the folder at her, he snatched up an elegant bowler hat from the table beside him and crammed it on his head. "You will be sorry," he gritted, and without further ado stormed away.

Farley trailed after him saying, "Sir, sir," then stopped and turned toward her, hand flapping like a helpless girl's. "He didn't pay for the coffee service," he said.

January sighed a resigned sort of sigh. "Put it on my tab."

She wasn't wrong about the news spreading, as she soon discovered. Every bit of business she contracted that afternoon seemed conducted by someone who knew about her and the terms of Joseph Flowers's will.

The first words out of Eli's mouth when, having dodged the clerk on duty, he knocked on her door along toward evening, proved the reports were even quite accurate.

"I ran into Milt Ferguson when I got back from the Pegasus Farm," he said. He leaned against the door jamb, his dark eyes concerned.

Pegasus Farm, he'd told her last night, belonged to the breeder who wanted Windswept's stud services. This interested her, seeing she and Eli were in the same sort of business back home at The Falls. "Did the fellow have some mares to suit you?"

"Had six, but could only afford a couple breedings." Eli smiled a satisfied looking smile. "He had me choose which two of his mares."

She could tell the choosing pleased him, and

opened her mouth to provide congratulations, but he'd already gone back to Milt Ferguson.

"Never mind that. Milt told me what happened this morning. About you getting shot at, then arrested."

"Except your policeman friend rescued me from one of the poorest excuses of a lawman I've ever seen." January got hot just remembering. "The exception being a certain, now terminated sheriff named Elroy Rhodes. But scoundrels, the both of them."

Eli smiled a little at this. "Worse than Dabney?" Dabney was the current lawman, known to dodge his duties whenever effort was concerned. Especially dangerous effort. He preferred to leave that kind of thing to sometime deputy January Billings.

"Dabney is useless, but not, I think, downright evil."

Eli straightened. "May I come in?"

She'd forgotten he was still standing in the hall where anyone who passed could catch their talk. "Please do." Even if Farley might think admitting a gentleman into her room improper.

He shut the door behind him just as someone entered the hall from the stairwell. "I heard another piece of news as I walked through the lobby."

"Oh." January's heart sank. Easy enough to guess what it concerned.

"Yeah. Oh." He walked over to the desk where a few of the papers Salter had brought were spread. The cardboard folder held more. Eli gestured. "About your banker friend. What do you make of all this?"

She managed a smile of sorts, though it cost her. "First off, one document is a blatant effort to bilk the heir—meaning me—out of the contents of one of Mr. Flowers's accounts. A large account, by the way. My signature would give the bank or its designated representative authorization to pay all incoming bills."

Eli's left eyebrow went up. "Designated representative?"

She nodded.

"Pay all incoming bills? Without consulting you?"

Another nod.

"Any word on who this representative would be?"

A shrug this time. "A choice was mentioned. Either Salter himself or—"

"Or?"

"Or Joseph Flowers III."

Eli stifled a curse. "What are you going to do about it?"

Instead of speaking, she took the document and ripped it in half, then in quarters, and those into sixteenths. The pieces fluttered into a trash can beside the desk.

"The next thing I have to do is find a different bank." She made a show of dusting her hands. "I thought this Grandfather Flowers person was supposed to be smart, but if he trusted Salter, he wasn't as smart as he thought. Unless this was part of his plan to begin with." January's voice took on a more sober note. "I wonder if he expected—and meant for me to be stupid and let Joe get hold of everything by wresting it away from me. To give him confidence in the taking of his inheritance by force. And most of all, I wonder if Delbert Avery is in on the deal. It didn't cross my mind before, about Avery, but all this..." Her voice faltered. "I just don't know who to trust in this town. If anyone."

"Ask Avery. Ask him flat out. And then talk to Salter again. See if you can tell if one or both are lying. It's probably best to get yourself a different lawyer. If Avery is on the up and up, he won't mind. He might even be relieved because otherwise this is a lot to put on his shoulders. Especially when you can count on the will being contested."

January's lips trembled when she looked up at him. "I never wanted any of this. Now, more than ever, I don't. But after meeting the cousins, they don't deserve to be rewarded with fortunes. It all just strikes me as wrong."

Eli smiled slightly and shook his head.

"Not that I'm saying I deserve it either," she went on. "I've done nothing to earn this...this...inheritance. I didn't even know I had a grandfather." Her shoulders drooped. "What's more, I wish I'd never found out. People here stare at me, as if their curiosity entitles them to learn every detail, every secret I might have. Plus, somebody wants me dead. Or at least gone." A thought occurred to her and her eyes sparked. "Although whoever fired at me this morning either isn't much of a shot or he missed deliberately. It was an easy shot seeing I was standing stock still. But people... witnesses...saw the shooter. They saw the man who pointed at me just before the window exploded, as well. Most of them ran before the police got there. Of those who stayed, not even one defended me when the patrolman tried to arrest me for breaking a window."

Eli didn't look happy. "Have you read the paper today?" he asked in what seemed a change of subject.

"No."

"Maybe you should."

January's stomach started to churn, this time, not from hunger. "Tell me."

"There's a summary of what happened in The Falls

last month, when Holzer and his gang were killed. Your name comes up, along with mine. There's also a mention of the kidnapped girls we saved from Peel in the spring. But right alongside of it there's a sympathy piece about the cousins. About them being cut out of Joseph's will. Spokane, and I mean that in an over-all way, is curious about you. They're not sure if you're a villain or a heroine. They want to know."

"I'm none of their business."

He smiled wryly. "Doesn't keep them from thinking you are."

She knew he was right. She'd lived with the proof of it from the time she was ten years old, her wound raw and fresh, and everyone stared at her. A good many of them weren't shy about asking what happened. Their questions used to frighten her back then, because she knew they frightened her father. These days too much curiosity just made her angry. The anger helped protect her and made her strong. Or so she told herself.

The reminder had let her drift off for a moment. When she finally heard Eli's question, she figured it wasn't the first time he'd asked it.

"I don't suppose you thought to bring a dress with you," he said, looking at her in a puzzled way.

She didn't understand. "A dress?"

He nodded. "Or maybe the nice outfit you wore to Avery's office. We'll go downstairs and have our supper in the hotel dining room. It is, after all, one of the finest restaurants in Spokane. Maybe the very finest. You can show off, let them see you. And January, try not to provoke anybody."

Her temper, already on a short string, started to smolder before she reined it in. He was right, her wiser self agreed. Let them look once and if she had any luck at all, they'd lose interest.

But she wasn't going to wear her pretty dancing dress in an effort to placate a bunch of people whose opinion she didn't really care about. Nor the walking suit. Back when she and Shay had faced a bright future together, she'd bought a couple dresses. The one she'd brought with her would do for tonight. She'd save the new green dress for a special occasion.

Provided she lived long enough to enjoy one.

# CHAPTER 11

ELI SUCKED AIR WHEN JANUARY APPEARED AT THE TOP OF the stairs and started down to where he waited. Seeing him, she smiled crookedly. His heart hammered.

He'd been to his hotel and cleaned up. Chin freshly shaven, hair brushed, he wore a starched white shirt under his suit jacket. He'd run a cloth over his boots as a finishing touch, and they'd taken on a shine.

But that was nothing compared to January's transformation. He'd seen her in many different guises, usually a bit unflattering. The outfit she'd worn to the attorney's office had been a surprising departure from her norm of dusty boots, plain split skirt, and a shirt. The shirts, he admitted, had been a little newer lately, a little dressier than her usual. He'd seen her previously in what might have been a cut-down left-over from her late husband's wardrobe. Quite frequently she bore smudges of dirt—or blood—and smelled of horses or gunpowder. Even so, she'd always been an attractive, maybe even pretty, woman if you discounted the scar. Which he did and always had.

But tonight? Tonight she was beautiful.

She'd done her brown hair up in a shining coil on top her head and stuck small gleaming earbobs through her lobes. She wore a swirly blue plaid skirt using a navy blue satin ribbon as a belt around her narrow waist, and topped the ensemble with a white blouse that bragged a row of lace down the front. Her erect posture made her queenly.

She approached, stared, then narrowed her eyes at him. "What's the matter?

The Lord knows what she read in his expression. He did his best to wipe it away, whatever it was.

"Nothing is the matter. Far from it." Did he dare mention her changed appearance? Probably best not.

"Huh. You're surprised to find me looking presentable. Admit it."

"Presentable?" He almost stuttered. "January, you look beau—"

He was saved when a man with a white towel draped over his arm approached and said, "Sir, your table is ready. Follow me, please."

The Silver Grill, the Spokane Hotel's famous dining room, occupied a commodious space enclosed within stone walls. An enormous fireplace occupied one wall, where a cheery fire burned. A silver serving cart toted a huge prime rib roast from table to table where a server carved off generous portions. Chairs large enough to easily support a man the size of his friend Milt Ferguson dwarfed January as the waiter seated her. Eli, with some effort, scooted his own heavy chair closer to the table where polished silver flatware gleamed. The waiter—or perhaps he was the *maître d'hôtel*—placed menus before them.

Eli noticed January eyeing the serving cart as it passed their table, pointing her nose toward the aroma rising from it. He smiled. "Prime rib? Or do you want to choose something else from the menu. Salmon is always good here. Or porterhouse steak."

"Prime rib." She touched the elaborate menu. "But I want to read this."

He laughed and gazed around the room where waiters and busboys dashed about. He took notice of the patrons, marking any who looked like they might cause trouble. Discounting the family groups and single women, he concentrated on lone men or couples, settling finally on one couple he recognized.

Reaching across the table, he tapped her hand to draw her attention away from the menu. "I want you to look to your right. Not fast and don't be obvious."

Caught by the changes in her facade, he'd almost forgotten she was no flighty girl overcome by the surroundings. She'd faced enough criminals, danger, and killers to understand the drill and remain calm.

Head barely turning, she reached up a hand as if to pat her hair into place and took a good look, peering between her fingers.

"Oh." She didn't seem particularly surprised. "John Byerly is here. I wonder if the woman with him is Mimi Jonque."

"It is. I expect she'd like a look at you considering her business partner will be losing their backup money."

"You don't think the saloon earns enough to support itself?"

"It should. But his gambling troubles are apt to drag

them in and out of the red. Remember? Avery said something about it."

She made her eyes widen as if woeful. "How sad. He's the only one who didn't threaten to kill me at the first meeting."

He couldn't help himself. He laughed. So, after a moment, did January.

\* \* \*

"I'M FULL TO THE BRIM." January groaned, eyeing morsels of this and that left on her plate. After soup, the roast, vegetables of two kinds, a baked potato smothered in butter, and a salad of fresh greens with tomatoes, she couldn't hold another bite. Where did they even find tomatoes at this time of year? Did the hotel have its own greenhouse? Although pretty, they hadn't had the taste of the fruit from her summer garden, but had still made a fine addition to the greens.

Eli winked and leaned toward her. "I didn't think a lady could eat that much."

She wrinkled her nose at him. "I was hungry." Then a little frown creased her brow. "Is it improper? Did I give these people something else to criticize? Because if it's improper, they shouldn't put so much food on the plate. Look at how much goes to waste." She made a "tsk, tsk" sound with her tongue, wishing she could take the leftover chunk of prime rib home to Pen.

"No. I was teasing. Look around you. Most everyone cleans their plate at the Silver Grill. It's—" He fell silent without finishing. Face hardening, he rose to his feet.

Reading tension, January turned to the side, where if she had to, she could reach her boot gun.

The clatter of silverware and the hum of conversation throughout the restaurant died as if shut off at a faucet.

She looked up as a man came to a halt beside their table. He stood just behind her and outside her field of vision but beside him, she could see the flare of a black taffeta skirt. Earlier, she'd paid particular attention to a woman wearing a gown with such a skirt.

Wadding the napkin spread across her lap into a ball, she set it on the table and stood as well, turning to face the couple.

"Mrs. Billings." John B greeted her. "Or may I call you cousin?"

She made a little flounce. "January is my name. I prefer that to 'cousin.' I'll call you John B, if I may, as I understand most folks do. And this," she looked past him to the woman, "must be Miss Jonque, your business partner." Business partner and more.

The woman let out a breath as if she'd been holding it while waiting to see how this meeting went. Along with the black taffeta skirt she wore a puff-sleeved white taffeta blouse, a rather modest outfit for a woman who owned a saloon. Her breast heaved as the air escaped her lungs. "My name is Mimi," she said, her voice curiously flat. She nodded at Eli, who nodded back.

Maybe she'd expected gunfire.

"How do you do," January said.

John B glanced around the restaurant, taking note of their audience. He smiled and nodded to a couple acquaintances. Their greetings hadn't been loud, but if anything, he went even quieter. "I heard about the trouble today. Me and about everybody else in town. I suppose they'll all draw their own conclusions."

January, following his gaze, didn't believe he was wrong. She nodded, even as she wondered exactly which trouble he referred to, the policeman or the banker? Or both?

"Anyhow, I wanted to say..." He hesitated. "I wanted to say, it wasn't me. I can guess the instigator and imagine you can as well. Simply said, I don't like what my grandfather did with us—any of us—we've always expected something a whole lot different and got kind of used to the idea. But it was his choice to make." Offering his arm to Mimi who placed her hand on it, he looked at Eli, took a step, then halted and grinned at January. "Oh, you should know I put our dinner here on the Flowers family tab. You'll be getting the bill. Since the estate hasn't gone through probate yet, you might want to start looking at charges like that."

"Good to know." She grinned right back. "I'll see the tab is closed as of tonight." Did he realize he'd done her a good turn? Or had the warning been deliberate, given as an intentional favor. Yes, she thought, eyeing him, he did. He just hadn't known the visit from Salter had already warned of the necessity to close all open Flowers family accounts.

The couple walked away, Mimi saying, "Ta," in a friendly sort of way. After a short pause, the sounds and motions of people dining began again. January plopped into her seat as if her bones had melted. She hadn't realized how tense the surprise meeting had made her. It was almost worse than trading gunfire with a band of outlaws. *Almost.*

Eli watched John B and Mimi until they left the building. The couple paused only once, at the coat room to pick up their outdoor garb.

"You're not putting your trust in him, are you?" he asked.

"Not a bit." Her shoulders slumped until she realized and straightened again. "But I don't think he was part of the ambush this morning. And if I hadn't already known, his warning about the open accounts was valuable. I'm sure Joseph and his wife are running up bills as we speak. Trying to, at least."

His expression asked a question and she answered with another of those little grins that curled her mouth up like a self-satisfied cat. "I closed every account I could find reference to after Salter's visit this afternoon. I'd love to be watching the next time Bethany tries to charge something at Mamzelle's Parisian Boutique," she added.

"Whoa," Eli said, his face showing concern. "You're not turning mean on me, are you?"

She couldn't help herself. She laughed.

At the desk, she cancelled the Flowers account, causing the manager to wince.

"Am I making more enemies?" she whispered to Eli as he escorted her to the bottom of the stairs. "They already tried to change my room to a suite." She snorted. "I turned them down."

"I doubt you're making any friends," he whispered back.

"That's all right. It'll keep me on my toes."

Before she slept that night, she wrote a lengthy—and expensive—telegram to Johnny asking him to stay in the house and take care of Pen and her cow and all the rest as she didn't know when she'd be back.

\* \* \*

HOURS LATER, in the dead of night, a fiery missile broke through the window of January's room, spraying glass all over the bed where she lay sleeping.

Awakening in a confused rush, her first realization was of a paralyzing bolt of pain in the vicinity of her knee.

Secondly, fire flashed through her closed eyelids and she smelled the reek of kerosene.

Thirdly, she realized the blanket covering her had already caught fire and if she didn't move, she'd soon be on fire, too.

With a gasp that drew in a lungful of smoke, she leapt from the bed.

Her leg gave way, tumbling her to the floor. She lay there, bewildered and panting in hellish pain.

*What the—?*

Within those few seconds of immobility, the curtains bracketing the window burst into flame and went up with a "whoosh." The flare of light showed her a thin shaft protruding from her leg.

*Ignore it.*

January crawled to the door on hands and the one knee she was able to make work. The other refused to cooperate, dragging behind and leaving a thin trail of blood. Pain flared with every movement.

*Don't think of it now!*

Once at the door, she fumbled for the door knob.

*No. The bolt first.*

Hands climbing the wall for support, she raised herself on one foot and thrust back the bolt. Groping blindly, she found the knob and twisted.

Smoke already filled the room, stinging her eyes, catching in her throat and making her cough.

Though the knob turned freely, the door didn't open.

*Wouldn't open.*

She rattled the knob. Banged the bolt back and forth. Rammed her shoulder against the door panel with enough force to rattle her teeth. Tried to scream "help"—not an action that came naturally to her.

The door, her fuzzled brain announced in a panicked moment, was blocked from the outside. Choked on a cough, she bent to the floor. Something, a wooden shim whose edge was just visible, had been thrust beneath the door to stop it from opening.

The bed was blazing by now, and helped by the kerosene, spreading toward the floor. She spotted her pistol on the nightstand where she'd put it. And laying alongside, the ruler she'd used to help read accounts and keep the lines straight.

Though her knee—she hadn't even looked at it yet —complained, she forced it to walk. She snatched up the gun and the ruler. Limped, leg dragging, back to the door. Her eyes burned from the smoke, streaming with tears until she could barely see. The ruler, when she forced the edge against the shim broke, but not before the shim moved.

She poked it again with the ruler stub.

And again.

The door opened. Smoke and heat poured out into the hallway.

"Fire!" Her cry was faint. "Fire!" she tried again, stronger, louder. She lunged across the hall, thumping her fists against the door opposite her own. "Fire," she yelled. "Help. Fire."

"What?" A man had heard. The door opened and a

grizzled head poked out. His bellow of "fire" awakened more people. Other doors along the corridor opened until the hall boiled with activity.

January collapsed against the wall and watched as both hotel personnel and patrons hurried to extinguish the fire. In only minutes, the peal of the fire department bell signaled their arrival. Men wearing uniforms swarmed up the stairs carrying a large hose. Presently, water flowed onto the flames, pumped by the fire wagon's steam engine. Men with axes in hand followed the water hose. In minutes, the fire was out, the room quite thoroughly destroyed.

Questions flew. So did accusations. She pointed out the shim that had locked her inside. Showed them the broken window. The burned blanket. And her leg, with an arrow still sticking out of it. An arrow just missing her knee joint.

A collective gasp resounded.

"A doctor," whispers went around. "She needs a doctor."

January fought with everything she had to hold onto consciousness. Holding her pistol in her lap, her hand tightened around the grip as if her life depended on it.

As it did.

Because someone wanted her dead. She didn't have to work hard to figure out who.

# CHAPTER 12

Eli went to sleep and was in the midst of a slightly salacious dream featuring, to his intense pleasure, January Billings dressed in her blue plaid skirt when a loud thumping on his room door startled him awake. He shot out of the bed, the gun he kept under his pillow already in hand.

"Pasco," a bass voice bellowed loudly enough to awaken every man, woman, and child on the third floor. And probably those on the second and fourth, as well. "Get up, Pasco. You're needed."

Overhead, a baby began wailing.

Oblivious to the fact he wore only his long handles, Eli opened the door to the limit the chain bolting the door allowed, stepping to the side as he peered out. As he'd suspected, the voice belonged to Milt Ferguson.

"What's happened?" Dregs of sleep made him slow. If given a choice, he'd have gone back to the dream. Unsurprisingly, he didn't get the choice.

"Your Mrs. Billings has had a bit of trouble." Milt

used his baton to batter at the door. "Get a move on. Seems as if she could use your help."

Eli fumbled for the electric light switch and pushed the button to on before loosening the bolt for Milt to step inside. Doors were opening all along the hall, the room occupants peering out. They were staring toward the policeman, alarmed expressions on their faces.

"Is the hotel on fire?" a woman quavered.

"Not this one," Milt said cryptically. "Go back to sleep. You're all right." He closed the door on more questions.

Eli had already pulled on his trousers and was stepping into his boots, stomping to set the heel. "What does 'not this one' mean?" he said to Milt. "You mentioned Mrs. Billings. Is the Spokane Hotel on fire?"

"Not now, I don't suppose." Yet another cryptic and uninformative answer.

Eli pulled a shirt over his head, emerging with his dark hair standing in peaks. "What are you trying to say? That it *was* on fire? Is January—Mrs. Billings—hurt? What's happened?"

Milt sighed. "I don't know the details. I got called to the station due to having helped Mrs. Billings out of a scrape earlier, and when I got to the hotel, she'd already been carted off to the Deaconess."

"The hospital? She is hurt then!" Making no secret of going armed this time, Eli situated his shoulder holster not to conceal the weapon but to make it easier to reach. Milt had nothing to say about the adjustment, for or against.

With an audible huff of concern, exasperation, and worry in a mixture not easy to describe, Eli jammed his Sunday go-to-meeting Stetson on his head. "Dammit,

Milt, what happened. How bad is she hurt? Who started the fire? Have you caught him yet? How did the fire start anyhow?"

"We're going to find out, Pasco. The chief of police ain't going to let this pass, even if it is due to the Flowers boys. Which it probably is. Let's go. I'll tell you what I know when we're out of here."

True to his word, once on the street, Milt burst into the tale. "Your woman was shot with an arrow."

"What?" Flabbergasted by the 'shot with an arrow' explanation, Eli didn't react to the *your woman* identification.

"She was shot with an arrow," Milt said again. "A fire arrow, to be exact. From the second story of the building next door. It smashed right through the window into Mrs. Billings's room and ended up in her leg. Seems obvious whoever done the shooting knew which room she was in. Think it was probably a lucky break it hit Mrs. Billings. Or unlucky, depending on how who's side you're on. Believe it or not, the arrow had a rag wrapped around it, dipped in kerosene and lit, probably meant to just start a fire. Turned out to be more serious than the archer might've thought. He got a two-fer-one."

"A fire arrow," Eli said in wonder. "Whoever would —" He shook his head. "How bad is she hurt?"

"Don't know. We're on our way to find out."

The streetcars weren't running at this time of night. Though Eli felt like breaking into a run, Milt's long stride kept a fine pace. They hurried over to Washington, then up to Second and the hospital. A guard stood at the door. He waved them inside when Milt's uniform bespoke authority to enter.

"They'll have taken her this way." Milt touched Eli's

arm, indicating a hallway where lights showed at the end. Otherwise, the building was dark and almost echoing with quiet. Their boot heels pounded on the tile floor.

Eli wasn't fond of places like this, although he'd been a patient in more than one. In the bounty hunter business, his prey were likely to fight him with bullets, knives and fists. The familiar odor of blood and alcohol reached him as they pushed through a set of doors with a sign that said, "Emergency Care. No Visitors Allowed."

A nurse clad in a dark dress with a stiffly starched white linen bib apron over the top, rushed over to them, putting up a hand in a stop signal as they entered the brightly lit room. "Stop where you are. You can't come in here."

"I'm the police." Milt started past her, but she stepped into his path. He couldn't stop. They collided with a jolt that set her white cap to quivering.

"You are not coming in here," she repeated, and poked a finger into his chest.

It would've been funny if Eli's sense of humor had been working just then. But he could see what he'd come to see. January lay flat on a metal table. A brightly glowing electric lamp hung from a hook above her. Except for her leg exposed from the thigh to the foot, blankets covered her. He could see her eyes were closed, her face very pale. Her brown hair spread across the flat pillow. She seemed to be asleep.

A doctor and two nurses hovered around her, the doctor with a sharp instrument in hand, one nurse with a tray of absorbent materials, the other with a tray of several sharper instruments, including a saw.

Eli sucked in a breath. A saw?

An arrow with a burnt and broken shaft was sticking out from her leg. He took special note of the remains of scorched red fletching. From where he stood, he couldn't tell if the arrowhead was imbedded in her knee or the fleshy part of her leg.

"Holy..." he started. Then, "January?"

The doctor looked up. "She's had ether. Get out of here and quit contaminating my surgery. I'll talk to you when I've got her fixed up."

The first nurse was still poking Milt's chest. He looked down at her as if he'd never seen a woman before. She was almost smiling.

"I'll show you the way to the waiting room," she said, and at last, Milt moved. Or his head did. He nodded.

The waiting area, Eli discovered, consisted of a row of hard chairs lined up against the wall of a small, cold niche off the main hall. The room already contained a lone occupant, a man sleeping with his head so far tilted to one side he must surely awaken with a broken neck. A strong odor of forty-rod clung to him.

Eli sat down as far away from him as he could get.

Milt, who still appeared gobsmacked by the nurse, remained standing even after she left. "She said it won't be long. She said removing an arrow is a simple procedure." No doubting the "she" he meant.

Eli wasn't so sure of that. The saw still bothered him.

"Ether." Milt squinched his face into dried apple wrinkles. "Mrs. Billings won't be making sense for a while even when she starts coming out of it. I've seen it before. I'm gonna go see what the detectives have found out, if anything. You stay here. Talk to the doc when he comes around."

Eli hadn't intended on going anywhere else. He nodded. "Let me know what you learn." He settled into the chair farthest from the man who stunk of booze and vomit. And waited.

Waited until the doctor, dark circles and heavy bags under his tired eyes, came to tell him January was out of danger and would be up and around before he—meaning Eli—knew it.

Probably, Eli thought, before the doctor knew it, too.

* * *

JANUARY CAME AWAKE SLOWLY and was promptly, exceedingly, sick.

"There, there," a gentle voice told her. "It's the ether. It most always turns one's stomach. You'll be fine afterward."

The woman—a nurse according to her garb—helped her sit up and kindly held her hair back for the duration.

January, to her everlasting shame, mewled weakly afterward, like a newborn kitten. Felt about as strong as one, too. She fell back onto pillows the nurse piled behind her, submitting to having her face washed and her mouth rinsed with peppermint water she was forbidden to swallow.

Once settled, the nurse asked, "Care to try a sip of water now?" and January, wishing her head would stop spinning, nodded. Since the water—plain, no peppermint—stayed down, she decided she was better. If only her entire leg didn't feel as if someone had set a branding iron on it. On the other hand—

Memory came back with a start. Someone *had* set

fire to it. With an arrow. A flaming arrow! She flipped back the blanket, but all there was to see was a rather bulky bandage with her foot sticking out the end of it.

The nurse, her name tag read Helen Schultz, smiled down at her. "The doctor removed the arrow, along with a few threads from your nightgown. He was very careful to clean the wound and it will heal up just fine within two or three weeks. There shouldn't be any lasting damage although you'll have a scar. It won't matter much on your leg. Nobody will see it." As if questioning prior visible scars, Helen's gaze drifted toward January's cheek, but she didn't ask for an explanation.

Which was good. January didn't think she could handle a discussion.

"You have someone waiting for you to awaken. Do you feel up to seeing him?" Helen asked.

A bit unsure considering the possibilities, January said, "Who is it?"

"Oh, I don't know." The nurse's brow puckered. "Do you want me to go ask?"

It occurred to January there was a simpler way. "What does he look like?"

At this, the nurse smiled. "He's very handsome, in a tough, masculine sort of way. And he's got the darkest brown eyes I've ever seen."

*Eli.* Relief surged through her. "Then yes. Yes, I do want to see him."

Smiling again, Nurse Helen promised to fetch him, and when she'd delivered her charge, left them alone with the admonition, "You mustn't tire her out. Mrs. Billings needs her rest to heal."

Looking up at him, January forced a smile. "My grandfather left me quite the prize package, didn't he? I wasn't expecting to be set on fire. What do you suppose comes next? Capture by men from Mars?"

He chuckled. "Knowing you, I wouldn't be surprised." Bending down, he touched her lips with his, featherlight and so fast she barely felt it. But he had. Eli had kissed her. Her pulse gave a startled sort of leap.

With no place else to sit, Eli perched on the side of the bed. On her good side, so he didn't disturb her bandaged leg.

"Shall I take you home to The Falls?" he asked. "Say the word and I will if that's what you want."

Did she want to go home? Oh yes. To her ranch. To her dog. To familiar work. But the words to say so wouldn't come out of her mouth. Allow herself to be run off by a trio of greedy relatives used to grabbing whatever they desired no matter who they hurt?

No. It wasn't in her nature. And somehow, she thought her stubbornness may have been what her grandfather had in mind when he wrote a will leaving her in charge of his massive wealth.

He'd expected his grandsons to protest. Had he expected them to try to kill her, too? Maybe. Delbert Avery had said her grandfather knew all about her exploits. About the outlaws she'd faced down. The justice she'd brought to her town. Knew she'd avenged her husband's murder.

He had left her to deal with a problem he no longer had the time, let alone the energy, to solve.

"What a despicable man Joseph Flowers must have been," she burst out. "I'm glad I never met him. He must have known this would happen." January was unaware she spoke aloud until she heard herself. "I understand now why my mother eloped with Dad and never went back to visit. And why my father kept him a secret from me."

"You're not going to do it, are you?" Eli chuckled again and, at her bemused look, added, "You're not going to go home. Your temper is up and you're going to fight your cousins claw and fang."

She rather liked that description.

From his expression, he figured it a foregone conclusion. He'd learned a great deal about her since they met in the spring. And she'd learned a lot about him. About his loyalties even to some undeserving folk, such as his father's ex-wife.

But she hesitated to draw him any further into *her* difficulties. She'd needed his advice about following up on the letter Avery sent, and he'd given it. He'd even played her champion at reading of the will. Since then, the situation had gotten a whole lot more fraught and it didn't seem fair to drag him any further into what was becoming a genuine fight.

"I don't know what I'm going to do. Right at the moment I can't think straight. But I'm mad as...mad as hell!" Even to herself she sounded querulous and unsure. "I'm tired. I need to sleep."

"I'll go then." He took her hand, warm fingers closing around her cold ones. "Your door is guarded. You'll be fine. Nobody can get at you here."

Fuzzy-headed as she was, she neglected to ask how that had gotten set up. Which was just as well as the guard consisted of Eli moving a chair from the waiting room for him to sit on outside her room. A private room, at that, the one set aside for patients of the wealthy variety.

Nurse Helen, who'd taken it upon herself to give the

necessary permission, didn't mention the guard either when she came to settle January for sleep. Upon which, still under the influence of the ether, January closed her eyes and drifted off until morning, when a different nurse awakened her by prodding at her bandage.

Unlike the gentle Helen, this nurse was brusque and more than a little rough. She set January's leg to burning again with her ministrations.

Temper not improved by the pain, January stared at the mound of gray oatmeal covered in canned milk that served as her breakfast and vowed whoever had put her in this predicament would be sorry.

On the third day, despite the doctor insisting she needed to stay off her feet and that the hospital was the best place to rest, January slipped away when no one was looking.

It had been Milt Ferguson who brought the carpet bag containing her possessions from the hotel when he came to question her the day before. Not just clothes for immediate wear, but everything, including her new green dress and the paperwork Salter had foisted upon her.

"You packed up everything?" She started to ask why, but Milt interrupted.

"You've been kicked out, Mrs. Billings. The hotel don't want anyone murdered while staying there, and they figure you're a risk. Said they'd help you find some-place else respectable, if you want. Didn't seem real happy to make the offer, I've got to say. Oh, and a Mr. Farley told me since you'd cut off the Flowers family tab, a final bill would be sent to the usual address, including an estimate of damages."

"Chicken-livered billy goats." Her comment was

almost, if not quite, dispassionate. "If they only knew, I didn't intend on staying on there, anyhow."

Milt made a show of applauding. "That's a girl." Then he frowned. "But where you gonna go?"

Mumbling under her breath because she couldn't get her boot on over the bulky bandage, she arched a brow. "I've got a perfectly good apartment waiting for me. I'd almost forgotten it until now."

Milt's mouth rounded as he caught the reference. "You're gonna stay in Flowers's place? By yourself? Mrs. Billings, in view of what's happened already, I don't think that's such a good idea."

She cut him off. "Why not? Eli has told you I can take care of myself, hasn't he? Besides, they tell me I own the whole building so I reckon I have every right. I'll just make sure my bed isn't directly under a window. Might as well get some good out of it." Or bad, she couldn't help thinking. But, at the same time, a question had been nagging at her from the first time she went there. Now she could look for whatever Joseph III and Bethany had been tearing the place apart trying to find.

And hope she found it first.

# CHAPTER 13

JANUARY SPOTTED THREE HANSOM CABS LINED UP OUTSIDE the hospital's front door waiting for any chance customers. Slipping out of the building while the doorman had his back turned to help another released patient hobble toward the nearest cab, she limped toward the second in line. She chose that one because she liked the condition of his horse, better cared for than the others, by far.

Lugging an over-stuffed carpet bag into which she'd crammed the stack of Avery's and Salter's paperwork, proved a chore. The driver hopped from his perch to give her a hand into the conveyance, shoved her bag in with her, and told his horse to walk on. Only a few minutes later they drew up outside the Flowers Building.

The driver jumped from his seat and helped her to the ground. He eyed the building. "You sure this is where you want to go? I can wait for you if you want."

"Thank you, but no. This is the right place." January studied the edifice and sighed. "I live here for now."

"You what?" Glancing at the scar on her cheek, sudden realization spread over the man's face. "Say, are you that Flowers granddaughter everybody's been talking about? I heard—"

He shut his mouth before he spilled whatever he'd heard. Probably, January thought, because it wasn't anything complimentary. Or maybe lowly cab-drivers weren't supposed to hear their passengers' conversations.

She forced a smile. "Afraid so," she said, offering him cash she found stowed in the pocket of her skirt.

Placing her bag on the walkway beside her, he drove away, leaving her to tote the bag herself. It was a very good thing she didn't feel compelled to bring half her wardrobe when she went anywhere, she thought, as sweat from the effort beaded her forehead. What if she'd been one of those misses who needed a steamer trunk full of assorted regalia for a weekend at an ocean resort? Not that she'd ever been to the ocean. Or owned a steamer trunk, for that matter.

The mere idea brought a weak smile to her lips as she slowly made her way into the Flowers building. Once inside, she faced the dreary climb up the stairs. Although several men passed her on the way up, none offered to help tote the bag. Good thing, she reflected, she wasn't some weak miss incapable of carrying more than a purse. Running a ranch built up muscle. Still, thankful to face a two-flight climb, rather than three or four, she horsed the bag along herself, bumping up the stairway with her limp becoming more pronounced with every step.

Shaking, sweat running into her eyes, January reached the top floor and twisted the brass key in the lock. Exhausted, she staggered into the apartment foyer, nose wrinkling at the musty, stale smell. A glance showed all remained exactly as she and Eli had left it three nights ago. Dirt from the plant pots still lay atop tables. The stench of cigar smoke still hung in the closed-up room from the one Joe had been smoking. Shards of glass from the broken vase still peppered the floor.

Ignoring the disorder, January locked and bolted the door behind her and made her way to the bedrooms. She chose not Joseph's, but the spare room where sunshine poured in through a street-side window and the lighter, plainer furnishings were more to her fancy.

Collapsing onto the bed without bothering to draw down the covers, she closed her eyes and slept. Right up until the light began to fail and the repeated sound of the door knocker jolted her awake. Seconds passed as she struggled to make sense of where she was and why she hurt. More thuds from the knocker demanded action. Memory returned. Grunting, she rolled off the bed to her feet. Her head whirling with dizziness, she cocked her revolver and staggered with it to the foyer. Once there, she hesitated before opening the door.

The knocker sounded yet again. Gathering a breath, she called out, "Who is it?"

"January? It's Eli," a muffled voice returned. "Let me in."

Was it truly him? January thought it was his voice, but a door as thick as this one had definite sound altering qualities. Unsure, but knowing she had to see, she released the bolt and flicked the lock, but didn't go so far as to actually open the door. Stepping to the side, she said. "Come in."

If someone bent on shooting her on sight tried to enter, she'd have the extra second it took him to turn the knob and come inside.

But it was Eli, bearing a picnic basket from which issued the enticing aroma of fried chicken, cinnamon, and fresh-baked bread. Vinegar, as well, she decided, sniffing the air like Pen anticipating a meaty bone, so there might be pickles. A pickle sounded good.

She released the hammer on her little Smith and Wesson.

His hands full, Eli cursed under his breath when she flipped the light switch. He took a moment to study her.

"You look terrible," he said with ruthless honesty. Evidently deciding she was all right since she was on her feet and carrying her pistol, he said, "Are you hungry?"

She considered. "Starving."

He pushed past her, heading for the kitchen. "A good sign."

In a matter of moments, he'd built a fire in the cookstove using the supply of kindling and chunks of wood from a nearby woodbox. As for January, she went to make use of the bathroom, delighting in hot water pumped all the way from a basement boiler to wash her face, and also, the luxury of something other than a two-holer.

When she got back to the kitchen, Eli had plates, knives and forks, and cups for coffee on a small kitchen table.

"I didn't think you'd want to eat in the dining room," he said, and she shuddered.

"No. The kitchen suits me just fine."

"Right," he said, "when we're having an indoor picnic."

They were down to serious portions of apple crisp before she got up the nerve to inquire as to how he'd found her. "I know I should've sent a message. But the opportunity to escape came and I took it."

"Escape?"

Embarrassed, she made a wry face. "Police hovering, nurses ducking in and out of my room every few minutes. Unidentified people walking up and down the hall all speaking at the top of their lungs. My nurses chased several away, some of them more than once. I suspect Joe sent a revolving crew to keep an eye on me. I imagine he was hoping I'd die."

She paused and laughed, hard and bitter. "Not that it would do him a particle of good. My grandfather, you see, made contingency plans in case I met with an untimely accident. Too bad he—and Mr. Avery—didn't make the contingency known to the cousins. It might have saved all of us some trouble. Especially *me*."

Eli paused with his coffee mug halfway to his mouth. "Is it a secret or can you tell me what this contingency plan is?"

"Sure. I'd tell them, too, if they'd ask nicely. Though I doubt they'd believe a word I said, even if they had copies of the codicil right in front of them."

His finger drummed on the table top.

"You remember," she said, "the part saying I can do whatever I want with everything after a year? Keep part, sell part, give some or all away?"

He nodded.

"As it so happens, there's more."

"For instance?" His dark eyes glinted behind narrowed lids.

"For instance, if I should happen to die or abandon the claim, the cousins still don't get to take over. Take Mr. Tanner, who farms the Palouse land and has been an excellent steward. He has first choice to buy the place, but if he can't, when sold the money goes to support the local orphans' home. The proceeds from the Airgead mine will bankroll a fund for disabled or out-of-work miners and their families. The horse ranch provides for abused or abandoned animals. Apparently a group here in town have been advocating for stray animals and they persuaded Joseph to their cause."

As if awed, Eli said, "I'll be damned."

She laughed. "When the city properties are sold, this building goes to a source that won't be revealed until that time. Generous donations will be made to build and support a park, provide for a couple new wells out in the valley area, and...and...I guess I forget anything else. Anything left over, it says, is left to the executor's discretion."

"And who is that?"

"I don't know. I haven't named anyone yet."

Eli sat back in his chair, the legs squeaking across the tiles. "That's a lot of money."

"That's a lot of goodwill and good deeds." January corrected him, but Eli was shaking his head.

"I guess I hear something different," he said.

Little vertical lines formed between her brows. "Aside from the possibility there'd be nothing left by the time the lawyers and courts got done divvying it up among themselves? What, for instance, do you hear?"

"Only about a million reasons for more folks than the Flowers boys to want you dead."

Like a snap of the fingers, January heard it then, too. It had taken her long enough, she thought in disgust. Sighing, she traced the scar on her cheek with her forefinger and met Eli's dark and worried gaze.

"For all these years I believed it was just my Shutt grandfather who hated me. Now I see this one did, as well."

"Hated you? I don't think he... Why would he?"

She shrugged, her shoulders stiff. "Who knows? I don't. But think. Someone must truly wish you ill when they concoct such drastic methods to foment hatred of you in others."

\* \* \*

A GREAT WEIGHT lifted from Eli's shoulders when he found January safe, sound, and holed up in Joseph Flowers's apartment. At first. What had been a companionable dinner turned sour in the recounting of the special instructions in Joseph Flowers's will and its peculiar conditions.

What had the old man been thinking, opening January up not only to the greed of his grandsons, but also each of the entities named as potential beneficiaries? Was she right in her grandfather's motive? Or had Flowers despaired of his grandsons' worthiness and devised all this as a test of their fortitude. Maybe he thought they ought to work for what they already considered theirs.

According to Avery, Joseph senior had thoroughly investigated January's exploits. Had he considered her, whom he'd never met, capable of making the inheritance a true test?

Before he could come to a conclusion, January's next utterance lightened the atmosphere. She burped. Loudly. Said, "Excuse me, please," while he chuckled.

She smiled, too, her face turning pink. "Good thing I didn't do that at the Silver Grill the other night. They'd probably have decided I was part of the rough crowd and thrown me out on my ear instead of waiting until somebody tried to kill me. Hah. Graveyard humor."

He hadn't liked the humor, if that's what it was, but he answered just the first part. "Doubtful. People from all over come to eat there, including sheepherders, loggers, miners, whoever can pay their prices. They aren't always the most respectable citizens."

"Outlaws?" Her forest dark eyes sparked.

"Wouldn't be surprised."

"Where did you get this spread, anyway? It was very good." She indicated what remained from the picnic basket. There wasn't much; a few soft bread rolls, a couple chicken thighs, three dill pickles tangy with flakes of hot peppers.

He felt a surge of satisfaction at having pleased her. "Found a little hole in the wall restaurant where the proprietor was willing to pack it up. She made me promise to bring the basket and containers back in the morning." He stood up and patted his belly as if it belonged to a plump Santa Claus. Not true since he was a lean man. "I'll get these washed."

"I will," she insisted.

"We will."

So they did.

He had more instructions for her before he left.

About locks. About something noisy to provide warning in case someone got in despite the locks. After all, they didn't know who all might have a key.

"Plot out an escape route," he told her. "This is a big apartment. Find a good place to take cover if you can't get out. A spot where you can make a defense."

January smiled a little and said, "I will."

He knew he didn't need to give so much advice. Or any. She'd been in danger before and fought her own way clear. But the thinking and the saying made him feel as if he was doing something.

She walked him to the door, yawning again with weariness even after her long nap. Time, he figured, for him to leave.

"Lock up the minute I'm outside," he said. "I'll wait until I hear the tumblers click over."

"I know the drill." January waggled the brass key she held. She smiled up at him as if...as if...

Eli knew he shouldn't do it, but he did anyway. Setting down the picnic basket, he took hold of her shoulders and drew her closer, until she was right up against him. She didn't fight any. Didn't protest. Just let herself be drawn.

And when his head lowered, hers may have risen a little. Enough so when their lips met, it seemed the most natural thing in the world. Most exciting, natural thing, and it ended much too soon for him.

She stepped back. "Goodnight," she said, all breathy-like.

As if dazed, he picked up the basket and walked away, forgetting to wait for the lock to click and the bolt to slide home, even after all his previous instructions.

Although, if he'd been listening, he would've heard them.

When Eli had gotten to the apartment, there'd still been people about. Lights had been on in the various offices with men bent over work spread across their desks, their doors still open to the hall. Not now. The halls were dark, doors closed and locked. Silent. The building was empty.

Except it wasn't.

He'd descended the first set of steps and started down the second when he caught a faint noise from overhead. Not the thud or a clomp of some innocent somebody openly taking the stairs, but the slither and slide of a sneak creeping after him. Stopping mid-stride, he tilted his head upward and listened harder. Had January come to see him out? No. She'd have called to him if she had. So who was this?

No one else should be in the building.

And come to think on it, shouldn't there be an electric bulb left burning over each staircase? He was a noticing man, and he knew there'd been one lit when he arrived, even though it hadn't been full dark yet then. Someone had either removed the light bulb or turned off the switch.

He had a good guess who, and figured it didn't bode well for him.

Another sound caught at him. There. What was that but the soft click of a gun being cocked?

Had they been waiting for him to leave January alone all the time he'd been with her? Anger roiled his gut.

Or was he the primary target? He'd been introduced as her bodyguard. The cousins' first thought might well be to get rid of him, thinking to make her into an easier mark without protection. He found the idea almost funny. The Flowers contingent was in for a surprise if they started a fight with Deputy Mrs. January Billings.

Whoever was stalking him must've gotten impatient. The footsteps started again, bolder n this time, much less hesitant. He moved, too, bounding two steps at a time to the bottom of the stairs. Very little light reached across the lobby to the stairway from the outside windows. His final step had been into deep dark.

Silently, he set the picnic basket down, positioning it just so, and drew his revolver from the shoulder holster.

He'd learned to be pretty good at creeping up on outlaws during his bounty hunter days. Could be he was a little out of practice now, but his boots neither slithered nor slid as he boldly crossed the lobby to the front entry and the grouped benches and hat trees standing there. Making a production of it, he unlocked the door and opened it, paused a couple seconds—time enough for a man to pass outside—and closed it again.

Hearing Eli's supposed escape as intended, whoever was following him rushed down the final six or eight steps, only to stumble over the picnic basket left at the foot of the stairs.

He—a loud grunt told Eli the sex of his opponent—hit the floor with a loud smack. A gunshot echoed in the enclosed space. A surprised—and pained—curse followed the shot as the contents of the basket scattered with a clatter and bang across the tiled lobby. Where the bullet went, Eli had no idea. If not for the man's fall, it most probably would've lodged in Eli's back.

At least it was easy to track his opponent by the noise.

"Drop the gun," Eli shouted, "and slide it over to the door."

He'd been standing, now he sank down behind one of the benches. A wise move on his part as a bullet followed the sound of his voice to where he'd stood. As it happened, a good five feet above where he now sprawled flat on his belly.

Afraid a shift in the darkness would show his location, he backed up and rose into a crouch beside the bench.

"You'd best drop the gun," he said, "because you're not getting out of here with it. Not alive, you aren't."

Another shot, nowhere close this time, possibly because January had come out of the apartment and called down, "Eli? What's happening? Are you all right?" It was enough to startle the man into firing again, *up* the stairwell, this time.

Fool woman. She was hurt. Exhausted. Why didn't she stay inside and let him handle the situation?

Instead, all she did was entice the fellow into getting up and go running back up the stairs.

Quick as a fox, Eli leapt to his feet and followed, slamming his pistol into the holster as he went. "Look out, January," he yelled. "He's on his way up."

The man snarled, looked back, the paleness of his face a blur, and snapped a shot over his shoulder. A clear miss.

Eli closed the gap between them as the shooter got to the landing on the second floor. A flying leap took the man down like a player in a game of tackle. His gun soared free of his hand to land tantalizingly just out of reach. They wrestled for it in the semi-dark, grunting, taking hits, giving them back twofold. Fists pounded into flesh with meaty thuds. Eli's knuckles turned slippery with blood, cut when he slammed a fist into the man's teeth. Then his cheekbone went numb for seconds before blazing up with pain. He was aware of the man rolling, stretching, reaching, and then a sixth bullet came close enough Eli didn't know why it didn't kill him. His shoulder rig came loose, dropping to his waist even as he slammed a blow into the man's gut that set him to coughing and puking.

Eli rolled to the side out of the way, grasping for the now empty, loose gun.

"Eli? Do you want some help?" he heard January call. She may have called before. If so, being otherwise occupied, he hadn't realized.

"No. Stay where you are. I've got him," he called back, panting and cross as a thwarted child. Truth to tell, he felt a bit of a fool having almost let the fellow get away with whatever he had planned. The whole episode showed he'd be better off if he ignored Mrs. Billings's undeniable charms, at least until all this was done with. He was no youngster to moon after the girl of his dreams. But that kiss—

On the off chance it might make him feel better, Eli clouted the fellow on the back of the head with the pistol barrel.

The would-be assassin, who'd been struggling to sit up, dropped like he'd been smote by God's own hand, eyes glazing over and his open mouth pressing against the floor. He wasn't a pretty sight.

Neither, Eli supposed, was he.

# CHAPTER 14

Wondering what was taking him so long, January stood at the top of stairs waiting for Eli to appear. The apartment door was open behind her and the electric light put her in a golden glow, her smile bright—until she caught sight of his face.

"Eli! You need stitches. Your cheekbone is cut to pieces," she said on a little gasp. "And your knuckles are bleeding. Are you sure you won?"

Eli scowled at her, dark eyes flashing. "Yes. I told you I didn't need your help."

Trying for an inscrutable expression, although none too sure she succeeded, January set her mouth into a straight line. "You could've fooled me. Looks like you took some pretty decent licks. Is he dead?"

"No." His scowl grew. "A good thing, too. If there's anything you don't need right now, it's having a dead man linked to you in any way."

"If there's anything I don't need, it's somebody sneaking into my building and trying to kill me. At least, I suppose that was his intention."

"Hmm," he said, agreement of a sort.

"Well, if he's not dead, where is he and what should we do with him? Shall I call for a patrolman?"

"Not a good idea. I figured I'd—"

Her startled cry cut short whatever he'd begun to say. "Eli! What happened to your shoulder rig? Are you shot?"

His brow creased. Fumbling at the holster where it sagged down around his waist, he stepped into the apartment foyer with its brighter lighting and uttered one of those indecipherable "hmms," again. "It's nothing much," he added, "except for ruining a good holster rig and a shirt."

"Here, let me see." January took hold of the jacket's arm from his opposite side and tugged gently while he tried to help.

"Ow," he said, almost absently when she hung the jacket on the hall tree. His thumb rubbed the ends of the strap that had gone over his shoulder and across his back. The freshly cut split showed raw leather where the bullet had burned through the strap to crease the top of his shoulder. *Only* a crease, thanks to the thickness of the strap. A thin trickle of blood leaked down his shirt and dyed the leather a rusty red.

He looked up, taking in her appalled expression. "Close call."

"Is that what you call it? A couple inches to the right and you might've been missing your head." January felt the blood draining from her face. "It's my fault you're here. It would be my fault if you were...if you were—"

Eli reached over and shut the apartment door. In case by some remote chance the lout he'd left below came to his senses, he didn't want him listening in.

Better he got away. "No, it wouldn't. You didn't ask me here. I came on my own."

Maybe she hadn't asked, but she'd most certainly wished for him to come with her. A pretty strong wish, in fact. And she hadn't sent him away when somehow, her wish was granted. She'd blindly accepted his help when she found him waiting for him in front of the attorney's office. Which hadn't, she admitted to herself, been fair.

"No," she said, voice creaking, "My problems have put you in danger. You don't want mixed up with these people."

But he wouldn't listen. Instead, he pulled her into his arms and patted her on the back like a child and said, "It's all right, January. I'm all right. We both are. Buck up, you're going soft. We've got work to do."

Eli was right. She'd turned into one of those gooey marshmallows T.T. Thurston stocked in his store at Christmas.

Leaning back, she peered up into his set, bleeding face. "What work?" It must, she decided, be her wounded leg making her act the weakling. She was stronger than this. To prove it, she pushed against him. Lightly.

He let her go and unbuckled the shoulder rig, setting it aside. "To start with, we need to pick that fellow's brain. He needs to tell us who sent him. Afterward, I figure to dump him down at the train depot and tell him to get out of town. And then, if you aren't too tired, I think you should try to find whatever Joe and his wife were looking for here the other night. It could be this one..." a tilt of his head indicated the fellow he'd left in the hall "...was just looking to rob the place. Maybe on Joe's orders, maybe on his own account."

"Meaning you think he might not be in the cousins' pay?" She'd taken it for granted Joe had employed him.

"The thought crossed my mind. Word is getting around about the Flowers heir, in case you didn't know. There's apt to be a good many pieces of trash like this one trying to cash-in thinking you're easy pickin's." He snorted. "Wait until they discover they're mistaken."

January pondered the idea, the trying to cash-in part, and found it lacking. The part about being easy pickings? Questionable. "You may be right, but I'd still bet Joe sent him. Or Calvin. Or Salter. Or even John B."

Eli chuckled. "Yeah, well, I'm not betting against you."

Minutes later January, rummaging in the bathroom as the logical place to find medical supplies, found a tin holding surgical tape and gauze. Thus armed, she stuck gauze and sticky tape over Eli's slashed cheekbone, and managed to wrap a bandage around the scrape on his shoulder. He sat unmoving, his eyes fixed on her worried face, and only flinching a bit now and then. Afterward, he donned his jacket, wincing as he settled his arm in the sleeve, and stowed his pistol in a pocket.

"I expect he'll be waking up about now," he said. "Leave him unguarded down there any longer and he'll likely make a run for it."

January agreed. Limping badly, she trailed after him to where he'd left the intruder. Eli's recommendation to hustle hit the mark. They found the fellow groaning as consciousness came back and on his hands and knees trying to crawl away. How he'd thought to manage the last flight of stairs January didn't know. Seeing the lump on his head, she figured he probably had a tremendous headache along with the goose egg and most probably wasn't thinking straight. Sympathy played no part in her first thought.

She surveyed the damage and managed a deliberate insult. "Was he always this ugly?" she asked Eli.

He snorted. "Don't know. He might not have been this bad but I wasn't paying attention to his beauty."

The man glared when she snickered.

Folding her arms across her chest, January stared down at him. "What's your name?"

He didn't answer. Making pained noises, and in her opinion going a bit overboard at it, he managed to roll onto his side and sit up. Eli allowed him the movement, letting him lean against the wall before nudging him with the toe of his boot.

"The lady asked a question," he said.

The fellow's split lip was still seeping a mixture of blood and drool, and taking aim, he deliberately spat a mouthful of it in the direction of January's foot. The one attached to her wounded leg.

Eli drew his arm back, prepared to punch the man again, but January waved him off. "Don't bother," she said. "I don't really care what his name is. He'd probably lie, anyhow. I'll just call him Ugly."

Eli smiled. "Works for me." He turned his attention to their prisoner who was gaping at January as if he'd lost his wits. "Tell me this, mister, and we might go easier on you. Who sent you to kill Mrs. Billings?"

January, before she could hide her reaction, sent him an uneasy look. Apparently, Eli didn't feel they had time to beat around the bush. The interrogation was going to be direct, and very likely harsh. Which suited her, she decided. Her leg was aching terribly and she wasn't in the mood to be gentle.

Ugly didn't say anything. His eyes, the white of one shot through with the red of a broken blood vessel, fixed on her.

Eli toed him again. "Speak up. Who sent you after Mrs. Billings?"

The man flinched away from the sharp poke in his side. "Who's Mrs. Billings?" he mumbled. "Don't know anybody by that name."

January shuddered, hoping Ugly hadn't noticed her reaction. "You notice he doesn't deny he's here to kill me. Just says he doesn't know my name."

"I did notice." Eli surveyed the man. "What do you think? Is that the same as admitting he was hired to kill you?"

"I'd say so." She was proud how utterly calm she sounded. Funny, since she didn't feel calm at all. "A cheap killer for hire." She looked at Ugly, and now she snarled. "Who is paying you? Joseph Flowers?"

He tried spitting at her again, but failed to work up a good slug of saliva.

Using an open hand, Eli slapped him. Plenty hard, just not hard enough to knock him out. Ugly yelped.

Down below on the ground floor, the front door began rattling as someone tried to get in. A man yelled, "Hie! Who's in there? Open this door."

Both she and Eli froze. January's heart gave a leap. Someone coming to finish the job on her? Or would this be the police, finally arriving to investigate? Ten minutes ago there'd been six shots fired. Would the ruckus be ignored in a city like Spokane? Officers should've been here by now. Or did they only investigate when paid to do so, or when enough gathered to make a gang? She had to wonder, remembering how they'd circled in on her like magpies at a kill when someone shot out the dry goods store window. Depended on who was paying them, she supposed. Reports on the reputation and efficacy of the Spokane Police left something to be desired.

Not for the first time, she found herself longing to get back to The Falls and home. To where *she* held the law to higher standards.

"Your name and the name of the man paying you." Eli's attention shifted back to their prisoner. "That's all we want. Afterward, you can take your chances with the police."

And now January cut in, her voice icy cold. "Think about this, sir. We'd be justified in shooting you dead, right here and now. There's two of us. We can swear that you broke into this building and tried to kill me, which is the truth. All we have to say is that we shot you when your attempt failed and you tried to get away."

Ugly blustered. "It didn't happen and you can't prove it did. I'm just a thief, looking to find whatever is laying loose."

She smiled. "A likely story," she said scornfully. "There's two of us. I'm the Flowers heir, plus someone— maybe even you—already tried to kill me. Who do you think they'll believe? Who they'd have to believe? You? I don't think so."

"No. That wasn't—" He cut himself off.

"Wasn't what?" Eli snarled.

"That wasn't me," Ugly burst out. "I didn't try to kill her before. I swear."

"Then who did?"

"I dunno." He looked away, seeming to steel himself in case of more punishment.

January caught Eli's eye. "Shall we just shoot him? He might go into the cemetery as an unknown when the county buries him, but I don't suppose it matters."

He winked. "Whatever you say."

"No," Ugly said. Or shouted.

Downstairs, as many as three sets of feet and three different voices made enough noise to warn that their company had found a way into the building and were heading up the stairs toward them. She heard a clatter, then someone asking what this picnic basket was doing at the foot of the stairs.

"Dang near fell on my face," he said. "I call that obstructing the police." He called it "*poe-lees*." Someone else laughed, then shouted up the staircase to them, "Hold your fire if you want to live. This is the police and we're coming up."

Hearing the warning, Ugly huffed out air as if relieved.

"Too late." He sneered at Eli with triumph. "You're too late. They'd know. That'd be murder."

January huffed out a bit of air herself. "Do tell," she said. "But is murder even a crime in this town?"

\* \* \*

EXHAUSTION DOGGED January when the police finally marched their prisoner off to jail. By the time they left, she truly did wish the intruder dead. All the intruders, as she painted the police with the same wide brush.

As it turned out, one particularly skinny patrolman had found a basement window unlocked. He'd managed to squirm his way in and run upstairs to open the front door. Afterward, the whole bunch spent more time looking around the building, being especially curious to get a good view of Joseph Flowers's sumptuous apartment, than they did doing any investigating. They looked her over too, maybe not impressed by a woman wearing a split skirt and a white shirt. Her scar drew a great deal of whispered comment.

When a detective put in an appearance at last, the same one she'd talked to earlier, he aimed his questions at Eli, ignoring January and the fact they were in her building and she was the intended victim. Only when finished with Eli did he turn his sights on her and ask her the same questions he'd already had answered. It didn't matter, she supposed. He didn't listen to her anyway.

January had a feeling he'd have liked to accuse Eli of assault, but didn't quite dare. The bullets lodged in the walls, the chip out of the railing, and even a hole in the floor all came from Ugly's gun, a .45. Eli's .38 hadn't been fired. Besides, his grazed shoulder, not that it amounted to much—or so he claimed—spoke for itself.

Being the Flowers heir, or even anyone siding with the heir, was proving a daunting prospect. January had no other words for it. One only a woman like her would tackle. And a man like Eli Pasco.

Eli stayed until everyone had gone, taking a head count to make certain no one got left behind. When they'd gone, he coursed through the building, checking door and window locks while she sat on the stairs and watched the front.

After a while he came and sat beside her. "I've been thinking," he said.

She smiled faintly. "Me, too. Thinking and wishing Joseph Flowers to perdition."

"Flowers senior or the third."

"Both." She shook her head. "I'm a cat's paw, not a real player in whatever game my grandfather set in motion. One that goes on even after his death."

Eli shrugged. "A man like Flowers, he probably figured you'd jump at the chance of money. Possessions. Prestige."

This struck her as amusing to the point of laughter. "Not to mention people trying to shoot me with arrows, set me on fire, and have me arrested. What's more, I suspect this is only the beginning."

"I'd like to say you're mistaken—but I'm afraid you're not." He took off his Stetson and, setting it beside him on the stair, ran his fingers through his thick dark hair. "You'll have to watch your every step, January."

"Yes. I'm aware." Silent, she thought for a moment, scenes running through her head. Finally, she said, "The police are holding back, acting as if they're neutral. Or at least, some of them are. I think they're waiting to see whose side to take when the boys' suit to contest the will is decided. Mr. Avery says it can't be done. Says the document is water tight, but that may depend on the judge."

Eli nodded.

"I have some experience with judges," she went on. "You have, too. They have bills to pay and families to protect, just like everybody else. Sometimes that weighs more heavily than settled law in the decisions they make."

He sighed, retrieving his hat and rising to his feet. "I'm afraid you're right. It's unsettling."

He left then, bidding her goodnight in a thoughtful kind of way. January had already reached the apartment on the third floor when she remembered she'd intended to clean up the scattered parts from the picnic basket and mop up the blood and other fluids Ugly had managed to smear the floor with. The occupants of the lower floors would not appreciate being greeted by signs of the invasion. But then, quite suddenly, all energy left her. She'd rise early in the morning, she told herself. Attend to it then, when there was daylight to see by.

On that thought, she lay on her bed and went to sleep, still wearing her street clothes and hugging a pillow to her chest.

# CHAPTER 15

JANUARY DREAMED OF A BROOM SWEEPING, OF A MOP swishing gently across a floor, of soft footsteps somewhere nearby. The sounds were not intrusive. She went on sleeping until a sunbeam struck directly across her eyes. It was, she instinctively knew, the latest she'd slept since she was a child, though still barely past dawn.

Startled, she sat up, yawning away sleep and remembering she had work to do before businessmen arrived to open their offices. She had no notion what any of them actually did. It might be in her favor to find out.

But later. Clean-up duty came first. Though an all-over bath in the big claw-footed tub in Joseph Senior's bathroom beckoned to her, she splashed her face with water that ran cold from the faucet this morning. Next came the familiar chore of poking up the fire in the cookstove, glad some hot coals remained from last night so she didn't have to start from scratch.

Her leg was better today—or so she insisted to herself—and gathering a broom, a mop, a bucket of water and some rags she found in the pantry, she made her way down to where Eli had fought the gunman last night. But when she got to where memory insisted the fight had taken place, there was nothing.

No sign of the fight remained. No blood. No spit. Not as much as a rumple in the rug. The only out-of-place thing she found was the carpet runner down the center of the stair, when touched, was slightly damp, the colors darker than the dry parts. Even the hole in the wall where Ugly's last bullet had penetrated had been plugged with fresh white plaster. Astonished, January touched the daub, smoothed perfectly into the original wall. It had to finish drying before it could be repainted.

Who had done the cleaning? The repairing?

Who had known cleaning and repair was needed?

Holding the broom like a rifle, she left the other implements on a step and went on down to the lower set of stairs. At the bottom, she stopped. Last night, the police had kicked the picnic basket out of the way as they transferred their unwilling prisoner to the black paddy wagon. Ugly had already stumbled over it, scattering the basket's contents far into the lobby.

The police, she remembered, had laughed about it.

But now, the basket sat on the bench by the entry door. Neatly closed and obviously cleaned, January felt certain if she chanced to open the basket, she'd find the plates, cups, and flatware all back in their designated places and ready to be returned to the restaurant.

The lobby gleamed, although with the sun shining through the spotless window providing extra light, she glimpsed another patched bullet hole on the wall above the door.

January didn't quite believe a Genie had popped out

of a bottle to help her. Didn't believe in fairy godmothers, or do-gooders eager to please her, either. Nor did she think for a second this was Eli's work. In the first place, he had no key, which meant whoever had done this possessed one.

Or did he even need a key?

The answer came almost as a bolt of lightning. Her dream before waking had not been a dream at all. She'd heard those things, the sweeping, the mopping, the footsteps. Which meant, now she had a clear moment to think about it, she was not alone in the Flowers Building. A caretaker must live on the premises, one who worked at night and slept, or at least disappeared until needed, during the day.

And where would he live?

In the basement, of course. This might be a good opportunity for her to get familiar with her newly inherited property.

Whoever had been the architect of this edifice, January soon discovered, had added a sense of playfulness to the design of the building. At her grandfather's request, she wondered? As a builder herself, she appreciated the effort. As someone with a sore leg, the task of discovering the basement's hidden staircase tried her patience.

But she had a feel for spatial awareness even in a building as large as this. Eventually, she found the door beside a brick chimney stack at the end of the lobby. The door took up the whole rear wall of a niche giving directions to the various offices holders with their titles and room numbers. The third floor, she noticed, simply said "private."

One accessed the door, she discovered, by pressing a

brass medallion, which seemed at first to merely be an award for the building's architecture, beneath the roster of names.

The door opened at her touch, silent on well-oiled hinges. She didn't step through. Not yet. Still carrying the broom, she drew her pistol from her boot, and stood listening.

Were those voices she heard, or the muted roar of a boiler? Why hadn't she wondered about the hot water before? And the heat rising from steam radiators in her apartment? And how clean the building always seemed to be? Of course, her grandfather hired someone to take care of maintenance. Someone on the regular payroll.

Standing still and silent at the top of the stairs, January heard a male voice below her curse, the word direct and distinct. Metal clanked and she felt a sudden gust of air rise from the basement's dark depths. Lights suddenly came on. Her eyes, adjusting, made out a sturdy rail and a mechanism to lift heavy objects up and down the stairwell.

Still she hesitated, until remembering this building belonged to her. The lawyer had told her so, so she guessed that meant she could go wherever she pleased. Which raised another question.

Just how many people had a key to this building besides her? And the janitors? Did each of the office holders? She supposed so, which opened the possibility anyone could enter the place at any time. Friend or foe.

The idea shook her. January had to admit it did.

Leaving the broom behind, January started down, holding onto the rail and taking care where she planted her feet. She stopped mid-way, perking her ears toward a slurred mumble coming from an enclosure where she spotted a large boiler burbling, gauges on the side of a large caldron tootling as steam rose up through metal pipes. There she spotted a skinny man clad in bib overalls and a sleeveless shirt jumped up and down while cursing a blue streak.

Doing a good job of it, too, January noted. Or bad, depending on how you looked at it.

"Consarned dim-witted, goat-eyed kids. You damn near blew the damn boiler," he was saying. At least, that's what she thought he said. As noted before, his speech slurred to the point of unintelligibility. From the way he weaved and peered nearsightedly at one of the gauges, she thought he might be drunk.

She paused, unsure whether to accost the drunken fellow. Who knows what he might do, especially as he acted like he was talking to someone. Although he seemed to be alone, he spoke of goats and kids in the same breath as if they were present.

The decision got taken out of her hands when the fellow collapsed. He sank down on the floor in front of the boiler's door, curled into a ball, and began to snore.

Eyes opening wide, January raised a foot to take another step and get down there to check on him, when another person did speak, taking her by surprise.

"About time," a girl's voice said. "I was beginning to think he'd never pass out. You take his shoulders, Jem. I'll take his feet."

"Yeah, yeah, I know the drill." A figure stepped into sight. A boy, clad in stained overalls and a shirt much like the ones the older man wore. He went around to the man's head and stretched him out, raising the arms to take hold of him under the armpits. It looked as though he'd done this many times before. "Pee-uw," he said, mouth curling. "He stinks like an old billy goat."

January, unobserved, grinned. Goats were apparently a common theme.

A girl came forward to stand at the man's feet. "He does. He probably puked on himself again."

She sounded resigned, January noted, as if she were accustomed to it. When the girl bent down to grab the man's feet, January got a better look at her. Younger than the boy, she, too, was small and thin, and like him, dark of hair and pale of skin, as if they might spend most of their time in this basement hidden away from the sun.

January was beginning to feel a bit uneasy. Were these youngsters captives of some kind?

Grunting, the girl got the man's legs spraddled and hanging down at the knee, and lifted. Impressed by the girl's strength when she appeared frail, January stayed where she was. She'd hate to startle the youngsters into dropping the drunk. He already appeared to be slipping out of their grasp.

They'd all moved out of sight when she heard a thunk, a double grunt, and two identical sighs of relief.

"He'll be out for hours," Jem said. "Hurry and get cleaned up, Hattie. We've got to get to school. The boiler will be okay as long as nobody uses all the hot water."

"What about the woman, the new boss, in the apartment? She might." Hattie sounded worried.

"Nah. She's one woman. She ain't gonna use the whole tank. Anyways, I can sneak out at noon and come check the boiler."

They were still discussing whether one woman—meaning her—was even capable of emptying the boiler tank when January hurried up to the center hall. Apparently, she'd found children who worked for her, which meant, if her head was on straight, she now had discovered at least two new dependents. A conversation was in order, just as soon as she figured out what needed said. And who it needed said to. Which of this threesome was in charge? If she had to choose, she'd take the girl. Or the boy. But not the drunk passed out on a cot.

Quietly, she gathered up the cleaning implements she'd left on the stair and retreated with them to the apartment. Time to complete the search Joe III and Bethany had begun. And although she'd never tell them so, she almost hoped there was another will. One that would take all this out of her hands and allow her to get on home where she belonged.

Surveying the apartment's disordered front room, January concluded cleaning this apartment was not part of the basement dwellers' duties. Eli had helped right the overturned sofa, taking one chore off her shoulders. They'd gone through the piece carefully, feeling and listening for anything out of place, but all seemed normal.

Pirouetting, January spun around the center of the room. Joseph had been standing at the fireplace when she caught him and his wife searching the apartment. As January recalled, he'd been puffing on his cigar, his hand poised on the mantel when his wife threw the crystal vase onto the hearth, shattering the vase and knocking off a tiny corner of the slate.

January picked her way through the glass, using the broom she already had at hand to stir through the sad dried remains of flowers, a bouquet left from before her grandfather died. She found nothing suspicious, and with the glass cleaned up, proceeded on to the fireplace.

It took no more than two minutes to find the cubby behind one of the almost black colored bricks. She'd been looking for such a hiding spot. After all, she'd built one into her fireplace at the new house, although she was still working on concealing the mechanism to open it. This one worked perfectly when she found the thumb-sized indentation to release the spring.

A single slip of paper lay inside. Excited by her find, January drew the paper out—and promptly dropped it, shocked when she saw her name scrawled across the fold.

Had her grandfather really thought she'd think to look for a hidden compartment? But then she remembered her dad, a master builder, had met her mother when he worked building a house for Joseph. That had been the ranch house in the valley to the east, she believed, and her dad had very likely been the originator of the hidden cubby built in this fireplace, as well.

So, the old man had paid attention to his son-in-law's talents, had he? If so, that must've been all he'd noticed.

Bending, she retrieved the paper and took it with her into the kitchen. Coffee might soothe her as she summoned up the will to see what Joseph had to say. By the time she sat at the kitchen table, her sore leg propped on a footstool with a pillow under her heel, she felt able to face whatever the note said.

*My dear January,* the note began.

Her grandfather's writing was shaky. Ill-formed, some words misspelled.

*If you're reading this, you probably figured out how I came to leave a note hidden here. You haven't read the letter yet, have you? I thought not.*

*I will always wonder why your mother and father named you after such a cold month. You're not cold at all, are you? From all reports, you're fiery and brave, able to hold your own no matter the odds against you. Supremely loyal to those you care for, as well, an admirable quality in either man or woman. That's why this sticky situation has landed on your shoulders. You resent me right now, and you're apt to resent me more when the year is up. I don't blame you. But after the year, you can give it all away. To my other descendants, if you want and find any of them worthy, or to the charities or anyone else if you don't. Take and use what you need first and I hope you'll make provisions for the ones who need it most.*

Find any of them worthy? Need it the most? January's brow together. What did he mean by that? And *other* descendants?

*I'm sorry for everything I did wrong. I raised and influenced your cousins to their detriment. They lost their parents, my own sons and daughters too young. Then I didn't protect or care for those who should've come first with me. I was cold and driven and lost out on the only one of those progeny who, in the end, I can trust. You. Live well. Let my legacy be known as something to be proud of.*

*Your grandfather.*

*Joseph C. Flowers*

*September 30, 1902*

January choked on a short sob, though for the life of her, she couldn't think why she should sob. The manipulative old coot. What was this letter but another attempt to coerce her into keeping together his vast empire? Hold the legacy in his name? Punish those who didn't live up to his particular standards?

After a while, she got up, found the leftover biscuits and chicken from Eli's picnic in the ice box, and after eating her fill, began the search for whatever Joe and Bethany had been looking for. Not the letter she'd found. January was certain of that much. No. Something else was hidden here, something too large to go in the fireplace cubby. Money? Papers? Artifacts?

Strange, she thought. Those kinds of things should've been left in a bank vault with Mr. Avery having access. Something else then. Something precious. But what?

# CHAPTER 16

AS SHE FELT QUITE PROFICIENT WITH THE TELEPHONE now, with help from one of the telephone girls, January got through to a locksmith who promised to come to the building that very morning and change the apartment's lock. A Mr. Burton showed up right on time. He appeared impressed with the honor of serving the Flowers heir, and installed a new lock within minutes.

"That all?" he wanted to know before he bundled up his tools when finished. He peered around the foyer and as far into the front room as he could see. "Isn't there another door to this place that needs seen to? There should be, you know, in case of fire. Folks have gotten a bit more careful since the fire in '89. How about the windows? Do they have locks?"

January stared at him. "We're on the third floor," she pointed out. "I don't expect a thief to try climbing the wall to get through a window. And a ladder that tall would be a bit obvious."

He took her seriously. "Yes, but there must be another door."

As she thought about it, she knew he was right. There should be. But she'd looked through the rooms and come up with exactly nothing. "Not that I've found," she said.

But just in case, with him trailing after her, they went through each room another time.

"I reckon as how you were right," he admitted when they stood in the foyer again. He busied himself stowing his tools in a leather belt. "No door." He shook his head in a cross between bewildered and sad.

But he still seemed puzzled by the lack as he left. So much so, she retraced their route yet again after he'd gone. And though there were plenty of doors, there was not one that led either outside or downstairs. The only way in or out appeared to be the main staircase.

At noon, although January hovered around the entry—and received more than one frowning look by people passing back and forth—the boy Jem didn't return home after all. Either that or he knew a way in besides the front. It stood to reason there was a way into the basement from the outside, for delivering items like coal for the boiler, or...or she didn't know what else. Her loss, she guessed, to be so ignorant of how city folks conducted business or home life. Could be she'd spent too much time alone after her dad died. Until Shay Billings rescued her and brought her into the light.

Late in the afternoon, she found her way into the bathroom, and filled the massive claw foot tub with piping hot water. Jem must indeed have made it home at lunch and stoked the boiler, she thought. Or maybe the drunken man—the children's father?—had awakened and taken care of the matter, because she then had to wait for the water to cool to a bearable temperature.

Since she knew it was time to change the dressing on her wound, she wasn't worried about getting the old one wet.

The huge tub proved as wondrous as she'd expected and she lingered. So long, in fact, that her freshly washed hair was still wrapped in one big absorbent towel and her body in another when a knock sounded on her door.

Should she pretend she wasn't home? It was her first reaction, even as she shook loose her hair and pulled on a robe still smelling of smoke from the hotel fire. Going to stand in the foyer, she heard Eli call her name. Staying to the side as far out of sight as possible, she opened the door. A crack. Only a small crack.

The look in his dark eyes as he stared down at her shattered her fragile composure.

"You shouldn't have opened the door," he said, very softly, as though not to yell.

She swallowed. "I wasn't going to, until you called to me. Then I was afraid if I didn't answer you'd get worried and break the door down." She gripped the robe tighter, aware of her face glowing red. "I changed the lock. At least, I hired a locksmith to change it."

Eli touched the door with a finger, pushing it a little wider. "I wouldn't expect you to do it yourself."

"I could have, if I'd had the tools." She backed away.

He followed her in. "I know you could," he said, but she'd already lost track of what they were saying because Eli'd kicked the door shut and had her in his arms. She felt his heart drumming against her cheek as he gathered her close.

\* \* \*

"I GOT A MESSAGE," Eli said when as he regained his senses, "from the fellow who contracted for Windswept's services. He won some—won a lot—of money in a poker game and insists on meeting me tonight to hand it over. I think he's afraid he might lose it all the next time he plays. He wants this done first before he goes back to his ranch."

"Wise of him," she said.

"I didn't want to tell him no."

"Of course not." January smiled, touching her lips. Thoroughly kissed lips. She wouldn't have minded more, except Eli'd gotten himself in hand and drawn back. "You could have telephoned me, you know."

"I could've." His voice came out husky. "But I wanted to see you. Make sure you're all right." He touched a patch of bare skin revealed above her collarbone when the robe had slipped, watching as the skin rose in goosebumps. "I think you are."

She'd forgotten her leg until then. Now she noticed it was throbbing. His kisses had caused her pulse to pound right down to her toes. Disconcerting, to say the least.

"As you see." She stepped back. "It'll soon be time for supper. Will you eat with me or the rancher?"

"The rancher." He hesitated. "He may want to make a night of it."

Nodding, she wondered if he'd expected her to insist he stay with her. But she was well aware of the way men conducted business, and was not so needy as to demand he coddle her.

*And I'm not ready for anything else.* She knew exactly what that 'anything else' might be.

"Then go. This is good business for you. I'm going to

search through my grandfather's bedroom to see if I can find what Joe and his wife were after." She didn't mention the two youngsters who evidently lived in the basement, or say the most important item on her docket for today was talking with them.

"You'll stay put? Promise?" Eli's grin twisted, his dark eyes flashing in relief. "Seems as if you have a habit of turning up someplace other than where you're supposed to be."

Solemnly, she crossed her heart. "I promise. The only way I'm leaving this building tonight is by brute force." Her eyes narrowed. "Oh, and Eli?"

He raised a brow in question.

"You watch your own back. My cousins, I doubt they care for you anymore than they do for me."

He nodded appreciation. "Good advice. I'll take it. Lock up behind me?"

January nodded, and with that he left, waiting outside until the lock clicked shut before she heard his departing footsteps.

\* \* \*

WITH ELI GONE, the apartment felt overly large and empty. Action striking her as the best cure for the lost feeling sweeping through her, January got busy. Aware she'd be staying in Spokane longer than expected, she wisely ordered a few groceries from Stenson's Market, the little store located on the corner, to be delivered to the apartment right away. They arrived promptly, delivered by same kid—the boy—who lived in the basement.

If he was nonplused by being greeted by a woman with a gun in her hand, he covered the surprise well. In fact, January decided, maybe she was the surprised one. Either way, it appeared the kid was ambitious and kept himself busy.

"You," she said. "You work in this building, don't you? And live here? You and your sister?"

He nodded, eyes lowered to study her pistol. If he wondered how she knew, he didn't let on.

She tucked the gun in the waist of her skirt, the slack there making her aware she'd lost weight in these last few days.

"I went to work making grocery deliveries in place of old man Stenson's son," Jem said. "He broke his leg a while back and don't get around much. I just brought these with me on my way home. No trouble."

"Would've been trouble for me," she said wryly. "My leg isn't broken but it has been injured. I find stair steps to be a problem."

"Yeah," Jem said. "I heard."

She supposed he had. Plus, anyone in the basement couldn't possibly have missed hearing the gunfire last night. The young ones had most likely been frightened. No wonder he kept his eyes lowered as he stared at her and her pistol.

"Did you know the man who lived in this apartment?" It occurred to her the kid might be a good source of information if he had known the elder Flowers.

"Sure. Me and Hattie, my sister Hattie, both visited with him sometimes." Jem shuffled his feet, seeming uncomfortable with the question although he answered willingly enough.

"Did you? Was he friendly?"

Jem frowned. "Friendly?" His lips pooched in a

thinking sort of way. "I dunno. Hattie..." he dropped whatever he'd intended to tell her.

"Would you and your sister care to come eat supper with me tonight?" The invitation came on a whim. "In an hour? I'd like to know about Mr. Flowers." Her mouth twisted. "He was my grandfather, although I never met him."

Jem's glance came up and immediately darted away. "Yeah. I know."

She supposed he did. She supposed everyone who had business in the Flowers Building knew all about her. "Please," she added, and fished a silver dollar from her pocket to give him.

Astonished, he stared down at it. "A dollar?"

"Um. A tip for prompt service bringing the groceries." And a sort of bribe, although she'd prefer to call it an incentive. It worked.

"I'll talk to Hattie," he said, "but I think she'll say yes. She said she wants to meet you." He smiled. "She read in the newspaper about you. About how you and some man saved those girls over on the coast. Was that him last night?"

"Yes. As for the girls, well, they needed our help." January was still uncomfortable talking about that time. Even had bad dreams featuring the maniac who'd meant to do unspeakable things to her. It had been kill or be killed. No choice, but not something she wanted to talk about. Especially to a boy child. "I only did what needed done. It just so happened Mr. Pasco and I were the ones in place to do it."

"But not everybody would've," Jem said, soberly enough she wondered what kind of experiences he'd had. He or Hattie. He turned smartly and dashed down the stairs, clutching his dollar.

Abandoning her search of Joseph Senior's room for the moment, she pawed through the box Jem had delivered, finding enough to make a pork chop, spud and peppered cream gravy dinner for the three of them. If the kids decided to come.

As it happened, the youngsters showed up exactly one hour later when January, moving a bit slower than usual because of her leg, opened the door. They were scrubbed, their clothing clean, though worn. Jem had slicked his brown hair down with water, and Hattie tied back her slightly darker hair with a dark green ribbon. Jem, at his sister's instigation, was rubbing the scuffed toe of his shoe on the back of his pant leg.

January smiled. "Hello. Come in. I'm happy to see you. Dinner is almost on the table."

She had to urge them as they turned shy.

Hattie whispered something to Jem and he replied, "I dunno, but she gave me a dollar and if she wants us to eat supper with her I ain't about to say no." He lifted his nose and sniffed. "Smells good."

"Thank you," January said. "I hope it is good. You brought some nice pork chops from Stenson's store."

"Stenson gives good value." Jem sounded as proud as though he were the one running the market.

"Oh, goody," Hattie crowed. "I love pork chops."

It seemed they were off to a good start, although January wished she knew what the girl had said to Jem.

They passed through the dining room into the kitchen, Hattie asking why they had to eat in the kitchen. Evidently, she'd been looking forward to the good china and the elegance of a dining room.

"Hush, Hattie," Jem told her quietly. "She's got a bad leg."

Hattie stared at January, but spoke to her brother. "How do you know?"

"She told me," Jem said. "Anyways, they was talking about it at the store when Stenson said I should deliver her order."

"Huh. Talking about what?"

Jem whispered his answer, though not so quietly January couldn't hear. "How her leg got hurt. She got shot by an arrow."

The girl stared at him, then at January. "An arrow? For real true?"

January nodded. "For real true." She forced an uncomfortable smile. "Listen, it's no trouble to move us into the dining room. Hattie, I noticed there are some nice plates and silverware in the dining room hutch. Why don't you set them out in there—and lay out a tablecloth if you can find one. We'll use the nicest things. Make this into a celebration. Jem, you can help me bring in the food."

She soon had them seated at the table, planning to get them fed before asking questions, a ploy she always found worked a treat with Johnny Johnson. Not, however, so much with Hattie. She had other ideas.

"Jem said you wanted to know about the old man," the girl said. She swallowed a forkful of potatoes drenched in the gravy, catching a drip on her finger before it hit her skirt. "How come?" She licked the finger.

"Because he was my grandfather, whom I'd never met. I never knew about him at all until last week."

"You didn't? Why not?" The girl eyed her. "Did you

do something wrong and make him mad? He got mad all the time at Joseph and Calvin. Especially Calvin," she added confidentially. "John B not so much. When John B irritated him, he just shook his head."

January stifled a laugh. "I'm not surprised." But maybe she was. Surprised the kids knew about it at any rate, if not at his anger. "And no. I didn't do anything wrong. I told you. I never even met him."

"He told us a little about you. Told us you'd be coming around after he died and we should meet you."

"He did?" Why? January wondered. Why tell them? But something else occurred to her. How to phrase it? "The man in the basement...is he your father?"

Hattie shook her head, giggling a little. "No. He's our uncle. Mama died of typhoid a few years ago and he had to take us in. Now we do all his work." She glanced at Jem. "He likes his hootch and kind of forgets why he's here sometimes. He's not really very good with the boiler. Jem has to tend it instead."

"You wasn't supposed to tell'er about Unc." Jem glared at his sister.

The girl lifted her napkin to wipe her grease smeared lips. "Oh. I forgot."

*Little minx.* January didn't believe for a minute she'd forgotten. Hattie had meant for her to know. But the way she'd phrased the mistake. It was almost as if she'd been trying to arouse January's curiosity. As if she wanted to be questioned. January, smiling inwardly, indulged her.

"Why do you suppose Mr. Flowers wanted you to meet me?" Her gaze flicked from one to the other.

Jem broke in before Hattie got her mouth open. "He

thought if you met us in person you wouldn't be as likely to throw us out."

"And hire somebody else to take care of this building," Hattie added. "He said that's what Joe would do if he knew we were here. Joe didn't want anything to do with us. He said children like us shoulda been drowned at birth." Her dark eyebrows drew together in indignation. "Because people like us aren't legitimate, according to him. He called us a bad word. It starts with the letter B, but he's the B."

"Hattie! You're not supposed to say things like that," Jem said, his face flaming red.

"Well, he is."

"Oh." January didn't know what else to say since she agreed with the girl. There were words for men like Joe III, but January didn't plan on stating them in front of the youngsters. The statement also went a bit overboard. Drowned at birth? Why should Joe care?

But then, as she gazed at the two, January caught a glimpse of herself reflected in the big gold-leaf framed mirror in back of the kids.

She blinked. Once. Twice. Her mouth went dry, as it became clear.

Oh. That was why. She'd been blind not to see it the minute they walked in.

# CHAPTER 17

THE WARY LOOK IN THEIR EYES FINALLY PUSHED JANUARY in the right direction, providing a last sudden leap of conviction. Those forest green eyes with their deep glints of brown. An odd color she'd never seen on anyone besides herself until she met the cousins at the attorney's office. And now on Jem and Hattie, though the kids' eye shape bore more of a tilt than her own. Looking into the mirror, she noted other resemblances between the three of them. She had more in common with this pair than she did with the older cousins, when she thought about it.

Hattie looked a great deal like she had, before the scar. The three of them shared the thin build, slight but strong. Hair color varied, but remained in the brunette range. The kids', she thought, was somewhat darker than her own, with fewer tints of red.

"What is your last name?" she asked, a general question she should've asked before. "You haven't told me."

Jem gulped the last of his potatoes, of which he'd had three helpings, forked up some green beans and gave a hefty belch. He cast a sideways glance at Hattie. She shrugged.

"Mother said it is Flint. Unc told us it was something else," he said.

"He said it *should* be something else," Hattie amended.

January's lips tightened. "What did your uncle say it should be?"

They were silent.

"Did your uncle say your last name is Flowers?"

Hattie bit her lip as January pressed on. "What did the old man, Mr. Flowers, say?"

"He said he made a mistake," Jem said. "And that it was a secret. The night he...died...he told us you'd do right by us. He said we should hide from the boys. They know we're around, but they wouldn't like it if they learned we was family. Real family."

"Huh." January snorted disgust. It didn't take a genius to figure that out. "You should just tell me what you know. Make it easier on all of us. Mr. Flowers left me a letter." More than one. Discovering Jem and Hattie made it imperative she read the one Avery had given her right away, since she hadn't had the fortitude to do so previously. What's more, she bet she knew what Joe and Bethany had been looking for the other night. They'd learned about Jem and Hattie and wanted to destroy the letter Joseph had left for her. Or, more likely, they hadn't known about the letter specifically, but had somehow discovered there was proof these children were Flowers heirs also, and that he favored them. And that depended on whether he could keep them alive long enough.

Or whether she could.

But were they— January drew a shaky breath. "Was

the old man your father or your grandfather?" How they could be unknown grandchildren struck her as impossible. That they were the results of an older man's declining years seemed more likely.

Hattie turned to her brother. "See, Jem. I told you she'd ask all these things. She's just doing it sooner than we thought she'd figure it out."

"It makes a difference, you see," January continued. A big difference. It seemed to her children of his body would have a far better claim on the estate than grandchildren, like the boys and her. Illegitimate or not. And her cousins would all know that as well.

She was shaking a little when she asked, "Do John B, and Calvin know about you or is it just Joseph III? About where you are? Who you are?"

Solemnly, they shook their heads no. "Joe poked and pried until he found out, but the rest aren't supposed to. The old man said only to tell you," Jem said.

"But he said not right away." Hattie shook her finger in his face. "He wanted you to get used to us first. And then you, Jem, went and spilled the beans."

January sighed. "This," she said, "is getting more complicated by the minute."

By the time she shooed the youngsters downstairs to their lair in the basement, she was too tired to think anymore. She'd have to check on the suitability as well as the safety of their living quarters first thing in the morning. The basement hardly seemed appropriate for Joseph C. Flowers's heirs—his closest born heirs, she meant.

Ingrained tidiness insisted she wash the dishes and put them away before falling into bed in the smaller bedroom. Exhausted, her mind went dark as a blown-out lamp.

* * *

JANUARY AWOKE with a gun barrel pressed to her temple and a rough hand covering her mouth.

She knew from the shape the cold metal belonged to a gun. Didn't even have to open her eyes to verify it. Questions flew through her mind. How had the gunman gotten in? How had she not heard the door being forced? Why hadn't she...

"Do not make a fuss," a man whispered. "It could be dangerous."

Whispered, as if anyone was likely to come at her call. Or did he intend to make the words more menacing? Anger, more than fear, got January's blood pumping. She lashed out blindly, clawing, writhing, thrashing. She tried to scream, unable to get much sound past the hand.

Seconds later, unable to breathe, she stopped fighting.

"For Pete's sake," another voice chimed in—a voice she knew—loud and rough. "Let 'er scream if she wants. There ain't nobody gonna hear her. Nobody's here but us."

The overhead light flickered on as one of them flipped the switch. She kept her eyes closed, as if only half-conscious.

A third man added his piece. "I'm paying you, not the other way around. If I don't want her screaming, I mean don't let her get her mouth open."

No danger of that, January realized. All in all, she

hoped they made up their pea-sized minds soon because the very large hand covering her mouth and most of her nose was about to suffocate her. For a moment she went slack, helping dislodge the hand enough to draw a decent breath, upon which, finally freed of the blanket, she kicked out with her good leg. Kicked out hard. Due to the fortunate circumstance of lying on her side, her foot struck one of the men in his unguarded nether parts.

He yelped louder than any girlish scream she could've managed and fell back, clutching himself.

One of the other men, she wasn't sure which, laughed. "Gotcha," he said. "That wasn't very professional. I thought you'd know how to handle a situation like this."

That one, his comment sure to egg Officer Rory Lynch on to further violence, seemed deliberately aimed to escalate the situation. And not in January's favor. No question who the unsympathetic voice belonged to. She'd heard enough of her dear cousin Joseph III to know him when she heard him. And the other? The first whisperer? She still hadn't opened her eyes but it had to be either John B or Calvin.

Calvin, she decided. So where was John B? He must be in on this, too.

"Get her dressed," Joe said. "Hurry. We need to get out of town before people start stirring. I don't want anybody remembering my carriage and telling Avery they saw it here."

"Or telling her paramour, Eli Pasco." Calvin again.

"Huh." Joe made a derisive sort of sound. "Who's he? A nobody."

Lynch, still bemoaning his damaged manhood,

managed to speak. "Him and her may be sleeping together, but believe you me, Eli Pasco is more than a nobody. He ain't no joke. You fellers sure enough don't want on the wrong side of him."

"Forget him. He's one man. We outnumber him," Joe said.

"You might think," Lynch agreed. "But he's friends with Milt Ferguson. Knows others, judges, senators, and such in high places. I'm telling you, he's dangerous."

One of the cousins, the one she believed was Calvin, reached down and grabbed her hair. Her eyes flew open. Yes. Calvin, since Joe stood over by the door and Lynch just out of reach of her feet. Well, foot, since one leg was in no shape to do much of anything.

"You heard the man." Calvin yanked her up and slammed her onto her feet. "Get dressed."

Gasping at pain fiery enough to bring tears to her eyes, she spoke for the first time. "Are both of you out of your minds? Or should I say the three of you, including this one." Her glare at Lynch would've stripped paint.

"Get dressed," Calvin repeated, "unless you want to walk out of here naked." He cuffed her on the cheek hard enough to send back onto the bed. A second later, he pulled her up again. "Now."

Wanting to tell him she wore a plain nightgown and wasn't naked, she refrained.

"I am not accustomed to dressing or undressing in public," she gritted instead. "At least have the decency to turn your backs. And get him out of here." She meant Lynch.

Joe and Calvin shared a look. To her surprise, Joe nodded at the policeman. "Go on down to the street,

Lynch. Make sure the way is clear and bring the carriage around."

"Me? What if she tries to get away?" Lynch seemed to hope that very thing.

Calvin snorted. "I figure between me and Joe we can handle her." He eyed her. "She ain't very big."

"She's got a reputation..." Lynch started, until Joe interrupted him.

"Go," he said, his impatience clear, and Lynch, muttering under his breath, obeyed. He limped worse than January with her arrow wound.

"Satisfied?" Calvin asked. Finding the clothes she'd worn yesterday tossed on a chair, he snatched them up and flung them at her. Her skirt fluttered to the floor, her blouse and drawers onto the bed. With that, he stalked over to the door by Joe. They turned and began a conversation. Not, if she was any judge, one of agreement.

It was easy to slip her drawers on while covered by her nightgown. Next, turning her back to the men, came a camisole. Then her blouse, which she managed somehow to drop to the floor and fumbled to retrieve it. She scrambled into the skirt, then, lastly, her socks and boots. She shoved her good foot home and drew a sigh of satisfaction.

She may not have had time to snatch her pistol from under the pillow when first attacked, but by golly she had it now, safely back in her boot. She might be down, but she was not out. Not until her dying breath.

Her cousins allowed her to pluck her coat from the tree in the foyer after Calvin searched the pockets and found nothing. Joe fumbled at the door. "No wonder we couldn't use this door. She changed the lock."

"We should go the other way," Calvin said, a statement January didn't understand at all.

"No. This is better. When they find her gone, there won't be a search. I can always get back in anytime I want." He bent over and peered at the lock. "Ah. There we are. Simple." The door swung open and he hurried them out onto the landing.

"Yeah, simple. Right." Calvin, possibly fed up by her tentative descent of the stairs, gave her a push. "Hurry up. We ain't got all night."

Caught by her cousins' inexplicable conversation, January hardly noticed the push. *Other way?* What did he mean? *Get back in anytime I want?* Same. She'd been all through the apartment. More than once, as a matter of fact. But Joe's words certainly implied there was another entrance, just as the locksmith had insisted there should be. But where? Did the children know?

At the street entrance, Joe produced a key and unlocked the front door. At that instant, a small, closed carriage pulled by two bay horses turned the corner and came toward them, stopping in front of the building.

Calvin hustled her toward the carriage, holding one arm twisted behind her back. Lynch sat beside the driver, a man bundled against the cold, his dark clothing and the dark night obscuring his identity.

Except, if January wasn't mistaken, Lynch was holding his service revolver on the driver.

"What the hell do you think you're doing, Joe?" The driver, ignoring the gun, gritted his question, staring down at Joseph III. "Are you out of your mind? What are you planning to do with Mrs. Billings? Leave her go."

"Shut up and drive," Calvin said. "All will become clear. Eventually. I'll see to it."

"You will? Since when did you—"

"Lynch?" Joe said in a tightly controlled tone.

Lynch poked his gun barrel into the driver's ribs. John B's ribs. January knew him now.

"Shut up," Lynch said. "I ain't afraid to shoot you. Caught you robbing the old man's place and had to prevent you making off with the goods before I knew who you was." He looked down at Calvin and Joe. "Didn't I? That about right?"

Mouth tight, Joe nodded. "Sorry, cousin," he told John B, and to Calvin, "Load her in."

Grunting with the effort, Calvin dropped her arm and lifted January, shoving her down onto the carriage floor. He piled in after her, his breath coming hard. So, she thought, he's soft. Soft and unused to work any more difficult than twirling his Colt revolver on his finger. Something to keep in mind.

As for her, she wondered if the lout had managed to break her arm. God knows it hurt enough. But probably not. Her fingers were tingling back to movement.

Outside, Joe said, "Go," and swung himself into the carriage, closing the door and lowering the curtains so they couldn't be seen.

January heard John B curse again. Then the snap of the reins over the bays and the vehicle lurched forward.

They proceeded, as far as January could tell, straight east. Headed, unless she missed her guess, to the ranch further out where the valley widened. Where there'd be no one near enough to help her if she yelled or the sound of a stray gunshot split the night.

The gun in her boot proved a reassuring lifeline. If she'd be allowed to reach it in time.

\* \* \*

*WHAT HAVE I DONE?*

Eli left January's apartment that afternoon with his blood thrumming through his veins like he'd been injected with heated moonshine. He only made it down the first flight of stairs before he asked himself the old 'what have I done' question. He'd kissed her, that's what, and he didn't mean a friendly peck. The kiss had been deep and full of desire. And she'd kissed him back. He'd felt her response and knew her blood had raged as hot as his own.

The kiss might've been a mistake.

A month ago they'd had a quarrel, a bitter quarrel unresolved at the time. Since then he'd decided she was right about Ruby Pasco, his father's divorced wife. Ruby was bad through and through and had no claim on him or the family name. It was time—past time—to put the evil woman out of his mind. Let her take the punishment her acts merited. Preferably, he thought, time in jail. If his father was embarrassed by having his name dragged through the courts—it had been bad enough at the divorce—so be it. No more than he deserved by marrying the woman in the first place. It wasn't Eli's responsibility to ease either Ruby's or his father's path. He knew that now.

When January showed up at his ranch asking his advice, he'd been floored. She hadn't asked for his company when meeting the lawyer, although he'd known she was grateful when he showed up at the office. The way her face lit, those remarkable forest green eyes of hers sparkling.

Now she'd inherited an unbelievable fortune. What

would she think? That he was a fortune hunter? It didn't seem to have occurred to her yet, but it would. There were people who'd make sure of it.

January had said she didn't want the Flowers properties. Been pretty adamant about the idea, in fact. He hoped she meant what she said. Hoped she'd turn it all down like she insisted she would. Then he'd see. They'd see.

Still pondering and lost in thought, he almost walked past Morton Thatcher, the rancher from Pegasus Farm, in the hotel lobby. Thatcher had to hold up a hand and wave to catch his attention.

Taking advantage of the fact Spokane had almost as many fine restaurants as San Francisco, they had a good dinner. Not so much to Eli's liking, Thatcher, full of bonhomie, ordered wine, and insisted he drink. Then later, at Thatcher's continued insistence, they moved on to the saloon the rancher preferred to visit when he was in town. Here, after a few rounds of stronger drink, Eli finally collected the breeding fees. Far too openly for his liking, as it seemed a dozen pairs of eyes watched the transfer of cash. He walked back to his hotel with his hand near his gun, sure every man he met contemplated robbery.

He was wrong. Only one stepped from the shadows with a billy club in his hand. Faster than the lout could raise it to club Eli's noggin, the click of his revolver gave warning that a bullet was always faster than even the downward swing of a club. More likely to be lethal, too. The fellow ran, saying, "Don't shoot. Don't shoot."

Eli, smirking a little, held fire.

When he at last poured himself into bed at his hotel, he went to sleep dreaming of January Billings. Right up until daylight and he awakened to a fist pounding on his door and a man yelling his name.

"Pasco, you deef son-of-a-gun. Get up."

Recognizing Milt's voice, Eli opened his bleary eyes, certain something had gone wrong. He was right. It had.

Milt lost no time in telling him what almost before the door opened.

"Hurry up!" Milt boomed, louder than Eli's head wanted to tolerate. He staggered to the chair where he'd dropped his clothes last night and yanked on his trousers.

"God only knows where they've taken Mrs. Billings," Milt continued. "Those kids didn't hear a destination mentioned. Said they know she didn't go willingly. She fought them all the way."

"Kids?" Eli echoed. "Taken January?" His head roared.

"Yeah. That's what I said."

"Who took her?"

"Dunno, but we'd best better find out fast."

Eli couldn't make sense of what he was hearing. What else had Milt said? *Kids?* "What kids?" He stared dumbly at Milt.

"Some kids who live with the building caretaker. They heard the noise and got up to see what was going on. They hid behind the basement door, scared they might be taken along with Mrs. Billings if they spoke up."

"Wise of them. Might've gotten hurt otherwise. Where was the caretaker in all this? Couldn't he do something?" Eli fumbled with his shoulder holster, fitting it in place, wishing in the worst way he'd brought his Mauser Broomhandle on the Spokane trip instead of the smaller .38.

"Naw." Milt scowled. "Says he was drunk and slept through the whole thing."

So had he. Guilt colored Eli's thoughts as they rushed out into the cold pre-dawn.

Ten minutes later, he faced two scared youngsters who sat side by side—and looking sadly out of place—on the satin damask sofa in Joseph Flowers's parlor. The girl's eyes widened as Eli strode in and glared around.

His gaze fixed hers. To his credit, he saw the resemblance right away, especially when Hattie's wide-eyed gaze stared back at him. No wonder they hadn't dared interfere in January's abduction. The pair, he felt certain, were the object of Joe's search. Or rather, he figured, written proof of their parentage had been the reason Joe and his wife had torn the place apart.

And here they were in the flesh, right under his nose on the premises. Under the Flowers cousins', too, had they only known.

Vulnerable. Too vulnerable.

He sat down across from the pair, making every attempt not to frighten them further. "What are your names?"

"Jem," said the boy.

"Hattie," said the girl.

No last name, he noted as Milt touched him on the shoulder and went to join another man, the detective, Eli assumed, in the room where January had bedded down.

He nodded and said, "Tell me what you saw," to the kids, unaware of how rough his voice sounded.

Hattie was not intimidated. "They snatched her."

Although no tears fell, they thickened her vocal chords, making her sound hoarse. "Sneaked right into her room and dragged her away. Are you going to find her?"

Eli's heart thumped faster. "I'll do my best. Do you know who took her?"

This time, Jem answered. "Joseph. It was Joe and his brother—"

Hattie had to correct him. "Cousin. The one...the one Mr. Flowers always said we should look out for."

Jem glared at her. "Brother, cousin, don't make much difference, Hattie. Shut up and let me talk for a change."

The girl pinched her lips closed with her fingertips.

"And some other feller," Jem continued. "He was the worst. He was hurting her. Even Joe told him once to ease off. They didn't want to carry her. Just make her walk, even with her hurt leg and all."

Hattie removed her fingers to talk. "Calvin called him Lynch. I heard him."

"Well, you got better ears than I do," Jem said. "Probably because you don't have to sleep in the same room with Unc snoring away like one of the saws down at the Sawmill Phoenix."

She merely nodded, as if it was a complaint she'd often heard before.

*Lynch.* Eli ground his teeth. Milt had mentioned him. Another member of Spokane's police force on the take. The one who'd already had a set-to with January.

Eli went through the standard questioning. What time did they hear the commotion, start to finish? The kids said they saw three men. Were they sure that was all?

"No," Jem said. "There was somebody driving the carriage. When they left the building, I looked out the side window. The bad guy, Lynch, was poking a gun in the driver's side. The driver was madder than hell."

"Interesting."

Hattie suddenly jumped to her feet. "Oh," she cried. "Oh, golly, Jem!" She bent to whisper in the boy's ear.

His eyes opened wide and he, too, leapt up. "You're right. I remember."

"What?" Eli asked, although he managed to remain sitting.

"Mrs. Billings changed the locks today. Nobody else has a key."

The girl stared at him and he stared back, thinking hard. "You know that?"

"Yes. Jem let the locksmith in. But with new locks, that means..."

Jem clenched his fists and took over imparting the information. "Means they know about the secret entrance."

Having returned to the parlor upon hearing the youngster's squeals, Milt stood in the doorway. "What secret entrance?" he demanded.

Eli felt frozen. Sick. January had never been safe in this apartment.

# CHAPTER 18

JANUARY'S BRAIN FELT AS SCRAMBLED AS A BAG OF LITTLE boys' marbles. She should've ignored that threatening letter. Both of the letters. Never have taken up the challenge they promised. A challenge more daunting than she'd ever figured.

Cold, hurting, more than it a little frightened, they'd nearly reached the outskirts of town where the valley widened before a troubling thought occurred to her. Straightening a little from her huddle, she looked at Joe. "How did you get in the apartment? I changed the lock."

Calvin brayed a laugh. "Hah, Joe. She ain't so smart. She didn't find the hidden staircase."

Joe's teeth flashed into a wide-mouthed grin. "You're right. She isn't smart at all. If she'd been smart, she would've stayed away in the first place. Or headed back to her little world when she learned the ups and downs of the inheritance."

"You're right," she admitted to both of the men's observations. "I should have. But here I am."

*Hidden staircase?* Where was it? Apparently, her grandfather had had a fetish of some sort when it came to hiding things. Including a great many items that needed clarification and should've been brought into the open right away.

"But in my defense," she added as both turned toward her as if surprised she'd grant the frailty, "I probably would've ignored Mr. Avery's letter, except for the one from someone else telling me to stay away. It raised my hackles and roused my curiosity. And as far as the staircase goes, you're right. I should've been looking for something like that. The locksmith told me there ought to be another entrance. If my leg hadn't hurt so badly, I would've made a more thorough search."

Calvin turned his head toward Joe. "Who did write that letter? You or John B?"

Joe shifted in his seat in an uncomfortable sort of way. "No. Neither of us. I'm afraid my wife took a hand on her own."

Shaking his head, Calvin cursed. "Time you took a hand with her, cousin. Or maybe a hand *to* her."

"And if you hadn't been so eager to shoot this one with an arrow and start the hotel on fire, *cousin,* she probably wouldn't have moved to the apartment and we'd have had time to discover where the old man hid those papers."

"The arrow?" Calvin mumbled. He had a shifty, smug look on his face, as if he knew something no one else did. Not even Joseph. "That was meant to just be a warning. The fire got a little out of hand, is all."

But had it? January wondered. There'd been a shim under her room door. A deliberate trap.

"Where are you taking me?" she asked, even though she believed she knew.

"You'll find out when we get there," Calvin said, and Joe nodded.

With the curtains down, it was quite dark, though not impenetrable, within the carriage. More like seeing in a moonless night. January had a good sense of direction and knew they'd driven almost straight east. The sound of rushing water traveled alongside them at times, loud over the rattle of the carriage wheels, so she knew they were following the river. In the packet of property descriptions Avery had given her, the survey map said the Flowers ranch lay along the river's front. When it came time to escape, she decided, it should be easy to make her way back to town.

To Eli.

*If* she made her escape.

The thought of him gave her some ease. Between the youngsters and Eli, they'd soon find she was missing and he'd be looking for her. But would he be in time? She drew in a breath, thinking it best if she handled this on her own.

Did they intend to kill her as soon as they were at the property, her body thrown in the fast-moving river? Because it seemed to her there could be no other answer for them. All she knew to do was to wait, then she'd just have to make sure they failed.

Settling back in the seat beside Calvin, she stretched out her leg and stuck her hands in the opening of the opposite sleeve, attempting to warm her cold hands. She was cold all over and if she had to draw on the men, she wanted her finger capable of pulling a trigger.

The drive seemed to last hours, although she realized it didn't. That was the situation taking its toll on her. They met no one else on the bumpy road and Calvin, over Joe's protests, soon rolled up the curtain in order to see out.

She grew colder, shivering violently enough to shake the seat. The men seemed not to notice.

Joe and Calvin argued, threatened, while she pretended to swoon—swoon!—and ignored them. For conspirators, her cousins struck her as remarkably ineffective. Not enough practice, she guessed, being more used to paying people to do their dirty work for them. People like Lynch, perched outside on the driver's seat holding a gun on John B.

Eventually, the carriage turned into a drive. Lynch dropped from the seat and pulled back a pole gate. John B drove on through, waiting as Lynch climbed back to sit beside him.

January heard John B grumbling and Lynch cussing, but soon river sounds filled the carriage and drowned their words. Both Calvin and Joseph perked up, as if anticipating a feast.

Sooner than expected, John B shouted, "Whoa," and the carriage stopped. They'd arrived at their destination.

Calvin flung open the carriage door and leapt to the ground, grabbing January by a handful of hair as he went and pulling her out with him.

Her bad leg wouldn't hold. She thumped to the ground, blazing with an anger she tried not to let show. Let them think she was cowed. Make it all that much easier to surprise them later on.

If she got the chance.

Surreptitiously, she pushed her little revolver, loosened by the force as she hit the ground, more securely into the boot holster until she could transfer it to her skirt pocket.

Meanwhile, Joseph, under the opinion he was in charge, yelled at John B and Lynch to take the carriage to the barn. "Get it out of sight before some curious farmer rides by and sees we're here."

But John B, with a confidence January hadn't thought he possessed, said, "Do it yourself. I'm not your lackey. And I still think this is a mistake." He jumped from the seat and headed toward her. For a moment, she froze, afraid he'd seen her movement with the gun, but if he had, he didn't show it. Reaching down, he offered a hand to help her up. Gratefully, she took it.

Their eyes met, his narrowed as he shook his head just the least little bit. "Hang on," he murmured, drawing her to her feet and holding steady until she balanced.

Her chin tilted, meaning yes. Yes to what, she wasn't sure. Depended on how much he'd seen. "Thank you," she said. Could she count on him as an ally? Or at least not an active opponent? Hard to know, she decided.

John B led her on an intricately paved path toward what she thought of as the front of the property. Behind her, she heard the carriage being driven away. By whom, she didn't know and didn't bother to look. She was too busy staring at the ranch house.

Growing daylight showed her a two-story farmhouse with a wrap-around porch and some kind of bushes, stripped now of their leaves, standing sentinel at the corners. Oddly sited, the building lay cater-corner to the road, making it easy to drive up to what could be the front on one side, but leaving plenty of room on the other to face the river view. The Spokane eddied around a series of large basalt and granite boulders here before continuing on to the Columbia with a tumultuous rush.

The house was large enough for the second story to accommodate three dormers, which she figured meant several bedrooms. It struck her as a home meant for a family. Plenty of room, January had the sour thought, for hidden staircases, fireplace niches, and secret rooms.

Trees surrounded it, and what she thought were gardens lay behind those. Beyond were barns and paddocks where she saw horse-shaped figures moving, indistinct in the gloomy morning.

John B, as it turned out, had his own key. He let them in at the back of the house where it faced the river, exaggerating a shiver as the chill of the unoccupied place struck them. Their breath steamed clouds as they exhaled. "Who volunteers to build the fire?" he asked. "It'll freeze a man's..." He stopped, shooting January an apologetic look.

"I'll do it." Calvin, acting put upon, shoved past January. "In the kitchen. It'll warm up faster in there. Besides, I could do with a hearty breakfast. We've been up most of the night and I'm hungry."

"Fix enough for everyone," Joseph ordered. Apparently, Lynch had been put in charge of concealing the carriage by himself.

"Me? I don't cook. Why don't you?" Calvin stared meaningfully at January. "On the other hand, I suppose our dear cousin knows how to fry an egg. I say she makes herself useful."

January flashed him a glare. "Useful? Really? And here I thought I was the guest of honor."

Calvin chuckled though he didn't appear amused. "Look at you. Awful sassy for someone without the power to back it up."

He had a point, as January had to admit.

Ignoring the byplay, Joseph rubbed his hands together and shooed them all through an enclosed porch into a large kitchen. "You're right. We're all a little at odds here. We'll eat first, then have ourselves a discussion. A serious discussion." He stood near enough to prod January in the middle of her back when she didn't move fast enough to suit him. "You'll find all you need."

"There's food here? Unspoiled?" She was surprised to hear the kitchen was stocked. The place was cold and empty, without the feel of being lived in.

Joseph's nose pointed up. "Naturally. This is no dry dirt ranch in the middle of the scablands. We have permanent caretakers, of course. A married couple. They keep the place in repair and tend to the horses."

John B gave a start. "Where are they? Some of your wife's relation, aren't they? You haven't—"

Mouth curling, Joseph saw where John B was headed with his questions and snorted. "Most certainly not. I'm generally not a man of violence. Or..." he gave January a meaningful glare "...only as the situation dictates. I made plans ahead and sent word for them to take the next few days off. I told them Bethany and I wanted the place to ourselves."

John B looked relieved. January thought he'd had his doubts. She still had them, not nearly as confident the man possessed any good intentions. Joe struck her as plenty capable of violence if he didn't get his own way.

As for Calvin, as he struck a match to the kindling ready in the big cookstove, a knowing grin plastered itself onto his face.

"Fire's ready," Calvin announced after a while when the fire crackled and the kitchen warmed. He beckoned to January. "Get to cooking. And fix enough for Lynch. He'll be hungry, as well."

January shrugged. "He can starve for all I care." Still, Calvin's expression warned her not to test his patience further. Exaggerating her limp, though God knows it was painful enough at best, she eyed the supplies, pushing aside a curtain to reveal a well-supplied, open-shelved pantry and an ice-box. Even then, Calvin followed her, not allowing her time enough alone to shift the pistol to her pocket.

She took her time, cracking eggs into a bowl and measuring out ingredients for flapjacks. If she'd had poison handy, she would've added it to the batter.

But when she took up a knife to slice ham, Lynch, back from barn duty, took it away and did the cutting himself. January took careful note when he tossed the used knife into the sink. It had been plenty sharp. Useful as a weapon of last resort even though she hated knives, the scar on her cheek reason enough.

They gathered around a well-used oak table to eat. There were initials carved into the wood at her place. A.F. Had this been the work of her mother? January's finger traced the letters and wondered.

Joseph finished his meal first. He laid his utensils neatly across the bottom of his empty plate and pushed it to the center of the table. It must've been some sort of signal, because one by one, the others shoveled last bites into their mouths and did the same. Lynch punctuated the moment with a belch loud enough to cause John B to lift an eyebrow and Joe to frown. Calvin smirked.

"Pardon me," Lynch muttered.

Joseph drew a handful of cigars from his pocket and passed them around, an indication they planned to smoke her out. January almost chuckled aloud at the thought. Even more so after the cigars were lit, all but John B puffing clouds to rival the logging train that passed through The Falls every two days or so.

"Now," Joe said, "we begin."

"We could have had a meeting in town," January said. "In a restaurant, by preference, which would've saved us all some time and hard feelings." She'd decided to play innocent—or maybe she meant naive—and waited for a reaction. It didn't take long.

Calvin blew a huge lungful of smoke directly into her face. "Hard feelings? You want to talk about hard feelings?" He huffed. "Lady, you don't know who or what you're dealing with here."

She waved the noxious vapor away from her eyes. "I have a good idea. Seems to me you've dug yourselves a hole and pulled it in after you. The list of charges just keeps getting longer. Threats, arson, attempted murder, grievous assault, breaking and entering, and now, kidnapping." She paused and wrinkled her nose, knowing it was dangerous to bait them but unable to stop herself. "Maybe the worst was setting that crooked bank manager onto me."

Calvin glared at Joe. "I told you she wouldn't go for that. Salter couldn't convince a starving man to take money for food."

"Shut up." Joseph's cheeks flushed.

"Attempted murder?" Lynch asked. "What was that?"

"Setting the hotel on fire," John B kindly explained, "and blocking the door so she couldn't get out."

"Ah." Lynch smirked. "I wondered about that. I heard Ferguson wanted to put a warrant out on Joseph, and the chief wouldn't let him. Not enough evidence."

"And, somehow, she did escape." Calvin scowled.

John B nodded. "Smart."

"Luck." January corrected him. She didn't want them getting too cautious an attitude toward her. If they thought her incompetent, her escape pure chance, all the better. "Tell you what, you let me go now and I'll drop the kidnapping charges. I'll say you escorted me here to show me the ranch."

"Nice try," Calvin said, "but you aren't going anywhere until we have what we want."

"And what, exactly, is that? You've read the letters your grandfather left you. You've read the will with all the stipulations. No matter what you do, nothing will change. It's all bound by law and the courts."

"We'll see about that. I have no doubt you can be persuaded to change your mind. And so can the courts." Joe smiled. "We have our methods."

A fist thumping the table rattled the dishes at John B's display of temper. "Rot it, Joe, this isn't right. I didn't sign up for this and you know it."

"Shut up. Stick with the plan, John B, or you may come out worse for wear yourself. Got it?"

John B didn't answer. Not to agree, but not to disagree, either. Could be because his lips were clamped down hard enough to keep the words corralled.

Joe, unfortunately, remained capable of speech. "Be quiet, all of you. Right now we have a bigger fish to gut."

Stomach seizing at the changed—and not for the better—simile, January barely stopped herself from reaching toward her gun. She knew very well she wouldn't stand a chance against the four of them.

There'd be a better time. Count on it.

# CHAPTER 19

ELI, TRYING FOR CALM BUT MAYBE NOT SUCCEEDING AS well as he'd prefer, thumped his fingers on his knee and eyed the Flowers children. Impatience tugged at him, urging him to hurry. To be out of this room looking for January.

Jem and Hattie, their last name unknown and perhaps feeling the same urgency, fidgeted on the couch across from him. They met his eyes unflinchingly.

Maybe, he decided, they weren't as childlike as their ages implied. They struck him as having dealt with more in their short lifetimes than seemed fair. The boy verged on manhood, caught somewhere in-between. The girl had the beginnings of, to put it delicately, becoming a young lady. Everyone's best interests lay in treating them as adults.

Their interests. January's. And his.

"Do you know where the men intended to take her?" he asked.

"They didn't say." Jem slowly shook his head, but

Hattie pooched her lips and leaned forward, elbows on her knees and brow furrowed, as if pondering.

A loud roar from the direction of the kitchen startled them all to silence. It was Milt, yelling something that sounded like, "Yowie." Then, "Eli, come look at this. Who'd a thunk it?"

On his feet and reaching for his gun, Eli stopped his draw mid-motion. Milt sounded surprised and unsettled, but not threatened. He strode toward the kitchen, following the voice until he ran right up against a blank wall in the maid's little room.

"Milt? Where are you?"

Jem, who'd followed him, gave an excited laugh. "By golly! It's true," he exclaimed.

Turning to look at the boy, Eli was taken by surprise when Milt tapped his shoulder and said from directly behind him, "Boo."

"What the..." Eli whirled, surveying the narrow opening that had suddenly appeared in the wall beside a free-standing closet. There were stairs leading down. Stairs more like a ladder, he decided, peering more closely. Steep and narrow. "Well. Guess it explains how they got in." His dark eyes flashed, glaring at Jem. "Did you know about this? Do you know where it comes out?"

Jem shrugged. "Heard about it. Never seen it though. I think it comes out at the base of the chimney stack, but he never said."

"Who never said," Milt demanded.

"Mr. Flowers. He mentioned it once when he was talking about fire." Jem took a moment. "Wait until I tell Hattie. She'll be surprised."

But Hattie wasn't exactly overwhelmed by the news,

even though it cleared up a mystery. She sat where they'd left her, her brow cleared. "You said they headed east, right?" she said to her brother.

He nodded.

"Well, we know what's in that direction, don't we?"

Jem's expression lightened. "Oh, sure. The ranch. Makes sense."

"Nobody is at the ranch now except for some second or third cousin on Joseph's wife's side." Hattie shifted her gaze to Eli. "It's always pretty quiet out that way. They might think nobody would look for them there."

"I heard mention of a ranch." Eli, with a sense of relief and almost certain she'd guessed right, grinned tightly at the girl. "Good thinking, Miss Hattie. It's worth taking a look. It's not far, is it? Do you know how to get there?"

Hattie blushed. "Of course. We used to live there."

Jem put it more bluntly. "We were born there. Ma and a couple of her brothers worked on the ranch for most of Hattie's and my lives. When..." he hesitated "... Mr. Flowers had to move to town, he brought our Uncle Bran, our only relative left, and Hattie and me with him. Mr. Flowers said we probably wasn't safe out there without him."

Certain things were starting to make sense to Eli, and when he looked over at Milt, he could almost see the wheels turning in the big policeman's mind, as well.

"My jurisdiction ends at the city limits." Milt spoke ruefully. "I have to call in the sheriff for this. In fact, I'll do it right now."

He turned to summon one of the patrolmen standing outside the apartment, until Eli stopped him with a word. "Milt, hold on a minute. I'm not going to wait. Like Jem says, it makes sense they'd take Mrs. Billings there. I'll hire a horse and go after her and I'd just as soon not have the sheriff horning in." He turned to Jem. "Which livery has the best stock?"

Hattie whispered something to Jem who nodded. She got up to stand beside Eli and plucked at his arm for attention. "We've got a horse. We brought her in from the ranch with us and she's a good'un. You can borrow her. Mrs. Billings has already been gone a long time. You better get going. Jem will go with you and show you the way. He knows a short cut."

Before Eli or Milt could voice a protest, Jem nodded and said, "I'll get my coat." But then he paused and frowned. "You got a gun, Mister? Because I think you might need one."

So did Eli. He patted his hidden shoulder rig. "Right here."

"I'll fetch Mr. Flowers's pistol from his office. Do you want the rifle, too, Jem?" Hattie darted out of the room even as Jem answered yes. In seconds she was back with a holstered .45 and a 30-30 lever action that appeared well-used.

Milt held up a hand, then dropped it.

Eli couldn't help but smile. Seemed as if little Miss Hattie was a commanding force. She reminded him a whole lot of January.

It was while Jem, with Hattie's help, put together his outfit, that Milt and Eli had a private word.

"If those youngsters aren't Flowers progeny, I'll eat my hat." Milt made no bones about his opinion. "Which one of the boys they belong to is the question. And why aren't they acknowledged?"

"Flowers progeny for sure." Eli nodded. "But it'd be

my guess they're the old man's own children of his old age. Probably born on the wrong side of the blanket right out there on the ranch."

Milt's eyes widened. He exhaled noisily through his nose. "Yeah? A well-kept secret then. First I've heard of them and a thing like that generally gets around. If true, no wonder Joe and the rest are searching high and low for them. Them or proof of parentage." He gave a short laugh. "Who knew the old boy had it in him? The grandsons are after January for now, but what they might do with those kids don't bear thinking of. This is apt to change everything."

Grimly, Eli agreed.

Eli and Jem left the apartment within minutes. Jem led the way through the dark, quiet streets to the livery where the horses were kept. The boy's mount, a nice sorrel gelding, shifted and stamped, protesting the cold as Jem got him saddled and a bit in his mouth. The sorrel was not the sort of horse usually allowed a lowly employee's young dependent, Eli noticed. The mare assigned to Eli, a near black without a trace of white, had been old Joseph's favorite, or so Jem assured him.

Hattie's description of the horse, Eli soon discovered, had been accurate. The mare was a good'un.

* * *

AT THE RANCH HOUSE, dishes with dabs of egg, syrup, and scraps of ham drying on them cluttered the middle of the table where the men had pushed their plates. Though it was only seven or eight o'clock, January had no accurate idea of the time, Calvin had found a bottle of cooking brandy in a cupboard and poured himself a generous portion. Lynch joined him. John B, though he sniffed longingly at the liquor's aroma, shook his head when the bottle came around.

Nobody offered the bottle to January, which she decided spoke badly of their hospitality. She, of any of them, probably could've put it to best use. Bolstered her courage, if nothing else, as it seemed in danger of failing. Or else the brandy would dull her senses. Not such a bad thing as she figured heavy abuse would be soon in coming. They seemed to be working themselves up to that point right now. Lynch, she felt sure, would be the administrator. He stared at her out of the corners of his rat-red eyes with a kind of anticipation.

Joseph passed on the brandy from the start. He rose from his seat, straightened his collar and jacket as if preparing to lead a meeting or make a speech and turned toward her.

Feeling at a disadvantage, she got up, only to have Lynch's heavy hand press her back into the chair. "Sit down. You're not going anywhere."

"I—" she started, but Joseph said, "Be quiet. We've gotten to the purpose of the meeting now, and I'll tell you what to do. And if you have any sense at all, you'll do it."

She let him go on thinking so, if even for only a few more moments.

Calvin, smiling and retaining possession of the brandy bottle, leaned against a short, solid table with a heavily scarred wooden block top. January diverted herself with the idea it would be handy in a kitchen, until the screech of Joseph's chair's legs as he scooted it under the breakfast table indicated he was ready for business. The time had come. Her fingers clenched.

John B sat erect and tense. He hadn't eaten much. Almost as little as January, whose stomach roiled and twisted with apprehension. Then, brushing aside a smattering of crumbs, Joseph drew a sheaf of papers from his jacket's inner pocket and spread them on the table. Self-important as a Supreme Court judge, he smoothed them flat with the side of his hand.

"Let me begin," he said. "Get this out of the way and be done with it. All it takes is a couple minutes and a few strokes of the pen. Just simple signatures."

"That's your signature he's talking about, Mrs. Billings," Calvin added, in case it wasn't clear to her.

January's insides began quaking, a sensation so strong as to feel as if the earth moved beneath her. She knew compliance was not possible. They'd have no choice but to kill her. The terms of the will pretty much made it clear only her death would give them a chance to regain control. And that was a chore probably left to Lynch, or maybe Calvin, the moment she put pen to paper. Like signing her own death warrant.

Was she scared? *Yes!* Did she want to draw her gun? *Yes.*

Not yet, she told herself. Not quite yet. They were all too close. Too aware.

John B drew in a breath. In the end, he didn't speak, no doubt because Calvin drew his pistol and aimed it carelessly at his cousin. "Sit still and be quiet, Johnny B." he said. "This'll soon be done. Then we'll all go home and wait for word."

January didn't have to wonder what word they

would be waiting for. She knew. Which is why she put all the scorn she felt for each and every one of them into what she said next. "What a disgraceful trio of men you all are. No wonder our grandfather passed over the lot of you. I only wish he'd passed over me, as well. God knows he ignored me for all the years of my life before."

The blow came almost immediately. Dealt to her, which sort of surprised her, by Joseph himself. The flat of his hand caught her scarred cheek strongly enough to scoot her, chair and all, back several inches. Still, it could've been worse. At least he didn't use his fist. Though her senses reeled, she didn't pass out. Didn't cry out, either. Her teeth chomped firmly together and prevented sound from escaping.

This time, John B did make it to his feet. "Stop it, Joe. She's right. We are a disgrace. Gramps was a hard old man but he didn't cheat people. Or hire killers to get rid of people who stood in his way." He glared accusingly at Lynch.

Lynch laughed. "He might've. Who knows?"

"Didn't cheat people? What are you saying?" Joseph shook his hand, evidently benumbed from striking her. "He cheated us. You, Cal, me. Me most of all. I'm the oldest. He always indicated I'd take over the business after he finally died. He groomed me for the position. You know he did."

January, as the immediate pain ebbed, wondered if that were true.

Calvin took another small swig of brandy before handing the bottle to Lynch. "He never said you'd be the one to take over, Joe. He just let you convince yourself and kept his own mouth shut."

Joseph whirled on him. "You know it was supposed to be me. He ruined everything when he brought her into it. I have to correct his mistake. *We* have to correct his mistake. What benefits me, benefits us all."

A loud hoot of derision resounded. John B, expressing his opinion. Under other circumstances, January might have smiled.

Snarling, Joseph pushed John B aside and loomed over January. "Save yourself the pain, Mrs. Billings. Sign the papers. You will in the end, you know. One way or another."

She drew a breath, firmed her mouth, and shook her head. "No."

\* \* \*

JANUARY HAD no idea how much time passed. Hours? Days? Maybe forever? She'd blacked out for a bit whether from fainting—heaven forbid—or from an actual blow that shut her down, she wasn't quite sure. Sound reverberated in her ears. Wisely, she didn't try to open the one eye she thought *would* open. The other, already swollen mostly shut, had become the subject of argument between Joseph, Calvin, and to a lesser degree, John B.

It hurt, she allowed herself to think, like hell.

Joseph had landed the first blow, as she remembered. The first blow after the one separate from the real beating, she meant. A slap on the unscarred side of her face this time, it hadn't been too bad. Then, just to keep the family in accord and show they were in this together, John B's participation was commanded. He pummeled her shoulder, whispering "sorry, sorry" to her.

But Calvin had no such scruples. "That didn't count," he said to John B, and telling Lynch to hold her, he landed a blow to her stomach that knocked all the wind out of her and left her retching helplessly.

Lynch laughed. "If she was pregnant, that should've taken care of it."

"Are you ready to sign?" Joseph asked. He sounded as if he really hoped she was.

Unable to speak, she turned her head away.

Lynch's turn.

After the first few blows, she lost awareness, except for pain. John B, stepping between them, finally forced him off, yanking him backward onto his butt. And now—

Regretfully, she drifted back to the light before they realized. Too busy quarreling among themselves. All, in January's dazed mind, to the good.

The first words she heard were from Lynch, calling for more brandy. "I'm thirsty," he was saying. "All this is hard work. I need a drink."

They seemed to have gathered over by the pantry. She heard a clink of a bottle and the pop of a cork, and guessed he'd gotten his wish.

"This stuff is hardly drinkable," Joseph said scornfully. "Cooking brandy. Gah!"

The bottle glugged. "Uh-huh. Tastes fine to me." Lynch again.

"He's already had too much," Joseph, as if he were somewhere off in the distance, said weakly. "He's getting careless."

"Let him drink." Calvin, his voice coming in waves,

seemed at first to be right beside her, then farther away. "Looks like his part is done."

John B was beside her for real. He lifted her chin, hurting her neck, although she didn't think it was intentional. Their eyes, or the one of her eyes that opened, met his, and he shook his head.

"Enough of this," he said. "Haven't any of you any sense? Mrs. Billings can't even open her eyes, let alone see to sign anything. Plus, she's bleeding. I'm sure you don't want blood all over those papers, Joe."

"No. No, I don't. Clean her up, John B, that'll be your job. Maybe fetch some ice or snow from outside to put on her eyes to take the swelling down. We need to get this done right away. We can't be away from town for much longer. Someone might notice when she..." He stopped.

*When she what?* January wondered. *When I turn up dead and they find my body at an inconvenient time?*

"That doesn't happen in five minutes. Lynch has damn near killed her." John B's anger threatened to overflow. In fact, he spoke so loudly he set her head to ringing again.

Not quite at the point of death, January figured to let them believe she was. She wouldn't speak at all. John B's protests were helping her case, as she was sure he knew. He shielded her with his body as she peered around him to see the others.

"You should've found a good forger, Joe," Calvin said, raising the idea out of the blue. "Instead of a hired killer." He scowled at Lynch who sagged against the work counter. "One like Lynch, anyhow. Look at him. He's drunk on brandy and has already bungled his job more than once. He's another loose end who needs dealt with. I could've handled our dear cousin myself and saved us the bother."

Even Joe appeared a little out of sorts at the proclamation. "Except we don't want our name dragged into it. Anyway, Lynch won't talk." He turned. "Will you, Lynch?"

"Me? Talk? Talk about what?" The words ran together. "This?"

"Listen to him. He can't even speak without slurring his words," Calvin said. "He's drunk. And stupid."

"Who you callin' stupid?" Lynch laughed. "Could be I should arrest you for insulting a police officer. See how you like it. In fact, I guess I will." He fumbled for his revolver.

Calvin glanced at Joe, who frowned. Joe's shoulders rose in a shrug, but before another word was spoken, Cal drew the pistol from his low-slung holster and fired just one shot.

A hole appeared between Lynch's eyebrows. Matter blew out the back of his head. He thudded to the floor like a bag of stones.

January blinked and gasped, a brief inhalation that went unheard in the aftermath. The killing took place so quickly it didn't seem real.

Joseph's mouth gaped open although no words emerged.

John B reached under his jacket, halting the movement when Cal aimed the pistol at him.

"Don't do it, Johnny B," Cal said. "I don't want to shoot you, too. I'm used to having you around."

John B wisely dropped his hand to his side, fingers spread. He nodded.

His face, January saw as she shot him a glance from

her better eye, the one not swollen completely shut, had gone pale with a greenish tinge. Thankfully, his body still hid most of hers from his cousin's gaze. Otherwise, she figured Calvin would've seen her shaking.

Old man Death seemed near, just then. Nearer than she'd counted on.

# CHAPTER 20

"WE'RE ALMOST THERE," JEM SAID. HE PULLED HIS sorrel to a halt a couple yards before breaking from the old deer trail through the woods they'd been following. They'd reached what appeared to be the main road. The river ran loud here, where the stream-bed narrowed and a level gravel landing provided a good watering spot for wildlife.

Jem's sorrel, sensing it had reached familiar territory, snorted, blowing a cloud of steam. The black mare Eli rode stamped her feet, wanting her home barn. They'd been pushing hard as the night faded. Full daylight set diamond-like glitters on the layer of snow, and Eli caught sight of the tracks of a carriage cutting through a fresh layer of frost. Tracks already beginning to melt. They didn't need them to follow now, anyway. Jem knew where they were going, the terrain as familiar to him as the bed where he slept.

Still, they rode forward cautiously, until they reached a rise where, when dismounted, they inched forward on foot to scout the buildings below.

The Flowers ranch sprawled along the riverbank, an impressive sight. Big house, big hay barn, big stable, big garden and yard. Made Eli's own place look like small potatoes. January's, too, although there was something to be said for the smaller ranches. Maybe the fact that Eli's place was his, worked for and paid for by the sweat of his brow. Or by the chances he'd taken rounding up criminals no one else wanted to take on.

The same could be said for January. Both her properties had been inherited, but she'd paid in blood to keep them and help them grow.

Now there was this, another legacy. How much blood was she expending over this grand inheritance she hadn't wanted in the first place?

And yet, on a soft sigh, he heard Jem say, "This is home."

Jem dropped to the ground and crawled to a better vantage point. "I don't see anybody outside. No horses in the corral, either.

Anxiety drove Eli. "Do you see anything out of place?" he asked Jem.

The boy pulled back from the boulder he was hiding behind and looked at Eli. "Like what?"

Eli shrugged. "Like a spot where someone might be holed up while he keeps an eye out for followers?"

Brows drawing together, Jem looked again. "No. But one thing, they drove the horses and carriage into the hay barn. That's kind of unusual. Putting the carriage in the hay barn, I mean. It should go in the stable unless they didn't unhitch the horses." He glanced at Eli. "Why would they do that?"

"Because they don't intend on staying long. Just long enough to force Mrs. Billings to do whatever they want."

"Why bring her here? Why not stay in town?"

"They wanted to terrify her. Break her spirit. Let her scream. A terrorized person is more apt to do as she's told."

"Beat her, you mean." Jem backed away from the boulder. "Then what? Will they let her go?"

Eli breathed in and out, in and out. "I don't know," he said, but he didn't see how they could. Not after what they'd done to her already. "You said somebody stays here to take care of the place. Any sign of them?"

Jem shook his head, then a worried expression took over. "You don't think the clan killed them, do you?"

*The clan*? Eli liked it. Shorter than naming the Flowers boys one by one. "Hope not," he said.

The boy took a breath. "I can sneak down and see what's going on," he offered. "I can do it without them seeing me. I got ways. Then we'll know what they're doing with January." His mouth twisted. "She told us, Hattie and me, to call her by name. I don't mean to disrespect her."

For the first time in hours, Eli felt like smiling. "I know. She tells most everyone to call her by her first name. She's got a hand named Johnny Johnson..."

Whatever he'd started to say was interrupted by the crack of a gunshot. It carried up to their boulder-strewn ridge, sharp on the morning air.

Jem's eyes grew big. Eli's heart shriveled. They were too late.

\* \* \*

JANUARY'S HEAD REELED, her eyes almost blind, with only one in fair enough condition to fix on Lynch's body and the blood and brain matter leaking from his shattered skull. It spread across the dull, copper-colored linoleum floor in a gentle bright wave. What next? If Calvin point his .44 at her right this minute, there wouldn't be a thing she could do to prevent him. If she reached for her boot gun, January knew she'd topple like a tree in the wind.

Prudently, she let her head hang, her hands dangle, her spine slump. Best if they thought her unconscious and unaware of the murder. John B, bless him, helped her out by standing in front of the chair where she sat. Standing motionless as a cemetery angel, she meant, as if movement might cause something to break.

Moments passed. Nobody spoke. Not until Calvin spun the pistol and shoved it back in the holster. Both Joseph and John B drew breath then. It surprised January they'd both been as tense as she. Or maybe she meant as frightened as she.

"Is he dead?" Joseph throat made an odd gargling sound, as if he was speaking past a blockage.

A snicker answered him. "What do you think? Nobody survives getting their brains blown out."

"Was that wise? The best thing to do?" Joe eyed John B as if seeking a fresh opinion. John B shrugged, a tiny movement of his shoulders.

Calvin's lip curled. "Better than letting him live. Lynch is noted for spending most of his time drunk and bragging about how dangerous he is. Best to get rid of him now before he got a chance to shoot off his mouth about any of this."

Joseph seized on the excuse with apparent relief. "True. He always was a loud, mouthy drunk."

"What about the woman he lived with?" John B asked quietly.

"Woman? What woman?"

"His common-law wife. She gonna raise a fuss?"

Calvin waved the idea aside. "She might a little. But she likes her booze just about as well as Lynch did. I doubt anybody'll take notice of anything she says."

Another worry struck Joseph. His hands closed into fists. "What should we do about the body? Where can we bury him?"

Calvin, as nonchalant as though he shot a man every day and never gave it a thought, shrugged. "Dig a deep hole out in the pasture and let the horses settle the ground."

"And just who is going to dig the hole in frozen ground? You?" Joseph's voice rose sharply. "I can't. You know I've got a bad back. And there's the blood and... the blood. Somebody will need to clean it up before the Peabodys get back."

"Always some excuse." Calvin looked down his nose at his older cousin. "Always wanting the dirty work done by John B or me. Or sometimes even by your wife. For instance, leaving it up to Bethany to shoot that fire arrow into the hotel room."

*Bethany shot the arrow?* Surprise startled January into a barely curbed jump.

"You were supposed to do it," Joe said, quick in his own defense. "I didn't know until after. But in the end, she was the best choice, the best shot."

"Yeah, well, she volunteered." Calvin grinned. "Said she was the only one able to get an arrow through that window from across the street. Besides, she wanted to settle the score after what Mrs. Billings did to her."

January's mind raced. A social climber like Bethany? An archer? Who would ever have thought? Maybe she shouldn't have taken quite so much satisfaction in Bethany being escorted to the police station in a patrol wagon. And maybe she shouldn't be so quick to write Mrs. Joseph Flowers III off her list of dangerous enemies.

Beside her, John B made a restless motion. "About Lynch—how about we load his body in the back of the carriage for now, and toss him in the river when we head back to town. Might be days before he's missed. Then nobody has to dig a hole."

Joseph, seeming much struck by the suggestion, voiced his quick approval. "I suspect you're right, cousin. Most folks hated him and he wasn't popular with the other patrolmen. They'll likely be satisfied to see him gone. Especially after the dust-up between him and Ferguson the other day. Sergeant Sullivan sided with Ferguson, so Lynch's days with the department were numbered anyhow."

"There's that rocky bluff right off the road," Calvin said thoughtfully. "The carriage can go right to the edge where it's only a few yards to the river. We can unload him from the carriage and carry him that far. Drop him off in the rapids where the water is high. Easy stuff. Could be the body won't be found until spring. If we're lucky, we can get back to town before anybody realizes we've been gone."

The other two nodded. January wondered if that would work to dispose of her, as well. Two for one, saving time and effort.

Joe put the binders on that, as it turned out. "I'm not

riding in the carriage with a dead man. Get rid of him now, before he starts to stink."

As it turned out, Joseph and the others still needed something from her. Signatures on those papers. But they'd have to wait. She feigned stupor very well.

Joe continued cursing Lynch even after Calvin brought the carriage around. And Lynch wasn't the only one in for a verbal flaying. Calvin and John B came in for their share, as well.

Calvin, taking charge, bent to grab Lynch's feet. "Take his shoulders, John B. And watch his head. You don't want his blood all over you."

"No," Joe, always officious, added quickly, "Put something down on the carriage floor first. I don't want his mess in there, either. And hurry." He glanced at January. "We're not done here yet. And this..." A gesture indicated the bloody smears on the floor. "...this still has to be dealt with."

But John B had a cure for that. "I saw some rags in a bucket in the pantry, Joe. You can 'deal' with that while we're gone. Shouldn't hurt that bad back of yours too much."

"Use plenty of elbow grease," Calvin added. "No half measures. We don't want anything left for Mrs. Peabody to find. Gather up the rags when you're done. We'll take them away with us when we go."

John B nodded. "And rinse the floor well, including the mopboards. Don't be stingy with the water. You don't want to leave any residue."

Calvin chuckled as he and John B lugged Lynch away. He was no light burden even for two strong men.

"Keep your eye on our dear cousin in case she's in better shape than she looks." Calvin called one more piece of advice as he went out the door. "I hear she's a wily one."

"Yeah, but Lynch didn't pull his punches when he knocked her out." John B shook his head like a doctor giving bad news. "She's probably got a concussion."

She didn't. No concussion, not even knocked out. But she did have trouble keeping up with John B. One minute he was giving good instructions on how to hide a flat-out murder, and the next minute, acting in her defense. All in all, she didn't know what to think.

The one thing she really knew is that she, for one, was glad to see them go. Sadly, instead of traveling with the body, the odor of blood and death remained.

She didn't mind Joseph's steady cursing. In between gagging and complaining, he aimed most of it towards Calvin and the fact he'd been chosen to clean up the blood. Inwardly, she laughed. Blame his own squeamishness. His reluctance to touch the body had brought this low chore on himself.

She choked back another laugh as Joe lowered onto his hands and knees, his trousers guarded with a rug, dipping into a bucket of water and some rags as if digging in manure with his bare hands. She found it a sight to behold.

Although not particularly diligent, Joe's scrubbing led him into a corner after a while, which forced him to fully turn his back on her. She'd been waiting for this opportunity. The job had taken him so long she'd begun to worry the other two would return before he reached this point. But now, he dunked his rag into water dyed a sad pink, and cast her a wary glance. Expecting it, she sagged as if too broken to move. Almost the truth, except January Billings was not, or so she told herself, one to let a little thing like being beat to a pulp deter her from acting.

Seeing no reaction, he muttered something and began scrubbing on the wall where polka dots of blood turned streaky red. His cursing began all over again.

Between the noise he made and the scritch of the rag on the wall, her slight movements made no sound. Drawing the small pistol from her boot, she rose from the chair and crept on silent feet until she stood behind him.

"Joseph," she said, her voice very soft and low.

He jumped as if Rory Lynch's ghost had spoken. The rag dropped, and he started to turn, but January poked the pistol barrel hard against the back of his head. He went still. "What..."

Funnily enough, his 'what' and her 'what' overlapped as she said, "What a fool you are."

Without taking notice of the wet floor, he reared backward as if to bowl her over. Instead, his feet slid out from under him. January skipped out of the way, her wounded leg blazing with the new pain. Her pistol bounced in her fingers as she struck out at him, hammering the barrel down hard on the back of his head when he grabbed at her. To tell the truth, she wouldn't have mourned if the blow killed him.

Without waiting to see if it did or not, as he slumped face down on the wet floor, she found her coat and fled the house. Where to go?

Once outside, she heard Calvin calling to the horses as he and John B returned, and knew she didn't have much time. Wherever they'd dumped Lynch's body, it must not have been far away. Not nearly far enough. Which meant she only had one choice of direction.

Running now, ignoring the pain flaring through her entire body, she turned right, toward the shelter of trees and the massive stones layered into the riverbank. The carriage turned into the drive, at which she flung herself flat into some frosty weeds. Her heart beat hard as she stifled breathing that sent a cloud of steamy breath into the air. Tucking her head, she blew into her coat.

January waited to get up until the horses and the vehicle rounded the house heading toward the barn. A short dash took her finally into the woods and, she hoped, safety. An odd sort of euphoria filled her. She'd escaped.

So far.

Back at the house, a shout announced they'd discovered Joseph laid out and her gone. She was pretty sure the shouted words were "Find her." Then a shot.

Why a shot? she wondered. Calvin blowing off steam? Had he shot John B? Or Joseph? Her curiosity may have been roused, but she didn't stop to inquire. Let them kill each other, if that's what they were doing. She couldn't bring herself to care.

Not until she stood above the river where a series of rapids drowned out most other sounds did she pause to take stock. A chill breeze dried the sweat on her face and as she faced the water, it seemed as though she smelled fish. Unless, she thought, it was the blood drying in her nose, the spot painful to the touch from where Lynch had landed a blow. At least her nose wasn't broken.

Pain made her want to weep. Anger kept her going.

Realizing it wouldn't be smart to stay too near the river, January angled her direction farther into the woods while keeping the river, narrowing as it swept around a bend, within sight and sound. The tree cover, she soon discovered, was sparse since it apparently there was more open area along here than there were woods. At every clearing she had to stop and scout whether the Flowers boys had gotten ahead of her. So far, she was moving at a good clip and figured she'd made as much as a half-mile.

While the distance satisfied her need to hurry, she wasn't sure she could keep up the pace. Her leg hurt badly as at one point, Lynch had deliberately kicked it. He'd missed direct contact with the wound, but had come very close. Her bruises hurt. Her stomach, her ribs, her head hurt. In a disturbing fashion, she was having some trouble keeping her balance, and it wasn't all the fault of the terrain. Trees seemed to whirl around her. Black spots floated through her eyes. When she lurched over the top of a downed log and almost impaled herself on the remains of a broken-off branch, she knew she'd have to rest.

Finding a clear spot where debris and bushes didn't poke her in the behind, January scrubbed out a place to sit where the downed log met in a tight corner with the stump. It sheltered her from the wind, a relief in itself.

*I'll close my eyes,* she thought. *Just for a minute or two. Catch my breath.*

And that was that until she woke, her body jumping right off the bare ground. Her sight returned in a blink and met the same forest-colored eyes she was used to seeing in the mirror.

January gasped, froze...and Jem grinned. "Found you," he said, a scout's triumph on his young face. "Told Mr. Pasco they'd bring you here. And he told me they'd be sorry if they hurt you."

"He did?"

Jem nodded enthusiastically. "Did they?"

She seemed to be having trouble catching up with the conversation. "Did they what?"

"Did they hurt you? Well, I reckon they did. I got eyes, don't I?"

January touched a wound along her cheekbone with a gentle finger, and found even the finger hurt. "Yes."

"Yes to which?"

"All." She felt too tired to say more and let her eyes drift shut again.

Hearing came back first. Birds calling, grass rustling, trees sighing, river running—ah, and people talking. *Who?*

January felt for her pistol, her hand creeping into her coat pocket and drawing the small weapon out. But then she realized it was Eli's voice she heard, telling Jem about his foray into enemy territory.

"Did you shoot them?" Jem asked.

Eli chuckled, and so did January, although her mirth was silent. *Blood-thirsty little man.*

"No," Eli said. "But I slowed them down. They won't be after us for a while unless they're more fond of walking than I give them credit for."

"Did you steal their horses?"

January didn't need to see Jem to sense the glee he felt.

"Unhitched them and ran them off. There are other horses in a nearby field, but it'll take them some time to gather them up. We need to get out of here before then."

"Should've taken one of the horses for January to ride."

"I don't think she'll be up to riding just yet, Jem, but don't you worry. I'll take care of her."

Eli's promise made her shiver. Then he was there, hunkering right in front of her when she opened her eyes. He looked tired. Whiskers sprouted along his jaw, lines radiated from the corners of his eyes. Those dark, dark eyes bored into hers with an intensity that almost frightened her.

"You've been crying," he said.

"I have?" She hadn't realized it. Or recognized it. She never cried.

He nodded. "Sweetheart, can you move? I'll help you up. You're riding with me."

She'd raised both hands for him to pull on when what he'd said struck her. *Sweetheart!* He'd called her sweetheart? That may have been why it seemed perfectly natural to press her lips against his when he raised her, holding her close until she steadied. Yes, even though her lower lip was split and the kiss probably tasted like blood. Although, when she thought about it, he didn't seem to mind.

Behind them, Jem guffawed. "Hah," he said. "Durned sister of mine is right again."

January didn't know what he was talking about. Didn't really care since Eli was kissing her back. Gently, though. Oh, so gently.

Then it was over.

Inside another minute they were mounted and on their way back to town. January rode on Eli's borrowed horse. His arms held her steady with her cheek resting against his chest. Safe at last.

# CHAPTER 21

THEY STOPPED THEIR HORSES AT THE REAR OF THE
Flowers building, and Jem, quick as a monkey, slid from
his sorrel. January and Eli watched as he walked
straight up to a chimney stack as if able to walk right
through it. He stood with his back to them and fiddled
around a bit. Soon, a portion of the brickwork swung
open revealing not a chimney flue, but a hidden
stairway.

Jem turned and bowed toward them with a magician's flourish.

He may have been a little disappointed with
January's lack of enthusiasm. She'd been expecting
something like this.

With Eli's help, she slid to the ground and hobbled
over to peer into the dark aperture. Barely able to spot
where a series of steps began, she shuddered at the
thought of climbing them. Worse, there were two sets,
one going up, presumably to the apartment; another
going down into the basement.

Jem grabbed a lantern from a wall-hook just inside

the aperture and struck a match, setting it to the wick. "This is how they got in," he informed her. "I guess Joe knew about it. Somebody should've told you."

Eyeing the steep, narrow stairway—the treads barely deep enough for the ball of the foot—January had a moment of weariness profound enough to wonder if she could manage.

But she would. She always did.

"Yes," she answered Jem's statement. "Somebody should have."

"You can't climb these, January. Let's go around to the front. Take the main stairs." Eli tried to direct her away, but she shook her head.

"I don't want anyone seeing me like this. Or only Mr. Avery. I'll clean up and pay him a visit right away." She thought a moment. "At least Joe's tricks prove Avery is following grandfather's orders and isn't trying to bamboozle anybody. But it's best done before the cousins get here. Whether," she added strongly, remembering Avery's clerk was a stickler for appointments, "Mr. Stone, his clerk, likes it or not." She was a little surprised when Eli nodded.

"Best thing you can do," he said. "And I'll go with you. From now on, you don't go anywhere alone. And you, Jem," he set a severe eye on the boy, "you and your sister find a place to hide out for a spell. Let us get this under control."

Jem shrugged. "Aw, Joe don't know about us. Or not about *us*, if you know what I mean."

January agreed with Eli. "Maybe not yet, but he will. Even he can't be dense enough not guess. Listen to Mr. Pasco. You two need to stay out of sight until all this is settled. One way or another." What January didn't say was that when she said settled, she meant Joe and Calvin either in prison for a nice long stretch or dead. As far as John B went, well, she hadn't yet made up her mind.

Eli sent Jem off to return the horses to the livery stable where they boarded, while he waited for January. Evidently, he'd meant it when he said he wasn't leaving her alone.

A warm, though quick bath in the sybaritic bathroom did a great deal to restore her. But nothing, she decided, peering into a steamed-over mirror, could hide the raw gashes and darkening bruises left from Lynch's beating. Frankly, she didn't much try, especially after she found a bald spot on her sore scalp where Calvin had yanked her hair out by the roots. Let Avery see what her cousin had done. Let the sheriff see, if he could be persuaded to take an interest. Unless, she thought sourly, he came down on the cousins' side of this business. What then?

Then the governor, that's what.

Eli was waiting for her when she emerged from the steamy bathroom. "Took you long enough," he grumbled, but then conceded, "I suppose the warm water helped loosen you up. I see an improvement."

"Better than a face painted with blood?" She's caught a horrifying glimpse of herself before the bath.

He didn't smile. "Yes."

This time, when January and Eli arrived at Avery's office, the clerk took one look at her battered face and went at once to knock on the attorney's private door. He whispered a message. They no more than had time to seat themselves when Avery escorted a disgruntled looking gentleman to the entry door and showed him out.

"Mr. Stone will arrange another meeting when we know more," Avery told the man and brusquely bade him adieu. He turned to January, studied her a moment and said, "My clerk didn't exaggerate, I see. Come in." He raised his voice to the hovering employee. "Bring coffee," he said. "And some of those pastries from Rose's Café. You," he told January, "look depleted."

She thought he might've been generous with his appraisal.

With his clients seated, he took his place behind the desk. "Tell me," he said.

Avery's face had paled before she finished, his fingers clenching and unclenching around his expensive Waterman pen. "Calvin shot Lynch? That's murder. It's time to bring in the sheriff. The Flowers boys can't be allowed to get away with this. I wish—" He hesitated. "I only wish the sheriff and young Joseph weren't so close. As for a judge, if Judge Merriweather is selected to preside, it means trouble. Joseph's and Merriweather's wives are sisters, you see. And I'm afraid he might not do the proper thing and recuse himself. You can be certain I can, and will, protest if that happens."

"Afraid they'll ignore murder, kidnapping, assault?" January voice rose. She started to shake her head in disgust, only to discover it hurt too much.

Eli reached over and took her hand. "Easy," he said.

She drew a breath. "I'm not really surprised. Joseph and Bethany were released almost as soon as they reached the police station the night they ransacked the apartment. The fire at the hotel barely drew police attention, even though I was shot with an arrow."

January paused and drew a shaky breath as she looked toward Eli. "I need to protect those children."

He nodded. "We will."

Avery eyed them warily. "Ah, you know about Jem and Hattie? Apparently, you've read Joseph's letter."

It struck her the attorney was relieved.

"No, I haven't read the letter you gave me, but yes, I'm acquainted with Jem and Hattie. They're smart, hiding almost in plain sight and doing a bang-up job of it." She sighed. "I've delayed too long with the letter. I'll read it as soon as I get back to the apartment. In any case, I'm prepared to contact the governor if the sheriff and judge refuse their duty."

"You know the governor?" Avery blinked rapidly. A turn he apparently hadn't expected.

"We've dealt with each other on a couple difficult occasions," she said. "That's not to say we're on a first name basis." That honor had belonged to her husband Shay.

Eli quietly chuckled. He, too, had received a commendation from the governor after he and January saved those young girls last spring.

Delbert Avery's telephone call to the sheriff ended in delay. "Gone?" he shouted into the receiver at one point. "Gone where?" A lengthy explanation followed, the attorney's eyes narrowing and his expression grimmer with every word. At the end, he said, "Pass him the message I called as soon as he returns. It's imperative I speak with him before he does anything." He listened a moment, his face reddening with anger. "And you, young man, may well see your career at an end if you don't. Immediately." At that, he slammed the receiver onto the hook.

Eli regarded him like a fox eyes a puffed up angry rooster; half wary, half amused. "I take it that didn't go well."

"Fools," Avery snapped. "The whole kit and kaboodle in city hall." Taking a moment, he seemed to gather himself. "I suggest you go home to The Falls, Mrs. Billings, Mr. Pasco. Those Flowers boys can run riot while the sheriff dithers over whether to tend his duty or cater to whoever pays the best bribes. Frankly, I suspect the latter. I believe you'll be safer on your home ground where strangers will be noticed."

January, who'd dealt with others of the ilk, simply nodded. She was ready—more than ready—to get home to her dog, and check the state of her livestock. And protect all, including people and property, in her care. With a gun, if necessary. She'd done it before. She could—she would—do it again.

Eli nodded agreement.

"All right," she said. "We'll take the first train."

And she'd make very sure the kids were on it with her, spiriting them out of this corrupt town whether their 'Unc' liked it or not. Best if he didn't know where they were going. She had no faith in a man who let his nephew and niece do his work while he spent his days and nights with a whiskey bottle. Now she'd just have to persuade Jem and Hattie.

\* \* \*

THE FLOWERS BUILDING lobby was empty when the cab dropped January and Eli off at the front entrance. Best, they agreed, not to have the tenants asking questions about January's bedraggled state. Eli had ruled out walking the few blocks home even if she'd wanted to. Which she hadn't. If he'd only known, she'd been about to suggest the cab herself. Exhaustion, she silently admitted, made her weak.

Circumstances changed when they found Jem waiting for them at the basement entrance. His hand reaching out of the dark and plucking at January's sleeve, made her jump. But not nearly as much as the sight of his ashen face.

"Jem, what is it?" January reached out to the boy.

He flinched. "It's Unc. Down in the basement." His voice faltered. "He's dead. Been murdered. Shot in the head. Just like you said happened to Lynch."

"What?" Eli glanced at January, then shifted his dark stare to Jem. "When? Who did it?"

"I found him layin' at the bottom of the stairs when I got back from the livery." Jem appeared not to hear Eli's questions and tugged at January's arm again. "We've gotta find Hattie. I don't know where she is."

What was he saying? That he thought Hattie had killed their uncle and was hiding? No. Impossible. An even worse thought occurred to her. Had Hattie been taken, just like she had been taken?

Eli's teeth gritted. "Have you looked for her? Called for her?"

"Looked." Jem's eyes were fixed on January. "Didn't call out in case whoever killed Unc was still here, but nobody is. Unc hasn't been dead for long. And Hattie is gone. She's not in any of the places just her and me know about."

And where, January wondered as she and Eli exchanged a look, would that be? More secret stairways or hidden rooms the cousins seemed to know about, and she did not?

"They took her." Jem's voice broke. "Joe, Calvin, and John B. I know they did."

"Best not to borrow trouble. Let's hope Hattie has found somewhere safe to hide." January sucked in a breath, wishing she really thought so. She eyed Eli. "How did they get back so soon? Why would they kill the kids' uncle and kidnap Hattie?" But she could guess.

"They figured it out." Eli's voice had gone stone cold. "They realized Jem and Hattie are Joseph Senior's own children and will play a role in the inheritance. They're using Hattie to force you to repudiate the will, January. Looks as if they caught up those horses faster than I thought they would, and ran them hard to get back to town." Eli grit his teeth. "As to why they killed the kids' uncle, I expect he protested them taking Hattie."

Jem let out something between a sob and a curse. "Yeah, Unc would've tried to stop 'em. He was good to us, you know. He just liked his drink too much."

"Steady, Jem," Eli said. "We need to take a look around the basement, both for your sister and to see what we can learn about your uncle. I'll call Milt Ferguson afterward."

Jem nodded, though his reluctance to descend those stairs showed clearly.

"It's all right." January sympathized. "You don't have to go down there again."

Eli, made of harder stuff, disagreed. "Best if you do, Jem. Save some time if we know where you've already looked for your sister."

Swallowing hard, Jem paused, then nodded. "This way." He took the stairs rapidly, Eli following on his heels. January, groaning under her breath, went after them as quickly as she could.

She smelled death the moment she reached the bottom of the stairs. Hard to miss the stench of fresh blood and bowels given way. Poor Jem. She felt like weeping for the boy. What must he have thought when he discovered his uncle's body? When he discovered his sister missing?

It was as Jem disappeared beyond a large boiler apparatus, and Eli strode into another room where she caught a glimpse of buckets and mops, that an idea poked sharply at January's subconscious.

Where else might Hattie try to hide? Perhaps the apartment? But then she remembered the new locks and the fact January had the only key. Unless—

An overwhelming urge sent her upstairs, then, seeing no one on the way, up to the third floor. Drawing her boot gun, she eased her way to the apartment door and listened.

*Nothing.*

The key was in her skirt pocket. Gun in one hand, key in the other, she got the door opened and pushed lightly.

The foyer, the parlor beyond, as far as she could see, everything was just as she and Eli had left it before their trip to Avery's office. The air retained a bit of humidity from her bath and she could still smell the scent of lavender soap.

No Hattie.

But there, on the floor, lay a scrap of paper someone had shoved beneath the door.

She picked it up.

The message was short and to the point.

*You know what you have to do. If you don't, this girl will die. Don't believe me? Proof is in the basement. Go home to that ranch of yours up north and wait. We'll meet you there. Bring the papers.*

Heat soared through January's body. Did those despicable cousins think to scare her? In truth, they were doing a bang up job of it. But it wasn't fear that brought the heat. It was anger, flaming like those men wouldn't believe.

They killed Lynch and she didn't much care. They killed the uncle and she didn't mourn.

But when they took Hattie Flowers and threatened to kill her, they'd made a terrible mistake. They just didn't know it yet. January had had all she could take of men who believed girls were fair prey in the games of men.

Footsteps pounded up the stair toward her, though she barely noticed the sound.

Eli stopped when he saw her standing there, the note in her hand, his face drawn tight with dread. "Is she in there?"

January blinked at him. "No. They have her. Tell Jem he can stop searching. He doesn't need to be down there with...with his uncle's body."

But Eli nodded toward the note. "What does it say?"

She handed it to him, her hand shaking a little, so the scrap of paper quivered as if about to blow away.

He took it. Took her, too, into the shelter of his arm as he read, then looked up, his expression grim. "Now we know. It's all in the open."

"And they have a head start." But January's brain had started working again. "You know what is faster than a train? The telegraph. I can send telegrams. One to Squirt to show to Marshal Southbrook, and one to Johnny at the ranch so they can prepare. My dear cousins don't know it yet, but they've boxed themselves in."

"I'll do it," Eli said. "And I'll tell Milt. You gather your things. I'll meet you at the train station in an hour. Don't be late. Bring Jem. We can't leave him here."

With that he was gone, calling to Jem as he went.

As for January, the time had come to read her grand-father's letter. Marching to the fireplace, she pushed on the correct brick and with a sharp 'snick' the compartment opened. Sighing, she took the envelope out and opened the flap.

*My dear January,* the letter began.

> *I'll say it again. I'm sorry I didn't get to know you. My own fault. Anita and I parted ways all those years ago. We quarreled and I disinherited her when she defied me. I was stubborn and unwilling to admit I was wrong when she insisted on marrying your father. She, it must be said, was equally stubborn. I didn't believe he was good enough for my daughter, but I discounted love. I know different now. Your father was a good man.*

Took him long enough to realize it, she thought sourly.

> *A better man than I,* the letter continued. *When I found out my grandsons were not the men I wanted or needed to represent my name, I started over. This time I chose a woman of hardier character than the women who fawned over me. Over my fortune, I should say. Nichola Flint and I*

*were married in 1887 in Colville, and she bore us two chil-
dren, Jem and Hattie. If you haven't met them as you read
this, I'm sure you soon will.*

*You can probably guess why I've kept my last two chil-
dren in the background. Their mixed parentage, for one
thing, and I can't trust any of my grandsons. I'm afraid for
the youngsters, should they come under the control of
Joseph and his wife, Bethany. Or Calvin, for that matter,
who has a strangely violent quirk. Or even John B, though
he'd probably be the kindest, as long as he stayed away
from the influence of the other two.*

*But now, before I, or the youngsters are ready, my life
is coming to an end. Tuberculosis has taken its toll and I
haven't long to live. My children and my children's children are in discord. You are the one who has made something of yourself. You've helped others, putting yourself in
great peril with no hope of reward. I hope, I pray, you will
extend these qualities of care to the last of my children and
raise them to be responsible citizens like yourself.*

January's mind stuttered. Take the youngsters and
raise them? Her? She knew nothing of children. Had the
old man been insane?

*I hope when the time comes, providing you can keep your-
self and them alive, you will eventually share the proceeds
of the estate with them. The estate is worth a great deal of
money and I am trusting you to do what is right. I have no
other choice. You are my, and their, best hope. I beg you.*

  *Too late, your grandfather,*

  *Joseph C. Flowers*

# CHAPTER 22

"I CAN UNDERSTAND," DELBERT AVERY SAID CRYPTICALLY when January, with Jem in tow, burst into his office only a half hour after her first visit, "why Joseph handed his assets and responsibilities over to you, Mrs. Billings, instead of the boys. Now, how can I help?" He waved away the clerk who'd protested yet another unorthodox entry, and eyed her companion.

January pulled Jem, whom she refused to let out of her sight—hers or Eli's, at a pinch—forward to stand beside her. "Have you met Jem Flowers?"

"No, but now we meet, I can see the resemblance." Avery extended his hand, which Jem met after a short hesitation. "How do you do, young man. Your father has told me about you. You and your sister." A thought seemed to strike him and he sent a wary look at January. "Where is she? Harriet is her name, I believe."

"Yes. Hattie. She's been kidnapped. Their uncle has been murdered."

Avery's jaw, concealed under his short beard, dropped. "What? Bran Flint is dead?"

"I'm afraid so. When Mr. Pasco and I got back to the Flowers Building, we found Jem in shock." She gave the boy a worried look. "He'd discovered his uncle sprawled in the basement with a bullet hole in his forehead. Although we searched the building, Hattie was gone." She sighed now. "I went upstairs to the apartment and found this pushed under the door." Handing Avery the note, her hand dropped to her side.

Avery scanned the note, then handed it back. "Well," he said. "Well. I didn't think the situation would go this far. Joseph, while he expected trouble and controversy, most certainly didn't anticipate this whole-sale violence. If he had, he never would have—" He stopped with a sideways glance at January.

Her upper lip curled. It struck January that for such smart men, neither had proven to be wise judges of character. Her grandfather had known his grandsons all their lives. Surely, he'd had some inclination of what their reaction would be at being more or less cut out of the will. Oh, not to expect murder and kidnapping, maybe, but strong protests at the least.

Or, it struck her, had he?

If Joseph I and Mr. Avery had investigated her activities these last two years, then they'd know about the revenge she took on her husband's killers. They'd know about saving those girls from white slavery. They'd know about how she, with help from Eli and Squirt, had captured a gang of thieves and killers who'd planned to take over and destroy the town. They probably even knew she was a deputy sheriff over in the next county. And most certainly they'd know none of the criminals had simply thrown up their hands and said, "I give up." Violence had been called for. And she hadn't flinched.

But one thing still puzzled her. If Joseph Flowers Senior, having thoroughly scrutinized her past knew so much, then why hadn't he simply asked her to take care of his younger children? Plain and simple with no subterfuge?

Because it wasn't the way his mind worked. And would she have? Even now, if given the choice, she didn't know what she'd have said.

Most probably, "no."

"Fool," she muttered, scarcely realizing she spoke out loud and not sure whether she meant him or herself.

But the reason she was at Avery's office now was to make out her own will, with certain instructions. "Just in case," she said, and the attorney, his face grim, nodded and bowed to her wishes.

A half-hour later, she, along with Jem, who'd sat outside Avery's office while the attorney and January conferred, met Eli at the depot where he'd gone ahead to send telegrams and purchase train tickets.

The recently completed clock tower rose above the yard where its four faces proclaimed the time. No excuse for being late and missing the train in this city, January thought. Even so, they were the last to board, with the conductor pulling up the steps even as Eli leapt to catch the door before it closed.

January, still a little breathless after her mad dash to the train—and her leg aching to prove it—collapsed onto a seat. Jem sank down on one side of her, Eli on the other.

"Did you get the telegrams sent?" she asked Eli. "Did you remember to ask for Johnny's telegram be delivered immediately by a messenger?" Nervous tension rose in her. Would Johnny be all right at the ranch? If the cousins went there expecting to find the place empty, would they kill her young employee and friend? Would they harm her dog? Would they set the place on fire?

"Easy." Eli, evidently sensing the chaotic thoughts roiling through her mind, took her hand, warming it with his. "I remembered. Johnny'll have time to clear out. Him and the horses and Pen. Don't worry."

But she did, and could tell by the little creases formed at the corners of his eyes and mouth that he worried too.

They were barely out of the city when Jem, like a plum dropping from the tree, slumped against her shoulder, his eyes closed. Despite her worry, January felt her own lids closing. It had been a long night, never mind the beating she'd endured.

"He's exhausted," Eli murmured. "He's a strong kid but this has been a rough ordeal. You, too, January. Go ahead and sleep. I'll keep watch."

"You?" She looked up at him out of bleary eyes.

"Don't worry about me."

Sleep beckoned, but she had one last thing to do before she rested. Pulling the letter from her skirt pocket, she held it up to where light still penetrated the dirty window and opened the envelope. Slowly, she unfolded the sheet of paper and, forcing her eyes to remain open, handed the letter to Eli.

"You should read this," she said. "It will explain a few things."

"Yeah?" Slowly, he took letter in hand. The reading didn't take Eli long. His eyes raced across the page until finally he glanced up at her.

"So, on one hand the old bugger gives you credit for

integrity, then offers a bribe?" One dark eyebrow arched.

"Apparently." January hardly knew what to feel. Maybe she felt nothing, or nothing for herself, at any rate. Except, perhaps, a sense of being fenced in. What would Jem and Hattie think when they found out? Or did they already know?

Odd, January thought, a wry smile tugging at her mouth. "Makes me wonder about the 'qualities of care,' he talks about. If that's the case, then why did he think he had to bribe me with promises of wealth?"

"I think he hoped to make you sympathetic." Eli poked his forefinger at the letter. "It's a situation that offers both reward for you, and a chance at redeeming himself."

"Gah," she said. "All he wants to do is use me."

"True, he is. But he's also doing his best to protect his young children." He shook his head. "And he hopes in meeting them and hearing their story, you will protect them, too."

Without meeting the youngsters, that outcome might have been doubtful. But she did meet them and somehow, sensed an immediate kinship. The old goat had known enough to exploit her. He'd known she'd do it, that she wouldn't be able to leave the kids adrift.

Did she resent it? Definitely. Would they resent her? Did they? The answer remained to be seen.

Joseph Senior had included three more documents in the packet. A marriage license, and two birth certificates, proof of Jem and Hattie's legitimacy and parentage.

January was too tired to think about all the ramifications now. The first thing to do was make sure Hattie survived. That all of them survived.

On this final grim note, she took the letter back, then slept, losing herself in the wish Eli would call her sweetheart again. And that when she woke up, this would all be over.

The next thing she knew, the train had pulled in at The Falls station. The whistle had blown, its piercing scream abruptly awakening her. She opened her eyes to see Jem stirring and Eli watching out the window.

"Wait," he said, grabbing the back of Jem's britches when the boy stood up. "We'll get off last."

Jem, his feet doing a tap dance as he fidgeted, probably didn't understand Eli's reasoning, but January did. One, to make certain the cousins weren't on the same train, the idea having occurred to Eli earlier, while they were still in Spokane and someone had walked past giving them a hard stare.

January, recalling the intensity of the stare, figured it was because he spotted her face, the damage being not only her S-shaped scar, but the new gashes and bruises of Lynch's and Calvin's handiwork, including a black eye.

"Might not be one of the Flowers personally," Eli had said then, "but Joe likely set somebody to keep an eye out for us. Probably just some no-good out to make a quick buck."

As for Eli's second reason, he told her he was fairly certain they'd have another bum watching the station here for them to arrive. He intended to locate whoever it was first and either avoid conflict entirely, or put the run on him. Or her.

And lastly, he wanted to make sure to find Squirt, as January had suggested in her telegram, waiting for them with Hoot and Windswept saddled and kept out of sight. Squirt would give them a high sign before they exited the train a minute or two before it pulled out again. The plan was to get out of town and to her ranch without being seen. By anybody, including the locals. Best, he thought, if nobody suspected what was going on. January agreed.

"There's Squirt." Eli tensed. Standing at the side of the window, he watched another moment before nodding. "Let's go. He says it's clear." He sounded surprised.

Jem barely withheld his impatience. January, the second she tried to rise, discovered she'd gotten stiff from sitting. A cramp hit her wounded leg, making her limp as they hurried to meet Squirt. She barely refrained from crying out.

Squirt noticed the limp right off and frowned. "What happened to you?" he demanded. Catching sight of her face in the waning daylight, his breath caught. "Holy sh...shmoke. Who did that? And why?" He glared at Eli. "Where were you? How'd you let this happen to our girl. And who," he turned to Jem, "is this? I'm guessing he's the reason for the extra horse."

January felt like hugging the older man, though she knew he'd be mortified if she tried. "I'll be all right, Squirt. Honest. I'll explain later."

Squirt switched his question to Eli. "You tell me now."

Meanwhile, she'd been busy counting horses. Her own Hoot, Eli's Windswept, and for Jem, the nice sorrel from Squirt's rental string. Plus two more, all the reins gripped in Squirt's helper Sam's gnarled fist. Bless them.

They obviously intended to play a role in this new adventure. She didn't know whether to be glad or reluctant to include them.

Eli did his best to answer Squirt's questions. None of which, going by Squirt's scowl, pleased him.

But Eli had questions of his own. "Where are they? How many men? Flowers is apt to have hired a few gunslinger types."

"Nobody showed up here. Not one single stranger." Squirt turned his head and spat, as Eli's expression froze.

"What?" He cast a puzzled glance at January. "Did they lie to you?"

Squirt held up a hand before she could answer. "I doubted if you was hallucinatin' about all this, so I took a notion to send a telegram to Bert Higgins over in Newport as it's the last morning train stop before The Falls. Bert runs the livery there. Sure enough, he had five yahoos he'd never seen before get off the train from Spokane early this afternoon. Well-heeled city slickers, he said, judging by the way the leader tossed money at him to hire a horse for each man. The feller said they'd need 'em for a day or two."

Squirt thought a moment. "Bert didn't seem real pleased when I told him I figured he'd be lucky if he ever saw his horses again."

Eli grinned.

"I wonder which of them thought to leave the train at Newport and take the road from there. Calvin probably." January moved to take Hoot's reins, caressing the horse's velvety nose as he blew a greeting at her. "Smart of him, and smarter of you to figure it out. We might have believed they'd had given up otherwise."

Squirt preened just a little under her appreciative gaze. "Quick as ole Eldridge brought your telegram to me this morning, I had Sam take it to Johnny. Johnny didn't much like your orders, but he said he'd drive the horses over to Cobb's east pasture, and settle your old dog there. I gave one more instruction, ma'am, seeing as I know how you care for that young feller. I had Sam tell him to stay put at Cobb's until this is over. 'Course, I doubt he—" He broke off before he said more, maybe because Eli moved to toss January up on Hoot. Finished checking Windswept's cinch, Eli swung into the saddle. Copying him, so did Jem. Not much to January's surprise, Squirt and Sam followed suit.

Silent now, they took the road leading to January's ranch.

# CHAPTER 23

PUSHING THE HORSES, WITHIN A HALF HOUR THEY ARRIVED at the crossroad where Shay Billings had been killed. January somehow always sensed his presence there, an eerie feeling. She called a halt, giving the horses a breather. The afternoon had grown toward dusk, and the feeling of doom this place induced in her grew with the dark. She and Eli had been caught in an ambush here not long ago, which led to a man dying.

Nowadays, she dreaded the need to travel this road. Usually, she hurried past, but today her thoughts cast ahead to what faced them at the ranch.

"Squirt?" She motioned her friend forward. "How would you and Sam like to take the back way around the hill, cross the stream at the ford and come out at the rear of the ranch? We'll catch them in a pincer movement."

Eli shot her a look and, evidently liking her strategy, nodded.

"You think they're waiting for you?" Squirt's face bore a ferocious scowl.

"With decent directions, they've had plenty of time to get here from Newport." January shifted in the saddle as Hoot stamped, eager for his own barn. "I worry if Johnny had time to get the horses and Pen away. And my cow."

Squirt guffawed. "You're worried about a cow?"

She smiled, cracking open the split in her lip, which formed a bead of blood. "She's a good cow."

All the sudden, Squirt started patting his chest as if trying to put out a fire, finally drawing a crumbled piece of paper of paper from an inner coat pocket. "Well, hell, Mrs. Billings, talk of Johnny reminds me. I forgot this. Came in the same time as Bert's." *This* turned out to be yet another telegram the telegrapher had entrusted to him. He handed the yellow flimsy to her.

Holding the paper up to the light waning in the sky, January glanced at the signature. "It's from Delbert Avery."

"Avery? Must be important news," Eli said. "Need me to strike a match?"

"No. I can see." She tilted the paper to a more advantageous slant, then gave a whoop.

"*Lynch's body found in river.*" January read the note out loud, leaving out the stops. "*Traces of guilty party left behind at ranch and with body. Sheriff knows killer. He will be at your ranch tomorrow. All is well. Avery.*"

She looked at Eli. "That's good news, isn't it?"

Eli nodded. "Sounds like good news to me. Unless tomorrow comes too late."

Exactly her own first impression, January thought, just as Jem, his voice thick with emotion, said, "Tomorrow? What about Hattie? Don't they care about her? Or Unc, seeing they murdered him, too? Or doesn't Unc dying matter as much as that stinkin' crooked policeman?"

It wouldn't do to let Jem get too bitter. January didn't want him getting carried away at the thought of vengeance and doing something stupid on his own.

"Nothing and nobody matters as much as Hattie, Jem, which is why we're here. We're going to free her and bring your uncle's killer to justice. We don't need the sheriff of Spokane County at all. I'm deputy of *this* county, and it's my job to take care of folks here."

Jem's jaw dropped. "You're a deputy? But...you're a girl."

She looked down at herself. "Why, so I am," she said, and Jem, at last, almost smiled.

"It'll take you a little longer to go around the hill now it's getting dark," she said to Squirt and Sam. "We'll give you a head start, then I'll ride down to the house. I'll try to see what's happening there and draw their attention while you come up behind them. Your friend said he supplied horses for five, which means at the least they'll have someone watching the road and maybe another either in the barn or the yard. Look sharp and we will, too. Our most important job—our *only* important job—is to get Hattie away safely, understood?"

"Yes, ma'am." Squirt saluted smartly, spurred his horse, and with Sam at his side, took off down the narrow trail through an overgrown pine woods. The sounds of their passage soon died away.

Continuing on, the three of them came to where January's unfinished new house loomed. Bypassing it, they crossed the bridge, the horses' hooves clomping hollowly over the wooden planks. All too soon, they reached the hill where the trail led down to January's home situated near the creek.

There'd been snow here, too, in the last day or two, and the smell of frozen apples rose from the orchard, mixing with the fragrance of woodsmoke. Sure enough, it appeared someone occupied her house.

She wished it was Johnny, safe and sound, but it didn't seem likely.

They stopped out of sight of anyone who might be watching the road.

"We'll give Squirt and Sam another ten minutes," Eli said, "then I'll head in."

But January had other ideas. She shook her head. "Not you. Me. Like as not Calvin would gun you down before you got close to the house. I'll go by myself." She made a motion that cut off Eli's protest. "They want my signature on their trumped up paperwork. They would prefer not to kill me until they have it. I'll have their attention while you, Squirt, and Sam move in on them. Wait until I'm inside before you approach."

The tightening of Eli's mouth hinted a dislike of the plan. But he didn't disagree, which indicated he approved the strategy, just not who undertook its commission. He nodded.

Jem, who'd sat quiet, made a noise. "What about me? What should I do?"

Just like Eli, he wasn't going to like his role. "I need you to stay back. Look over there. See those?" She pointed to a cluster of boulders about halfway between the trail and the house. "The minute Hattie is free, she's going to run to you. Grab her and you kids get out of here, fast as that horse can run. Use your spurs. At the bridge, stay on this side of the creek. Go past the first bunch of buildings, and on to the second. That is Bent Langley's place. Tell him and his wife what is happening and they'll keep you safe."

She'd been right. Jem didn't like this part. His head hung.

Eli dismounted and started a series of stretches, arms, hands, fingers. Gradually, his motions smoothed as Jem watched. After what seemed a long time, he said, "Time to go. Jem, you know what to do. January—" He swallowed. "Be careful. I'll be listening. Scream and I'll come running."

Jem nodded. "Me, too."

"No." January shook her head at the boy, cutting his argument short. "Hattie is the reason we're all here, Jem. You've got the most important role in this whole shebang. Just follow the plan. Your job is your sister. Do it."

She dredged up a crooked smile from somewhere and aimed it at him. "I'm counting on you. This will soon be over. One way or another."

Aware of Eli muttering something, she toed Hoot and urged him forward. First a trot, while she dug out her deputy's badge and fixed it to her coat lapel. They went faster then. Hoot's smooth lope took them down the hill to her house where yellow light shone through the windows.

As she drew closer, she saw Hattie through the window. The girl, back-lit by the lamp, sat curled in the rocking chair, her shoulders bowed as though trying to make herself small. Small enough to disappear. January knew the feeling well. Once upon a time, she'd done the same to hide from the grandfather who wanted to hurt her.

Anger boiled within her. Maybe at herself, for becoming embroiled in this mess, but mostly at the man who stood behind Hattie, one hand pushing her shoulder and a tied-down holster hanging low on his hip. Calvin. Standing alongside him, she had a partial view of another man. Joseph, no doubt. Where were the others?

Drawing Hoot to a halt, January dismounted. Looking around, she hardly had time to question the set-up before John B stepped up on the side of the porch. Carefully stepped, staying in the deep shadow of a bush where Joe or Calvin couldn't readily spot him. Or anyone in the barn or yard, for that matter.

"You shouldn't go in there," he said, so low she could barely hear him. "I think they've gone crazy. They mean to kill those kids, you know, and either blame you for it, or kill you, too."

Her heart thudded. Well, it wasn't any more than she suspected. "I know. But I can't let it happen. These young ones have become my responsibility, one I don't take lightly. And this," she waved her hand, "is my property. My home. You, and they, have invaded it and threatened me. You should all know I defend what is mine."

John B shook his head. "Ride away," he said grimly. "If you want to live, set spurs to your horse and go. You can't win."

January shook her head, smiling a little. "It's clear you don't know me. What about you?"

"I'm caught, aren't I? Calvin will kill me, too, if I don't go along with them. He's already made that plain. And if I do go along with them, I suspect they'll kill me anyway. "

"Then why are you still here? Why don't *you* run?"

John B made a noise deep in his throat. "There's a guy in barn, right now, who has orders to shoot me if I do or say anything. There's another down by the watering trough. He's got an open view of the whole yard, including anybody approaching from the road. He was ready to put a bullet in you until Calvin sent me out to tell him to hold fire and let you in."

*Dear Lord. What about Eli?*

She dropped the reins, trusting Hoot to stand where she put him. She patted his neck, then stepped up onto the porch. "What are you going to do, John B? Who do you support? Them? Or me and these youngsters?"

A second passed, two. No answer, and it came to her John B had gone as silently as he'd appeared, creeping away as if he'd never been there. A coward's decision. But probably wise. The most she could hope for was that he stayed out of the fight he, and she, knew was coming.

That meant no one was close enough to hear the shaky breath she took as she reached out and opened the house door. No drawn gun, no dramatics, all being a good way to invite a slaughter. She stepped through the entry into the light.

"I was beginning to think I'd have to go outside and get you." Calvin stood facing her, a grin twisting his lips. Perhaps his hand tightened on Hattie's shoulder, because the girl flinched. A little poof of sound escaped from between her teeth.

January let her gaze drift around the room before she spoke. John B stood near the kitchen door with his back to it, his eyes riveted on her. On her badge. If he carried a gun, unlike Calvin, he made no show of it. As for Joseph, he'd walked over to where a fire crackled in the fireplace and a shotgun leaned against the wall.

Nonchalantly, as though he considered himself completely in control, he leaned with one arm resting on the clear pine mantle she'd put up a few months ago when she refurbished the fireplace stonework. Shay hadn't been the best brick mason she'd ever encountered.

But she couldn't let herself think of him, of his work, now. *Or of Eli.*

"Make yourself at home," she said, her tone, though not the words making the sarcasm obvious. "Have they hurt you?" she asked Hattie.

"Yes. He did," Hattie said, indicating Calvin, at the same time as Joseph said, "Of course not. She's just a little girl."

He did frown as he looked over at Calvin. "She has served her purpose, you know. Why don't you send her outside? She..."

"What purpose?" January let her lip curl with scorn. She didn't want them quarreling over Hattie for fear an argument would prove dangerous to the girl.

Calvin smirked. "To get you here, what else? And it worked. Quit your bitchin', Joe. The girl stays."

January forced a laugh. "Here's a first. I'm going to agree with Joe. Hattie," she directed her words to the girl. "There's a group of boulders about halfway up the hill. You run on up there and see what happens." *Pray God Jem followed orders.*

Hattie, at least, seemed to catch her meaning. The girl sat up and put her feet on the floor, perched like a bird ready to fly. Her eyes, a match to January's, sparked with hope.

"No you don't." Calvin shook his head. "There's a document on the desk. The girl can leave when you've signed your name to it and not before." He indicated a single sheet of paper lying on her opened roll-top desk.

"What does it say." As January walked toward the desk, Calvin turned, unwilling to take his eyes off her. But as she passed between Hattie and the men, she stopped, knelt down in front of Hattie and pulled the girl toward her.

John B, she noticed, had still not said anything, but when she moved forward, so did he, inching toward the front door. What were his intentions?

Still, it was now or never.

Hattie's eyes widened as she threw her arms around January. "Jem's at the boulders," January whispered.

"Enough." Joe didn't care for this show. "Sit down, girl. As for you, Mrs. Billings, Calvin is right. We take care of business first."

January, rising to her feet, gave Hattie a little push in the right direction. "Then what happens?" she said to Calvin while ignoring Joe. "Will you leave if I sign? I don't trust you. None of you. She goes first or I don't sign. You may have noticed I'm a bit stubborn." She smiled at them and headed for the desk, adding, "Brute force doesn't work well with me."

She was at the desk now, and picked up the paper, reading quickly. Calvin followed her. Joe eyed her avidly. The silence in the room felt like fog.

Until her head jerked up and she laughed. "You can't be serious."

Calvin put his hand on his gun. "Sign it," he growled. "It'll go easier if you do. I'll take grandfather's papers. We'll destroy them first."

Shoot her quick instead of slow? Is that what he meant? Meeting Hattie's eyes, she nodded. She bent, picked up the pen waiting there, and wrote on the signature line, ending with a flourish.

Calvin stepped toward her to take the paper, but as he did, Hattie broke for the door. She swerved as John B lunged forward. But not to stop her. He swung open the door. Hattie ran out without pausing, and just as quickly, John B slammed it shut as Calvin drew his gun. He fired twice, the first bullet thudding into the thick wood door where the girl had been a half-second before.

But the other bullet went elsewhere. John B made a sound, blood welling from the gash opened in his upper arm. Deliberate?

January didn't know, and didn't stop to think. Calvin was already turning his gun toward her.

He hadn't expected to see her with a .25-caliber boot gun in hand, and he hesitated.

January didn't. She fired one shot, aimed straight into Calvin's heart. She whirled toward Joseph who stood as if paralyzed, one arm still on the mantel gawking as his cousin tumbled to the floor.

His face turning white as milk, Joseph stared at her blankly. "You killed him."

"I can kill you just as easily," she said to him, shifting her gaze to John B. He faced her, his arms spread, hands palm out in submission as if he didn't realize he'd been shot.

"Thank you, John B," she said.

Slowly, Joe's arms rose in the air. Giving up.

Gunfire sounded from outside, then a whoop of glee in Sam's deep voice, followed by a bellow of rage and a loud thud as something—or someone—dropped onto her porch.

The door, which January was beginning to think should've been installed on a revolving axis, let in more cold air as Eli charged into her front room. Beyond him, a burly guy was lying in front of the door writhing with pain, one leg turned under him in an awkward position. Probably, she thought, the person who'd been hiding behind the trough. Or maybe the one from the barn.

Eli stopped, surveying first her, then the scene. Finally, smiling just the least bit, he said, "I see you have the situation under control, Deputy Billings."

"Did you doubt it, Mr. Pasco?" She smiled back and if the curve of her lips wobbled a little, well, Eli was polite enough to pretend he didn't notice.

He took a breath. "Nope."

Squirt's head poked inside, took in the body on the floor, and John B's bloody arm. He retained his main observation for January. "You all right, Deputy Billings?"

They were, she noticed with some amusement, being extremely punctilious in using her lawman's title.

She took a breath. "Fine and dandy." She told the lie with a straight face just as Eli, able to see the weariness on her face, gathered her into the crook of his arm and took charge.

# CHAPTER 24

"TEN MONTHS TO GO," JANUARY SAID TO PEN, WHO LAY with her head resting on January's slipper clad foot. The dog heaved a great sigh and so did she. She'd been doing a lot of sighing lately. Almost two months had passed since that day at the ranch, and it felt like years.

One of the dog's eyes opened and blinked up at her mistress.

"You'll be glad to get home, won't you, old girl?"

Pen made a whuffing sound.

"Yes. Me, too."

As though to prove it, the dog got up and went to the door.

"Soon as can be," January said with another of those heartfelt sighs, "but not just yet."

The last couple months had been trying, to say the least. There'd been no real trouble over shooting Calvin Flowers. It had taken place while freeing a kidnap victim from his clutches, and she was, after all, a deputy sheriff on her own property. Even Joseph, after negotiating for a lesser charge, had verified the circumstances.

Kill or be killed. Reason enough. Apparently, events had shaken even Joe's sense of entitlement. Unfortunately for him, aside from being the main instigator, the murders of two men made him an accessory to the crime. All the crimes, including the beating January had endured with his active participation. It had figured largely, but most telling was Hattie's abduction and the murders of Rory Lynch—no matter how deserved—and Bran Flint.

Also the document written in Joe's own hand he'd insisted she sign under pain of death.

The judge had laughed when he read it. She'd written *No Signature* on the signature line.

In the end, Joseph had confessed all. He'd soon begin doing his time in Walla Walla State Penitentiary. John B would join him there, if only for a few months on lesser charges. As for Bethany? It tickled January no end that Mrs. Joseph III would also be seeing the inside of a jail cell.

One might think the bad days were over.

They'd be wrong.

She spent most of her waking hours nowadays with lawyers, including Delbert Avery, but others as well. Like a gathering of jackals, bankers, with boards of directors and supervisors, with tenants of the buildings, with repairmen, maintenance men, and tax advisors encircled her. All were men involved with the Flowers empire, all of whom demanded something from her. The list went on and on.

Then there were the kids. It made her laugh, when she didn't feel like sobbing, to think of Jem as her uncle, and Hattie as her aunt. Ridiculous.

As if her thinking conjured them, a key sounded in

the lock and the two bounded into the apartment. Pen's head lifted and she struggled to her feet, happy to see them.

"School is out until next year," Hattie announced gleefully. As if she hadn't been counting down the days for a couple weeks already. "Can we leave for The Falls right now?" She knelt down to hug Pen and give the old dog a scratch behind the ears. "See? Pen wants to go, too."

Jem, pausing to deposit a couple books on an already crowded foyer table, shook his head. "The train leaves at noon tomorrow, Hattie. You know that."

The girl flashed a grin. "Never hurts to ask. We don't want to miss the dance on Saturday, you know. I'm going to dance with Eli. And Johnny Johnson. And Art Langley. And I'm going to make Squirt dance with me, too, and maybe Sam."

Clearly, Hattie had been impressed with January's friends and neighbors when they'd come forth to save her from the evil relatives. Especially Art Langley.

January had to smile at the girl's anticipatory excitement. "A dance in The Falls isn't exactly a debutante ball, you know, Hattie. It's more like a—" Like a what? What did she know? She didn't attend such functions either, on a regular basis.

"Thank God," Jem muttered, just above a whisper.

"I know. It will be more fun than a formal ball," Hattie said, sobering for a moment. "People don't like me here. Or when they act friendly, that's what it is. An act. Because they found out my last name is Flowers and my family is rich."

Smart girl. Wincing, January had to agree. The upper echelon of Spokane wasn't wasting time currying *her* favor, either. She'd brought too many of them down in the aftermath of the cousins' crime spree. Made known the accounts from which the banker Salters, with Joseph's help and sometimes that of the businesses involved, had managed to embezzle thousands in the months both before and after Joseph I died. Salter, along with his wife, had been prominent in society. His downfall had tarred several of the best families with the same dark goo. So no, January wasn't popular in Spokane.

"I'm going to go wash my hair and pack my new traveling bag." Hattie, perhaps more aware of the repercussions than January had thought, dashed for the bathroom.

Pen, meanwhile, ambled back to January and laid her head on the slipper again. A comfort. Jem hustled down into the basement and the room he'd taken over since his uncle Bran died. A new man had been hired for caretaker duties, but Jem hadn't quite flung off his habit concerning the boiler's state of efficiency. He took seriously the realization that within a few years most of this would be become his responsibility. His and Hattie's. January had been upfront with the steps she was taking regarding the inheritance.

And January could barely wait for the next ten months to pass so she could complete the final process. A trust taking the inheritance out of her hands was ready to be signed as soon as the year was up.

But she wasn't giving up the care of Jem and Hattie. They were her family now.

\*\*\*

Snow stopped the train about halfway to The Falls. Men, including Jem, piled out of the cars to clear the track, upon which January and Hattie took Pen outside to do her business and stretch their own legs.

Hattie threw snow into the air in a cascade of powdery white. "Gonna be a white Christmas," she said gleefully. "We'll have presents, won't we, January? Father used to give us something every year. But not too much. He didn't want to cause talk."

The last sounded a bit wistful and made January's heart hurt. Nothing she had learned about her grandfather made her like him. But she kept up an act. "Aren't presents supposed to be a surprise?"

Her wink was meant to relieve Hattie's mind without giving anything away. There were presents tucked away in her portmanteau she hoped her young relatives would like.

They were only an hour behind schedule when the train finally pulled into the depot. As if they were important visiting potentates, they found people waiting for them. Squirt, leading Hoot for January, along with a spritely little mare pulling a sleigh for Jem to drive with Hattie, Pen, and their luggage. Johnny was there, too, escorting Evie Langley, who was ever curious about Jem and Hattie. T.T. Thurston from the mercantile welcomed them home, as did Bo Cobb, come to town to pick up a load of supplies.

"Hope you'll be staying home for a bit," Bo said to her, grasping her hand in his big, calloused paw. "I been missing Johnny these last months."

Seemed he was bound to make her feel guilty.

Then, glancing away, she saw at the edge of everything, Fat Mary from the brothel down by the river waving surreptitiously to her.

Equally surreptitiously, January waved back.

But of Eli, though January looked for him, there was no sign.

She tried not to let her disappointment show. Tried not to feel the disappointment. After all, Eli was a rancher. He had livestock to care for, especially after a storm strong enough to shut down trains and freeze the stream where he'd have to break ice for his cattle to drink. His duty to them came before meeting her train, as she well knew. Besides, storms always hit a little harder on his side of town, where the mountains began to rise.

But still, the next day as she prepared for the dance while competing with an excited Hattie for space at the mirror in her bedroom, some of the girl's excitement couldn't help rubbing off on her.

And finally—finally—the green dress came out of its wrappings.

Hattie gasped. "Ooh, I saw this dress in the window of Mamzelle's Boutique and thought how pretty it was. So, you're the one who bought it!" She helped January slip the dress over her head and shook out the skirt. Stepping back, she said, "You look beautiful, January. The green is perfect on you. Just beautiful. Eli is gonna turn a cartwheel when he sees you."

The idea of Eli turning a cartwheel, let alone one over her, made January force a small laugh. "Doubtful, Hattie, but thank you. He may not even be at the dance, you know. Mr. Pasco is not always very sociable."

And yet, why else had she donned her green dress? And the hair ornament? And the dancing slippers?

She studied herself another moment. She wouldn't put the doodad in her hair just yet. The velvet flowers and netting would be crushed under her Norwegian cap. She just hoped the dress would stand up to the drive into town.

She turned to the girl. "You look mighty fine yourself, Miss Hattie Flowers. I'm sure Art Langley will be impressed. His brother, too. I hope you don't start a family feud!"

Hattie giggled and preened a little. Her dress, pink and frilly, set off her dark hair and forest green eyes almost as well as January's dark green complimented hers.

Then, when they were ready to go, Jem, with slicked back hair, a Stetson hat, and a crisp blue shirt under his coat, took the reins of a couple of January's fine Belgians, and they were off. The women-folk bundled under furs, and Jem wore a woolen scarf over the top of his new hat to keep his ears warm.

Hidden by the bearskin rug, January's hands twisted nervously in her lap. Would Eli attend the dance party? Would he ask her to dance? Would he like her dress? What if he ignored her? When he'd helped her with the Flowers men, he'd been open with her. Attentive. *More than attentive*. Had it meant anything, aside from neighbor helping neighbor?

What about those kisses? What about after Joseph's trial last month, when not only John B and Calvin had been judged guilty, but also his wife Bethany? Joe had screamed his rage more than once, interrupting January's testimony. He called her a thief, an interloper, and, of all things, a scarred whore. And right there on the stand he'd vowed to kill her as well as, quoting him, "those mixed blood bastards my grandfather thought to put in my place" as soon as he went free.

Considering his outburst, as it turned out, he might never be free. January sincerely hoped not.

Afterward, when she, shaken and white and trying comfort both Jem and Hattie when she herself was almost in as bad a case, had looked up to find Eli making his way to her. He'd embraced her right there in public, looked her in the eye, and said, "You hang tough a while longer, Deputy January Billings. You can do it."

Just like she was someone who could manage all these cares put upon her, ignore the stories told about her, most of them crude and untrue, and not turn a hair.

She guessed he'd been right, mostly, although in the month since it hadn't been easy.

Back then, she remembered, as he noticed people watching their meeting out front of the ornate Spokane courthouse folks were so proud of, he'd stepped back. His features cooled, and as he turned away, she heard him murmur, "This is not the time."

Time for what?

She hadn't seen or heard from him since. Would he be at the dance tonight?

Her fingers clenched hard enough her newly buffed nails dug into her palms. She guessed she'd find out. Or not.

At the cut-off where Shay had died, January's heart wrenched as the twin Inman ladies, one of whom had married the previous sheriff who drove their rig now, pulled out from the crossroad. They traveled together then, which helped January cease her fretting. Somewhat.

Hattie chatted over her shoulder to the newcomers,

sometimes shouting over the bells that adorned both sleighs. And at last they reached the schoolhouse where community dances were held. Lively music already trilled into the night. A large bonfire lit up the yard, smoke rising into the cold and clear starlit sky. Men stood gathered around the fire, and even in the uncertain light she noticed flasks being passed around.

January caught sight of Bud Knowles, owner of the Barefoot Saloon, backlit by the fire, drinking from a bottle of something. He'd closed down the saloon for the night, a rare occurrence.

With Jem and Hattie turning shy at meeting so many new people eager to draw the Flowers youngsters —the very rich Flowers youngsters—into their midst, January let the Langley boys, helped by Johnny and Evie, introduce the pair around.

Dora Dabney came forward to shake first Hattie's hand, then Jem's. From the way she clung to Jem, January guessed she'd gotten old enough to flirt. His cheeks turned red.

Inside the schoolhouse, January shed her coat, hat, and mittens, changed from boots to dancing slippers, and anchored the doodad in her hair. She was ready. Walking across the school's newly waxed hardwood floor to join the ladies on the women's side of the room, she was aware of indrawn breaths and whispers. Straightening her spine even more than natural, she smiled at Pinky Langley. She felt safe with Pinky, her first female friend here.

Then a new song began. Couples changed partners amidst talk and laughter. Dancers whirled about the room in an energetic polka. January turned to watch when, at a sudden hitch in the sound, she caught sight of the latest arrival.

*Eli!*

He was looking for her. January knew it like she knew her own name. As she watched, his gaze drifted past her, then snapped back, traveling from the top of her doodad adorned hair, past the froth of her lace skirt, to her light dancing shoes.

Inside those shoes, her toes curled.

His approval was instant. A small smile lit his face and he started toward her, his steps firm and measured.

She waited, barely breathing. She heard no music, saw no dancers, smelled no food or liquor or smoke. Everything faded into the distance until she only saw him.

*Eli.*

And then he stood before her and reached for her hands.

"This is the time," Eli said, his eyes so dark they smoldered.

And January, swallowing hard and shaking, said simply, "Yes."

# ACKNOWLEDGMENTS

My thanks, as always, goes to my publisher Mike Bray and his staff at Wolfpack Publishing.

Included in my thanks is the Red Inkers critique group, who help keep me honest and prevent some of my more egregious mistakes. I hate finding errors in my work, and as readers, I know you do, too.

And to my family, thanks for being there for me. You make it all worthwhile.

## A LOOK AT BOOK SIX:
THE WOMAN WHO WENT FOR
BROKE

**SPUR AWARD-WINNING AUTHOR C.K. CRIGGER'S FAN-FAVORITE THE WOMAN WHO SERIES IS BACK WITH A JAW-DROPPING CONCLUSION.**

January Billings is entangled in a web of family drama and danger after inheriting the Flowers fortune and guardianship over her young cousins, Jem and Hattie Flowers. With an inheritance that isn't just wealth—but also a legacy of trouble—she must navigate the treacherous waters of societal expectations, hidden family secrets, and a tangled past that threatens to unravel her newfound responsibilities.

When Jem is falsely accused of theft and a mysterious girl named Wren seeks refuge in her home, January vows to protect her family and unearth the truth. Joining forces with rugged bounty hunter Eli Pasco, they confront relentless attackers and work to unravel the dark secrets of a notorious brothel where Wren's mother once worked.

But with a final confrontation looming on the horizon, and January and Eli drawing closer amidst the chaos, January makes her biggest gamble yet—risking it all for a life of normalcy.

*AVAILABLE NOW*

# ALSO BY C.K. CRIGGER

### *The Woman Who Series*

*The Woman Who Built a Bridge*

*The Woman Who Killed Marvin Hammel*

*The Woman Who Wore a Badge*

*The Woman Who Beat the Odds*

*The Woman Who Inherited Trouble*

### *Western Short Stories*

*Aldy Neal's Ghost*

*Ask Parrot*

*A Deal's A Deal*

*Double Deal*

*Left Behind*

*Memory of Blood*

*The Whereabouts of Miss Nellie Thistlewaite*

### *Novels*

*Ault's Heir*

*Black Crossing*

*Hereafter*

*Letter Of The Law*

*Liar's Trial*

*Lost Girl Lake*

*Madame's Daughter*

*The Yeggman's Apprentice*

*Yester's Ride*

*The Winning Hand*

# ABOUT THE AUTHOR

Two-time Spur Award winner C.K. Crigger lives with a wild Pomsky (Arctic Spitz) pup, and a reclusive Persian cat. Born and raised in North Idaho on the Coeur d'Alene Indian Reservation, she is a long-time member of Western Writers of America, and reviews western genre books for WWA's *Roundup* magazine.

Imbued with an abiding love of western traditions and wide-open spaces, Ms. Crigger writes of free-spirited people who break from their standard roles. In her books, whether westerns, mysteries, or fantasy, the locales are real places. All of her books are set the Inland Northwest, the westerns with a historical background. Her short story, *Aldy Neal's Ghost,* was a 2007 Spur finalist. Her western novel, *Black Crossing*, won the 2008 Eppie. *Letter of the Law* was a 2009 Spur finalist in the audio category. *The Woman Who Built a Bridge* won the Spur Award in the Western Romance category in 2019, and *The Yeggman's Apprentice* won in 2020. *Yester's Ride* was a 2020 Western Fictioneer's Peacemaker Finalist, and *Madame's Daughter* is honored as a 2022 Spur Award Finalist.